*Houghton Mifflin* BOOKCARDS

# BURNING HOUSES
## A NOVEL BY
# ANDREW HARVEY

*We at
Houghton Mifflin
feel that special
books are meant
for special people.
If you enjoyed
this one, share
your thoughts
with a friend.*

© 1986 Houghton Mifflin Company, 2 Park Street, Boston, Massachusetts 02108
Jacket art and design by Dale Gottlieb © 1986

**BURNING HOUSES**
Andrew Harvey

*Houghton Mifflin BOOKCARDS*

# BURNING
# ·HOUSES·

# BURNING
# ·HOUSES·

◆

## ANDREW
## HARVEY

◆

HOUGHTON MIFFLIN COMPANY
BOSTON · 1986

Library of Congress Cataloging-in-Publication Data

Harvey, Andrew, date.
  Burning houses.
  I. Title.
PR6058.A6986B8  1986    823'.914    85- 24924
ISBN 0-395-40426-6

Printed in the United States of America

S 10 9 8 7 6 5 4 3 2 1

For Simonette Strachey

·ONE·

had been living and writing in Paris for five months, staying with my friend Anna at her flat in the rue Jacob. In the middle of a night in June, the phone rang.

'If you don't come over this minute and read your new novel to me – Anna says it steams like a dungheap and that we're all in it – I'll never lend you my tape of Maria's Mexico City *Aida* again. I'll never tell you my Garbo stories so you can steal them, never buy you that Versace jacket I promised, never tell you exactly what Bokassa ate with baby flesh and how many diamonds he gave Giscard. You'll die provincial, ignorant, and as badly dressed as you are now.'

'Adolphe . . .'

'You're going to say it's two o'clock. You're going to say you've been writing all day and the pain of it has turned the bristles of your hairbrush white. You're going to say you're with someone divine with the mind of Erasmus and muscles like Gary Cooper.'

'It's four. I'm alone. I'm exhausted. The young need their sleep.'

The telephone trembled.

'I may be sixty-seven – fifty-five in candlelight – but I'm not old. Writers start old; film directors never age. The juvenility of their medium, its bad taste, keep them young for ever, like divas, old soldiers, and some mythical varieties of the Himalayan pine. If you can't come now, come tomorrow night. You're going to say you're dining with Cécile, and le tout Paris will be there. Cancel her and cancel them. I'm the most interesting person in Paris. Have been for years.'

'OK.'

9

'OK? I'm not the editor of a minor rag, or some bat-eared professor from Tulsa. Hemingway used to beg to read to me. Cocteau . . .'

'I remember.'

'Be here at nine. Try and wear something luminous. There'll be just the two of us. And Maria. I've got the most gleaming new tape of her, very late.'

'I'll be there.' I paused. 'You don't know what you're letting yourself in for.'

Adolphe waited one long, practised moment.

'Neither do you.'

He laughed and hung up.

And so it began, my journey with Adolphe . . . Adolphe, who once described himself in *Paris Match* as 'the worst film director in the world (after Ingmar Bergman) – and the most famous – with the green, wind-washed eyes of a Breton choirboy, the penis of a stevedore, and the long fingers of a tropical night animal fed on musk and faeces', adding to the nervous reporter, 'If you think "faeces" too extreme, put "blood".'

That is one beginning. Another is a strange incident that occurred a week before Adolphe rang.

I had just written the last pages of my novel, and was at a dinner-party of Gioia's, a friend of Adolphe's and mine. Gioia is rich, bone-thin, Egyptian, married to a dealer in Polynesian art. She is given to saying things like, 'That salad looks like a still life by Soutine,' throwing back her head and laughing noiselessly. The party was to show off a new table of Diego Giacometti's that she had bought. It had spindly bronze legs and grinning lions at three of its four corners, the fourth being 'bare'. Gioia was in well-rehearsed ecstasies.

'Diego,' she was saying, 'is not only a genius, he is a beautiful soul. He is a . . .' I did not hear what Gioia said. I heard the word 'fool' repeated three times as if in front of me in a deep male voice, and not derisively either. The apartment which a moment ago had seemed so substantial with its red-lipped masks, ultra-modern chairs, sky-lit white on white walls now seemed unreal, as if improvised in a coloured gauze I could put my hand through.

I was back in a winter afternoon in India four years before. In Mathura, by the Ganges, I had run down an alley to escape the noises of the city and stumbled on the river glowing in the later afternoon light. A small boy had appeared and offered to take me on his raft. As we moved out into the heart of the river, the sun slowly changed colour to a deep blazing red and all the noises of the city – the horns, the hundred thousand clanging, clashing bicycle bells, the shouts of the street-vendors – receded into the light. We were moving in a silence both delicate and extraordinarily dense. The water around us was on fire. The boy was thin and beautiful: he had a turquoise bandanna round his forehead, two silver bangles round his left ankle that chimed and flamed as he swayed from foot to foot at the edge of the boat. We had been on the river for about twenty minutes when we came to a stretch of white sand that burned evenly in the late sun.

It was then that I saw the sadhu walking naked across the sand to the river. He was about sixty, white-haired, broad-shouldered, with a body that glistened as if it had been rubbed with oil, and the high cheek-bones and deep-set eyes you sometimes see in the holy men of India. He saw me looking at him, smiled, and started to dance slowly and point at me. I had no idea at first what he was doing. Then, I understood. He was mocking me: mocking my clothes (making strange butterfly movements with his fingers down his body); my nervous melancholy (jutting his head out like an ostrich, twisting down the edges of his mouth); my spectacles (making two large Os in the air with his thumb and forefinger and blowing noisily through them). I began to laugh. He mocked my laughter too, catching exactly its scared intonation, and throwing it back at me. As he mocked, his dance grew faster, wilder. The raft drifted to the bank. The man stopped dancing, came to the edge of the water, and gazed out at me. His look changed,

11

became kind. He spread his hands, cupped some of the Ganges, and let it fall in long fiery strands back into the river. He waved his palms in the air, showing they were empty, then brought them together and raised them to his forehead. He had mocked me; now he was worshipping me. I laughed again. He laughed back – a clear high laugh ... Gioia was tapping me on the shoulder to ask me something: the chairs and red masks reassembled, the sadhu's laughter faded. But for the rest of that evening, and much of the night that followed, I saw his face clearly, his hands open above the river ...

After Adolphe called I went back to bed trying to imagine what he had been wearing ('I always change for the telephone – it alters the atmosphere'). His blue shantung Anna of Siam? His pink Maharani of Jaipur with the antique silver earrings in the shape of maple leaves? I fell asleep and dreamed I was walking in the place Saint-Sulpice where he lives. It was a winter night; I was going to the Cinéma Bonaparte that faces the church. The cinema was boarded up, but a small book-shop beside it that I had never seen before was open. An anti-quarian bookshop, cramped, musty-looking, lamplit. I could see an old man shuffling about in its shadows. As soon as I entered the old man said, 'I have just the book you are looking for,' and shambled up and placed in my hand a large khaki volume. It was the encyclopaedia I had loved as a child in India. It was my copy too – it smelled of the rosewood cabinet I had kept it in, its pages were riddled with insect holes; it had my scrawl in its margins. As I flicked through it – past the drawing of the duck-billed platypus, past the illustrations of Tibet that had thrilled me – I came to a blank double page. A colour photograph fell out of me as a child at a fancy-dress party. I was dressed as a clown in white satin with red woollen balls down my front. Behind me stood a bored-looking elephant and a date tree hung with fruit. The one startling detail was that I was holding the hand of a fat man whom I did not recognise. He had the naked pot-belly of a priest and the

12

swirling cloak and plumed feather hat of a maharaja. I pored over his face. It became Adolphe's.

The next evening I walked to Adolphe's in Saint-Sulpice. All the moods and images of my five months of work went with me. I remembered the afternoons walking restlessly from one room to another in Anna's flat, rearranging the cushions and staring out of the window at the yellow shutters opposite. I remembered my midnight wanderings around Montmartre, the ritual of morning coffee in the cafés of Saint-Germain. I remembered one hot Sunday afternoon in early May in Saint-Germain-l'Auxerrois when the purple windows of the nave had trembled as the organ pealed out Bach's 'Descent of the Holy Spirit', and an old woman in a tight black dress sitting next to me suddenly began to sway as if at a southern Gospel meeting. The last months had been lonely, tiring, but full of a secret, somehow premonitory richness. Outside the Deux Magots that evening, a young gypsy was swallowing fire, surrounded by tourists. His eyes were laughing, and he kept wiping his mouth with a red towel as if delighted to find it still there.

When I reached the place Saint-Sulpice, it was almost nine o'clock. The air was chillier now; the first stars were appearing in a mauve sky; the cars parked in the square looked squat and furtive in the dark, like familiars. Adolphe's apartment is in the corner of the square by the church. I walked apprehensively up its ill-lit, eighteenth-century steps with their green-bronze balustrades. What could the old queen be planning? I remembered the other occasions I had come to see him – the parties, the soirées, the long luncheons with countesses and cardinals, and cardinals dressed as countesses, and young men with foxy faces and bulging muscles just out of prison ... The names Anna and I had given to Adolphe's apartment came back to me: 'Haroun al Raschid's Cave of Strange Delights'; 'The Kitsch-Kultur Palace of Khorsabad'; 'The Circus'; 'The Star Chamber'. 'Anything could happen there,' Anna once said. 'Anything already has.'

The front doors to Adolphe's palazzo are tall, stark and white. I never stand before them without a moment of panic. Even the knocker – a dolphin with an open mouth – is white. Even the secret recesses of the keyhole are white: white, Adolphe says, as the space around the ace of spades. The white is so brilliant that you can see your face in it, elongated, as in a circus fun-fair mirror, and pale, as if a clown had poured flour over it. Adolphe's visitors know where to touch the doors so that they open. 'Open' is too tame a word. They spring, they fling open, as the doors in dreams do, or in the *Arabian Nights*. It is all electronic, Adolphe will claim if you ask him, something to do with hidden electrical eyes and laser-beams. The doors close noiselessly behind you. You are in an oblong, bright-red room with high red walls and a vast long window with a long red curtain. It is the most disruptive, incongruous room I know, half shrine, half playpen.

In the middle of the room is a Louis Quinze sofa with bug-eyed sphinxes struck along its back, covered with leopard-skin. Sometimes Adolphe will tell you that the animal was shot by Princess Anastasia in the Caucasus when she was six; sometimes he will say that he bought it in Montparnasse from a rag-and-bone man. Above the sofa a chandelier hangs askew. From its gilt legs sashes of bright saffron silk dangle, with small red bells at the ends of them. The bells, designed by Dali in the shape of open lips, tinkle when the window is open.

In all four corners of the room there is a large gold Buddha in the attitude of bestowing Protection, each one from a different part of Asia ('For the Rice Queens, darling'). Each is lit by surrounding candles; each has seven cracked Sèvres saucers in front of him, filled with water; each has stuck to his circular base a photograph of a clown. Burma has Buster Keaton staring out and scratching his armpits in imitation of a monkey; Thailand has Barrault in the scene from *Les Enfants du Paradis* when he turns the rope he was going to hang himself with into a washing-line; Tibet has a reproduction, stuck on with adhesive tape, of Nasruddin the Sufi turning somersaults in the dust; Sri Lanka has Chaplin making the spoons dance on the table in *The*

*Gold Rush*. Chaplin and Barrault have quotations underneath them, written in red ink in Adolphe's shaky hand. Chaplin's is 'Great straightness seems twisted'; Barrault's is a quote from Fuseli that Adolphe loves to intone: 'Can the reptile joys of the bee rival the lion's colossal pleasures?'

In front of the red sofa stands a large black marble sculpture about four feet tall, in the shape of a tear. It is shining from the water that is poured on it at intervals throughout the day. The water, Adolphe will tell you, comes from the Ganges – 'a little village I know, down-river from Benares . . .'

Behind the black tear, behind the red sofa, there is a long wall, entirely covered by three vast photographs. The first, ten foot by ten foot, is of Garbo in the scene from *Camille* when she looks down from the balcony at Armand for the first time. 'It is *the* look in films,' Adolphe says. 'She is looking at a beautiful man wild about her and knows already that she will love him back and that their love will be fatal.' The second photograph, ten by ten also, is a still from the final scene of *The Titanic*. An obviously toy-boat plastic *Titanic* is sinking with its bow sticking up in the air. 'Don't miss the iceberg to the right. How sweetly it stands by, now it has done its worst – just like God and most of one's friends.' The third photograph, the largest of the three, twelve feet by twelve feet, is of Callas in a scene from *Medea*. She is lying prostrate on some marble steps, her right hand raised as if to kill, glaring murderously. Adolphe has had painted on her little Doris Day spectacles. 'Why do you have these weird photographs on the walls?' a young American starlet once asked him. 'To surround myself,' Adolphe replied, 'with the delicious energies of destruction and despair.'

There on the sofa, waiting for me, smiling, flanked by his sphinxes and Buddhas, backed by the *Titanic*, Garbo and Callas, with his legs crossed like Claudette Colbert in *The Sign of the Cross*, an ebony cigarette holder and passion fruit juice in one jewelled hand, three African silver bangles on the wrist of the other, a turquoise shirt slashed to the middle exhibiting a pink belly with a forest of curling grey hairs, is Adolphe: pug-faced, chubby-cheeked, Empress of the Demi-Monde, spiritual adviser to cardinals and princesses, pimps and taxi-drivers. Adolphe, alias Alphonsine, René, Maria, Rapturosa, Dulcinea the Thirteenth, Alexandra the Great, Buddhetta, Lulu, and many, many others.

Adolphe was about to rush over and embrace me when the phone rang.

'Oh God', he groaned, rolling his eyes, 'she's been at it all day . . . I can always tell when it's her. The phone gloats.' He picked up the long slim white phone as if it were burning. 'Marlene! Haven't heard you for twenty minutes. I was getting quite lonely . . . What have you decided? Happy about it? Oh, darling, of course I don't mean "happy" – a figure of speech. Not totally *un*happy . . . Well, that's a lot in life . . . Ring me when you get back . . . I'll be here. I'm not going anywhere ever again . . . What am I wearing? If I told you you'd die of jealousy . . . No, darling, no one wants you to die  .  .  .' Adolphe sat on the sofa, making small barking noises.

'Will she make this television film with Shell or won't she? "Adolphe darling, tell me frankly, shall I appear?" I told her she should just be a voice. "Me, a voice? Just a voice?" That was the first call. Two hours. Then I lay down and did my exercises. The second call . . .'

The phone rang again. Adolphe screamed.

'If it's her I'll do my Haile Selassie imitation and say it's the wrong number.'

'You wouldn't dare.'

'Wasted effort anyway. She wouldn't notice.'

Adolphe picked up the phone gingerly, grimacing. His face exploded into a smile.

'Jimmy, Jimmy, my poodle-bear . . . Where are you? Australia? How original! Are the deserts marvellous? . . . You've got a girl? A real one? Does she know you spent five years in jail for rape? I think you should tell her . . . Oh, Jimmy, I thought this was a love-call . . . I haven't a sou, I've given it all away to a rest home for the rich . . . It's the rich who need help, the poor can survive anything . . . I'll send it . . . Is there any point in

saying this is the last time, positively the last? I suppose not . . .
I love you, too, every lying inch of you, every tattoo.'

Adolphe put down the phone. 'Poor little Aussie girl! What
does she think she's getting? Remember Jimmy the garage
mechanic?'

'Of course.'

The phone rang again.

'Tell me it can't be happening! The last call I'll answer.
Promise.'

He picked up the phone, adjusting his African bangles.

'Hank . . . Is it raining in LA? "Fuck the rain"? Wash your
dentures out. You don't want a polite conversation? Ring
Ingmar then . . . Hank, I can't do it . . . Let someone else cringe
all the way to the bank. I won't do it as a musical. I won't do it
in Japanese. I won't do it even if Jimmy Dean comes back from
the grave specially. I'm retiring. Is that clear? . . . What am I
doing with my life? Hank, darling, I'm living it!'

Adolphe hung up and threw the phone down on the floor. It
rang again. Adolphe walked to it and pulled its lead out of the
wall.

'No one will interrupt us ever again. I can't save lives all day.
Now is my time for you. Come here and get a big sloppy hug.'

He hugged me. 'I've been so looking forward to this. I've
been thinking of nothing else.'

'Liar.'

'Almost nothing else. Your opus – it's time for your opus . . .
How I love the word opus. Short for "octopus". I had a pet
octopus once, you know, but it died. I took it up in a plane so I
wouldn't be lonely and it asphyxiated. I want to get Messiaen to
write a requiem but I know already what he will say. "Birds,
yes. Octopi, no. I do not know what noises they make." Such a
literalist – and I could make the noises for him.'

Adolphe came over to me and, folding his hands behind his
back, said, 'Darling, what's it like really, this new masterpiece
of yours? See, now we can focus on you entirely. Must make
you feel marvellous.'

'A poor thing, but my own.'

'It's dangerous to quote one's betters. And ugly in someone as vain as you. Try again.'

Suddenly, he screamed. 'My dear, your clothes! Their full horror has just registered. Black on fawn. You've never known how to dress but this is insanity. Take them off. Don't look at me like that. You know I don't have "designs". I just insist you change into one of my robes. When you read to me, I want it to be as a good imitation of a young god and not a bad imitation of David Bowie, himself a bad imitation. Don't worry, I'm not going to have you Greek and naked. You'll be Mesopotamian. I've got the perfect thing.'

Adolphe ran through the red door into his bedroom and ran out again, with a long flimsy red robe flung around his shoulders.

'Cruella left it.'

'Cruella?'

'A Texas oil executive I met in the Opera Baths. A bore but deliciously violent.'

'I thought you'd renounced sex.'

'Nothing as one-dimensional. I've transcended it. But I like to go back to it sometimes just to see it's the same as it was.'

'You want me to wear that?'

'Haven't you given me long lectures on the Androgyne? Didn't you give me that copy of the Tao with "Opening and closing the gates of Heaven/Can you play the role of Woman" underlined in green? With this on, God only knows what voices will skip from you. Red for passion, red for Adolphe's room . . . And I'm dead sure that anything you've written is *very* red. Am I wrong? I don't think so. Take those dreary things off at once. Make-up?'

'Adolphe!'

'Sorry. I forgot. One can't go too far with the English on the first night. Simple missionary position with the lights off . . . Cocteau used to wear make-up when he read me things. Purple round the eyes and always a green line down the centre of his nose. Said it made him feel other-worldly.'

'I don't want to feel other-worldly.'

18

'Well, you've come to the wrong place. You are in the cave of miracles, the Alhambra. Don't go Brit on me. One thing you should know now is that one may not be able to leave the earth exactly, but one can keep on arriving on it from different directions. Change. Or I'll get Cruella to get his boys to wrap you in a cement kimono.'

I changed.

'Well,' Adolphe said, stalking around me, 'that didn't hurt too much. You look very Joan Crawford. Now we should sing something to freshen the air.'

'Sing?'

'Maria used to say to me, "With a voice like yours I would have gone places".'

'You can't sing a note.'

'It's not the notes, it's the feeling. Billions of hoi polloi have the notes. Three or four people at any one time have the feeling, the whatnot. I have the whatnot.'

Drawing himself up to his full height, flexing for a moment his surprisingly broad shoulders, opening his ringed hands, Adolphe, with no musical instinct at all but with an eerie lyrical grace like that of an elephant dancing in a ballet by Fokine, sang the first lines of 'Casta Diva'.


*Casta Diva*
*Che inargenti . . .*


'Why "Casta Diva?"' I interrupted tetchily.

'In honour of Maria. Because I feel like it. Because we need something casta around here. Because Bellini's grace of line is an inspiration to us all. And most of all because . . .' Adolphe skipped across the room and swept open the curtains, '. . . there's a full moon. Plop in the middle over Saint-Sulpice. Wrapped in nature's own finest indigo. The moon shines on Diana Vreeland and Mother Teresa alike, and who can be sure which of those two enjoys it more?'

'You've said that before.'

19

'Naturally. It's perfect. Like Bach, I use my best inspirations again and again. It's a kind of humility. Why are you
laughing?

'Here I am, in a red robe, having just heard you sing "Casta
Diva" . . .'

'Stranger things have happened here than were dreamt of in
your philosophy. Whole cultures have changed in this room . . .
Go and stand over there, with the full moon and Saint-Sulpice
behind you, and your red shoulders casting heroic shadows on
the window-sill . . . Oh for a camera! No, I swore last week. No
more cameras! The simple life from now on . . . Straighten
them shoulders! Clear that long swan throat of yours. Gallé
should have done that throat, in smoked blue glass, with
dragonflies . . .'

'Am I really to begin?' I said stiffly.

Adolphe giggled. 'You sound more like Queen Mary every
day. Though you haven't quite got the bust for the part.'

I went to the window, trying not to trip up in my red dress.


'How to begin?'


I began, with my 'reading voice', very calm, very measured,
the sort of voice I used to read lessons with at school, a voice to
get right to the end of the hall with.


'I suppose what I have to tell . . .'


'For God's sake, Charles. How old are you? Thirty-one?
Twenty-five in candlelight? One can "suppose" up to twenty-
four. After that a little brio, dear.'


'It begins,'


I began again,

'It begins with Anna's letter . . .'


Adolphe screeched. 'Darling, how is Anna? Tell me everything. Haven't seen her for ages. What's Anna doing in this novel? I thought it was going to be a saga of heartbreak and parting, a homosexual *Tristan und Isolde* set in Saint-Germain. That's what you said on the phone.'
'I did not.'
'No, you did not. But that's what . . .'
'Will you . . .'
'Give the Created its place and shut out the din of Life for a while? Certainly. I'm game for anything.'


'It begins with Anna's letter, and here is the letter.'


'No, no. You cannot say, "and here is the letter". This is not the eighteenth century. We can't lumber any more. We have to skip. Give us the letter neat.'
'If you interrupt me, Adolphe . . .'
'You'll leave? Egomaniacs never leave when they have a captive audience, even if this one talks back. Just take an imaginary Valium and accept with grace whatever black pearls I throw your way!'


'It begins with Anna's letter,' (I began again.)


Adolphe screeched again.
'Oh, do stop that dreary schoolboy voice of yours and do Anna's voice. You are in a red dress . . . And she has such a wonderful voice. Such an I've-had-it-all, knock-me-down-and-drag-me-out voice. She should be here, this minute, poured into one of those black Saint Laurent numbers, sitting on that sofa as she always sits with her legs tucked up under her like a unicorn, and smiling. That smile! I'd give my rings to be able to smile like that! Half sphinx, half Little Red Riding Hood.

21

Anna, where are you? We need you. Fly through the window on one of your Cardin broomsticks!'

I put down my slim manuscript pointedly.

'What's the book called, anyhow?' Adolphe drawled in a slyly conciliatory tone.

'*A Burning House.*'

'Too simple. There's a title Firbank flirted with and didn't use, *In the Dusk of the Dawn*. Couldn't you use that?'

'Not really appropriate.'

'Ah, I see. Yours is a realistic novel . . . Pity. *In the Dusk of the Dawn* is the greatest title I know. If I could write I'd write a book with that title myself. But my function is not to write. Did Socrates and Jesus write? They did not. They talked. They were. I talk. I am.'

Adolphe's face suddenly became blank and childlike. He took off one African bangle and sat down on the sofa.

I began again.


'Anna's letter is as good a place as any to begin.'


Adolphe clapped his hands.

I waited.

'What kind of paper was it written on?'

'Oh God . . .'

'I'm trying to help you be a great artist. Very important, the paper. Anna uses different paper for different occasions. Mauve for invitations, black for scoldings . . . All revelation is in detail. Didn't they teach you that at Oxford? Didn't Blake tell us to see heaven in a daisy?'

'Not a daisy. A flower.'

'I always hoped he hadn't written "daisy". Can't stand the things. The simple life is fine but one must draw the line somewhere. I draw it at daisies. But then the nearest I've ever got to nature is a salad.'

I glared at Adolphe, cleared my throat, and started yet again, trying this time to imitate Anna's voice.

22

'You're welcome to stay,' Anna wrote. 'Get the keys from the concierge. She's a Moroccan with a face like a Bellini "Madonna" but the manners of an Old Etonian, and a tow-haired dwarf for a husband. The keys are on the key-ring you brought back from Turkey — remember the one? With six wrinkled fat beads that look like dog's balls left out in the sun? If anyone rings up while I'm away do one of your Indian accents and say there is no one called Anna who lives at this number. Make up anything you like. There's an American producer who's crazy about my new songs (la la) and I want him to chew on his cigar for a while. On no account tell anyone where I am or who I am with. Especially not Daddy. You know how vengeful he gets every time he thinks I might be having a good time. Not that I will be. Hans will be a disaster (all seven foot of him) but I want him to be my disaster, private, personal, to be shared with no one but you.

'If you do find someone nice (you sound as if you need to) do anything you like in any or all of my four over-decorated jewel-box rooms but see that he (it will be a he, won't it? No more she's, I hope, after the last one ...) see that he doesn't steal any of my mother's silver spoons. My father counts them each time he comes. Anyone would think he'd loved her. She was crazy and did, it's true, try to kill me in my sleep — but why should I hold that against her? We're all human.

'Be happy. I'll write that again, California-big. BE HAPPY. Have my flat and have a whale of a change in it. What did Colette write? "Being happy is a way of being wise." Malicious bitch. So sad it isn't the other way round ...

'PS Throw all the bills away.'


'I adore it!' Adolphe cried, '*Very* Anna. And did you notice your voice was beginning to sound like hers! What a red dress can do for one. Why had you written to her in the first place? Why were you coming to Paris?'

I picked up my manuscript.

'Don't read, tell me,' Adolphe wheedled. 'It's much more direct. No, let me guess! You had just fallen out of love. You were doing your usual escape act. You wanted to walk up and down those freezing Jap-haunted corridors of the Louvre and cruise in the Tuileries ... Sorry. Slipped up there. Not your thing. Too virtuous. No, not too virtuous. Too desdichado. Not even a good wriggle with a Tunisian could cure

23

your ennui that year. It was too too absolute. Right?'
   'Half right.'
   We smiled.
   'Then don't read me the bit where you explain to the reader
how miserable you are. I remember. I've had quite enough
Mahler to last a lifetime.'

   'I was nearly thirty, feeling with a sharp intensity that I had failed
in everything.'

   'You had. We all do.'

   'I had started insulting old friends at parties, and putting down
the phone on editors ...'

   'Never put the phone down on an editor! The voice of the
editor is the voice of God.'

   'I had taken to listening to Brahms in the middle of the night.'

   'Oh, my God. Brahms – in the middle of the night. Bad
enough in the middle of the afternoon. You poor weasel. How
boring you must have been in that period.'

   'I was falling into the states of self-pity I most despise myself for.
Only a bout of solitude could help me.'

   'Well, I congratulate you on your choice of a monastery.
Anna's flat on the rue Jacob. The crotch of Babylon.'
   'Shall I go on?'
   'Who's stopping you?'
   'Anna's ringing from the south of France ... I've just put my
bags down in her tiny red hall.'

   'You should never have begun it,' Anna barked down the phone
   ...

'Begun what?' Adolphe interrupted. 'Oh, I get it. The affair you were fleeing from. Unconvincing. Anna would never under any circumstance – especially the worst – say that you should not have begun an affair.'

'That time, Adolphe, it was with a woman.'

'Oh my Lord. A woman! What will they think up next, these youngsters ... I remember now. Anna was furious, she called her, "That crazy Italian with a squint and smelly armpits." Women are so charming about each other. Almost as charming as fags. Why are the damned so damned clear? It's the flames – they light up things ... And what do you say about the Squinter in your narrative?'

'Nothing much. Enough to hint at Disasters Past.'

'The massacres of narrative! She nearly kills you and you nearly kill her and the whole thing ends up in five snappy lines as a transition to some other story. Go on. No, don't. Don't go on with the remorse and psychologising. We all know what that's like. Arrive in Paris, burnt and palely loitering.' Adolphe paused dramatically. 'So it is autumn. You are recovering from a tempest with an Italian Squint. You are staying in Anna's flat surrounded by its painted screens and brocade cushions and ivory elephants with cracked tusks. You wander through the flat on grey mornings musing on private and public disasters. The light from Anna's windows falls on to the rue de Furstenberg in sad white oblongs ...' Adolphe giggled. 'No, not oblongs, obelisks, sad white obelisks. More *you*.'

'Don't be foul.'

'Not foul, inspired. Not that there's always a difference.'

'I had just put down my bag when the phone rang ...'

'Anna! I'm famished for her! I don't want to hear another word about you! And I want you to come closer to me, here on the sofa, take a deep breath and really *do* Anna this time.'

'How are you?' Anna boomed.

25

'Short-haired,' I replied. 'Dirty. Longing for a drink . . .'

'The booze is in the imitation bookcase to the left of the dining-room door. Under Tolstoy.'

I went over to the 'bookcase' dragging the cord of the telephone with me and poured myself a vodka.

'How are you? Who's paying for this call?'

'Oh, don't worry. I made a bundle on those songs I wrote in Haiti last year. Remember the ones? You thought them obscenely cheerful. They've been bought. The Yank market loves banana-boat optimism at the moment, as we know. Who's paying for you?'

'The end of the end of an advance.'

'Oh, our elegant brinkmanships . . . How am I? I feel that elation I always feel just before I am about to be left. Hans will leave me, I know. But only after the hols. I'm paying, after all. Or rather the Banana Songs are paying.'

'I thought he was rich.'

'Rich? You know perfectly well the only rich men I ever meet are pot-bellied, and into partouzes with Brazilians. Hans has two suits, both threadbare, and lives in a room the size of Sarah Bernhardt's coffin off the rue de Pont. He can't stand up in it. (He's six foot four — why do I always fall in love with trees?) He reads occult manuscripts for some obscure occult publisher called L'Avenir Rouge or something. Why am I with him? He's good at *it*.'

'Anna, don't despair,' (I assumed my father's military voice). 'He might be the one.'

'Hans only loves Hans. And Herman Hesse. Could you spend your life with a man who thinks Hesse is the greatest writer of our age? And he loves his mother.'

I groaned. 'How many hats have you bought so far this trip?' Anna buys hats when she is depressed.

'Don't try and get me off the subject of his mother. It is too absorbing. Guess what she is.'

'A prostitute.'

'Too Zola.'

'A duchess.'

'Too Proust. Charles, clutch your sides and gasp for air. She's a . . . medium.'

'I'm proud of you. A man ten years younger than you, who's dirt-poor, pseudo-religious, with a medium as a mother. Anything less implausible or self-destructive would have been out of character. What about this mother then? Is she vast, like one of those Hawaiian queens, with a moustache and bangles? Does she really produce ectoplasm?'

'She's huge. She has a moustache but she doesn't have bangles.

She doesn't just produce ectoplasm, but whole people. Warts and all. For a fee, of course.'

Anna sounded hoarse, strained.

'You're scared.'

'Yes I'm scared. I love him. No, to be accurate I love *it* with him. You're scared too.'

'Yes.'

'I'm scared and you're scared. A great pair.'

'Come back to the rue Jacob and we'll be a pair,' I said expansively and insincerely, winding the grey telephone cord round my wrist.

'Absolutely not. I'm going to see this thing through. Six weeks I said and six weeks it will be. It's warm down here, anyway. I'll get a tan if nothing else.'

She gave a short laugh. 'Hans spends his time reading sutras in the restaurant. He makes love like a tiger all night and spends his days avoiding me and writing phrases in his diary like, "Nothingness is the only thing there is." He says I'm corrupt and not at all New Age! Well, he's got that right at least.'

'What does he write about you?'

'One entry: "She has the eyes of a snake that has swallowed a goat."'

'Remember the lover who used to tell me I had hands like crows?'

'Dear John. A real Genghis Khan, that one. One of your best. Remember Simon who told me that I had the ugliest ankles in England?'

'In England? The world!'

We laughed our 'survivors' laugh.

'Tell me.' Anna's voice grew serious suddenly. 'Is there anyone in your life?'

'No, and I don't want anyone.'

'I've heard that one . . .'

'I mean it. I get down on my knees every night and pray, "Please Lord, don't send any disasters my way for at least five years." All I want to do is stare out of the window and read trash.'

'You should find someone under forty and relatively unsyphilitic and have a fling. Make love in the afternoon. Go to old Marlon Brando films . . .'

'I can't tell you how little I want to make love. I think if I saw anyone naked I'd vomit or throw myself out of the window.'

'What? In my house?'

'What if The Tree really does leave?'

'I'll cheer myself night after night with thoughts of suicide, and

27

go on. Life as usual. What else?'

'You could come home and write songs by day and read Balzac by night.'

'Look here, I'm thirty-seven with one wretched marriage behind me and God knows how many bad affairs. I'm getting plumper, more lined, every day. I have my forties for Balzac.'

'You'll never be plump. You'll never finish Balzac. There'll always be another Hans.'

'And why not? When I'm fifty I plan to have a go at educating les jeunes. Aimez-vous Scarlatti ... I'll do it well.'

'You'll be married, Anna, with three children.'

'No one in their right mind would marry me.'

'I'm not in my right mind. I'll marry you.'

'I am. I refuse. When we're in our seventies, perhaps. Not that either of us is going to make it that far.'

'Oh, we are. What did that man in Benares say to me? "If you love Death, he will make you wait a long time."'

'So even Death is a man. Oh God, I was relying on death.'

'So that's how you and Anna talk to each other,' Adolphe said. 'Snap, crackle, pop. How amusing.'

'We strive to please.'

'No, amusing for another reason. I mean, talking so coldly, as if you had no illusions and being full of them. Staggering from crisis to crisis with nothing but a handful of epigrams as fig-leaves against the wind. But that, I do remember, is how the smart, burnt young do talk.'

I glared at him.

'Don't sulk. I'm adoring the book. Who else could have written it? I've dreamt of such an art for years and now, as the shadow of death ...'

'Don't overdo it.'

'Are we feeling better with the flattery? Are we?' Adolphe let out a strange curdling yodel, tapering at the end to a few short rattles. 'That is the kiwi bird surprised by a predator over its nest of eggs. Perfect, isn't it?' Adolphe has an entire repertory of animal noises.

'Perfect.'

'Look, we have the scene now, the place. We have Charles in

28

despair in Paris and Anna in itinerant despair. We have the air alive with scorched epigrams – but is anything going to happen? Not that I'm an addict of happenings. Good God, I know there are years when nothing happens at all. One empties the garbage, goes to the opera, eats too many Bath Olivers. And living in Paris has taught me to cock a snook at plot. Is the dance of language itself not enough for us? Can man not live by tropes alone? But – where is Tristan? I want to get to the meat. One wants to get to the meat immediately at my age!'

'No doubt.'

'And,' Adolphe swept on, 'I want to see Charles in love. You *are* going to be in love in this novel, I trust? It's not going to be one of those dreary modern novels, is it, when all that happens is that people talk to stones occasionally and dream of murdering their mothers? I once read ten of them at a stretch when I had herpes. Never again!'

'I'm going to be in love, and you may even suspect with whom.'

'Not with that blond with the sad eyes and the Conscience? Not with . . . My dear . . .'

'Wait and see. I swear to you, that as I am your friend, there will be in this novel everything that you like.'

'No talking to stones?'

'No talking to stones.'

'Any visions? I like the odd vision.'

'Visions galore.'

'"Galore" sounds a bit dangerous, but heigh-ho. Read on. It is 1980. You are in Anna's flat. Misery reigns . . . I'm sitting comfortably.'


No sooner do I arrive anywhere than I want to leave. It is an hysteria I have had since childhood – a fear of walls closing in on me, of objects storing a dark power in the silence they have stewed in too long. In London I had longed to be in Anna's flat; nearly every time I had been happy in Paris I had stayed there. Yet this time, Anna's clutter oppressed me. The flat, with its tiny poky rooms, its pink and green painted cupboards which didn't shut properly because the wood was warped, its mish-mash of objects,

Buddhas and reliquaries, small jewelled crucifixes festooned with old beads, row on row of nineteenth-century leather-bound books all jumbled together, bound me in and dispirited me. I wandered from room to room, angry at the confidence each object had, the smirking opulence of the masked revellers in the screen in the dining-room, the smug smile on the bronze Tara in the bedroom, the sweet smile on the face of the Raphael 'Madonna' above the mantelpiece. Things I had loved of Anna's — the Persian carpet in the drawing-room with its whirl of birds and flowers — now seemed vulgar to me.

I walked over to the drawing-room windows. I had forgotten that Anna's flat did not look out on to a square. In London I had imagined spending the solitary autumn looking out on to the place Furstenberg, watching the light on those faded pink and silver walls. In fact Anna's flat looked out on to another flat: this red and greeny-gold mirror that she lived in gave on to another, with hardly a breath of space between. I felt hemmed in by mirrors, saw a Paris in which there were no wide leafy avenues, no Tuileries, no bridges sweeping the Seine, only windows that peered into other windows, interiors that could find no relief in sky or wind or the play of light on water, but only gave out endlessly into other interiors, worlds of vast, stacked, mirrored playing-cards reflecting each other . . .

A man was playing a guitar on the place Furstenberg — badly — twanging along to 'A hard rain's gonna fall!' The hard rain had fallen all right, or rather the soft bleak mushy grey rain of the seventies. Neither Anna nor I, I realised, standing there, had known what to do with ourselves when the euphoria of the sixties had ended. Others we knew had collected their 'wits' or what remained of them, rolled up their prayer mats and stashed away their yashmaks, and settled, without too much chagrin, for a life of ambition and pseudo-glamour — but we had not been able to. Not from virtue, and not from any continuing faith in the ideals of the sixties — but from a fear of being contained and conditioned that was also a fear of being committed to anything.

Anna and I were both still running, I saw, listening to that trite ancient song, still running, with no idea of where we might be going or what we might want. Sometimes we would congratulate each other that we were free. Free for what? We would pretend that we were less corrupt than the friends we knew. This was not too hard a game to play since everyone we had been brought up with, all the Oxford cronies and New York drug partners, all those encountered on the flower power and hippie trails, all the old inamorati (now getting their first wrinkles and children and paunches) were by any standards defeated, uncreative . . .

30

Yet were we really very different? Anna wrote her songs. Many were good, the bitter ones were very good; but the songs that kept her in Saint Laurent dresses, that kept the paint on her warping walls fresh, were the upbeat little numbers she despised herself for writing, the "I never thought I could feel this way" numbers that the men in New York adored, but which she called her Banana Boat Bangs. I, to finance my fantasies of integrity, wrote novels and travel books. Who bought them? The stay-at-homes whom we slanged, the solicitors dreaming they too could spend a summer with yogis in the Himalayas if they really wanted. Anna and I used to say we only worked to win one more space of 'freedom'. But it was they who paid for our extravagances, our upper-middle-class luxuries. We were their parasites, their kept fools.

'And a hard rain's gonna fall ...' Now the man's voice was rising, out of tune. If it had been a hard rain we would have been hardened, made clearer, but that too was a fantasy, Dylan's fantasy, our fantasy, that the apocalypse was coming when everyone would have to change and be transformed. There had been no transformation.

'Historical Weltschmerz,' Adolphe drawled. 'One of youth's luxuries. A little too enjoyably expressed to be quite genuine, but I get the picture. Our hero is in a bad state. Good. Lay on the greys and blacks.'

That first night, I undressed listlessly. Anna's sheets smelt of powder and old scent. Every time I sat up in bed I saw myself in the mirror Anna had placed opposite. My face disgusted me by its pallor, its theatrical hollows. I hardly recognised it; it looked misshapen in the moonlight, filled with a trouble I did not want to acknowledge. Once I shouted and sat up and started tearing my hair, hoping by that miming of my misery to be able to laugh at myself. All I saw as I did was a thirty-year-old trying to pull out his hair in the mirror, sitting up in a bed smelling of powder and Arpège. Not pulling too hard either, in case it did come off, not shouting too loud in case the shout really turned ...

Adolphe giggled. 'You'd never pull out your hair. You know it's one of your best features. Mind you, it could *fall* out.' Adolphe ran his fingers up and down his bald shining skull. 'I had hair like Jean Marais, and now look. Promise me you won't

31

do any more hair-pulling in life or fiction. It makes me angry just to think of it. Promise me you'll bury me in one of my furriest wigs. I want to have hair when I meet those butch blond archangels. No more misery, Charles. I need a stiff dose of Anna.'


'So what have you been doing?' Anna's smoky, inquisitive voice, at noon, three days later.

'As little as possible.'

'Oeufs au jambon once every two days at Lipp?'

'Yes.'

'Long walks by the river with the collar of your coat turned up like Jimmy Dean?'

'Yes. Do I hold no mysteries for you?'

'Have you seen anyone?'

'No one knows I'm here.'

'What's up with you?'

'I'm exhausted. Aix — we're in Aix now — is exhausting. Hans' sutras are exhausting. How much Nothingness can a woman stand? Hans' mother is especially exhausting. She rings him every night just when we are about to make love and they talk for hours on the phone.'

'Come back.'

'No. Six weeks I said and six weeks it will be. At school they always used to write on my report, "She's too flighty to finish anything." Ever since then I've finished everything. Hans isn't stupid, you know. Yesterday he said to his mother over the phone, "It isn't my spirit she is interested in." Stop laughing. He's not clever enough to pun . . . Dead right. I do not love his spirit. When did I last love a man's spirit? When did I last believe a man had a spirit? Why am I talking like this?'

'Because you're depressed, slightly drunk, and because your birthday is in a week.'

'Sweet of you to remember. Thirty-eight! Shelf-time! And how old are you? I keep forgetting.'

'You know perfectly well I'm thirty.'

'Oh, past it, darling.'

'In the Gay World you're past it at twenty-five. And I wasn't in it until I was past it.'

'Keep doing those neck exercises that old Indian dancer taught you and wear dark colours and you'll have a few years yet.'

'Thank you.'

'Thank Time. Dear, tender-hearted Time. You need a little false levity and that's why I've rung. Tomorrow night Adolphe is giving a party. He adores you. You need only stay for an hour . . .'

Adolphe gave his kiwi cry. 'Oh, I'm in it and I'm coming soon! I want to dance round and round, but I'd better not because of the hip operation.'

'You forget I've been to Adolphe's parties before. After one of them anyone with any intelligence wants to commit suicide.'

Adolphe chuckled. 'As long as you're accurate I don't care how cruel you are. Of course my parties are dreadful. I give them just to make certain I still know the worst people in the world.'

'You must go. You are a writer,' Anna said, drawling the word 'writer'. 'Remember that famous old fart you took me to dinner with once? Who lived in Streatham with three indistinguishable mistresses and bicycles in the living-room? Remember him saying "One must experience everything," and then falling flat on his face?'
    'Look where it got him. Twenty bad novels later . . . Life is like writing — it's what you leave out . . .'
    'Get out of the flat. Go to Adolphe's party. Even if it's bad it'll do you good. Find a nice heroin addict or something. You know Adolphe's bathroom . . .'

'My bathroom! That had Peggy Guggenheim burning her cobra-skin petticoat with chagrin!'

'The one with the circular gold tiles and pictures of Serge Lifer all over the ceiling?'
    'Yes. It's one of the only bathrooms,' Anna said, 'I have ever wanted to make love in. There seems to be a craze for making love in bathrooms. Princess Whatsit did it at Orly airport and then there was that scene in *Rich and Famous* . . . Why don't you go and do it for me?'

33

'I have not come to Paris to make love in the bathrooms of ancient queens under pictures of Serge Lifer.'

'Ah,' said Anna, 'The life of the lonely spirit must go on. On your own cross be it. The real reason I want you to go to the party is that I want to hear you on it. Won't you go for my sake? Just to bring a little corrupt amusement to your spiritual sister.'

'I will not.'

'You will. I know you too well.'

Anna paused.

'Charles?'

'What is it?'

'Look after yourself.'

'Look after yourself. I am not with the son of a medium who reads sutras in the bath. I am not thirty-eight next week. I have not had three too many Martinis already tonight.'

'Good,' Anna said. 'I thought you were getting so depressed you couldn't even be bitchy. Enjoy Adolphe's party.' She rang off.


Adolphe stood up, opening his arms wide.

'Do I come next? No pun intended.'

'You do.'

'I feel faint. I can't possibly take in all this brilliance and my appearance in one night. We must stop. It's three. And my face-lift's slipping. Let's go on tomorrow. Now I want to go and have a nice hot bath in that bathroom you were so rude about and listen to Caballé sing something soothing. She goes so well with bath-salts. Can you come tomorrow?'

'Well . . .'

'Don't play elusive. You're too old. Where's the look of tender gratitude that should be flitting across your features? Flit it briefly please . . . There, that's better. Europe has such satisfying rituals.'

Dazed from Adolphe, from exhibitionism, from exhaustion, from the memory of these tangled days I was writing about, from the several vodkas that I had been sipping while I was reading, I was about to walk out of Adolphe's palazzo still wearing his red dress.

'Darling,' he drawled, 'you look absolutely ravishing, it's true – but do you really want to be raped by a gendarme?'

34

·TWO·

was late. It was already nine-thirty. A friend working on Schiaparelli had rung up at seven and talked for two hours about her buttons. 'Elsa's genius was in her buttons. Not her scarves, not her boleros, but her buttons. Piano buttons, scarab buttons, insect buttons . . .'

Adolphe was famous for the splendour of his rages on set when anyone was late. I had never seen him angry, but I could imagine it: the blotched hands clenched, the face purpling, those eyes of his, usually so lidded with amusement, staring and flaming, the *coloratura* of his long periods turning into short, all too savagely connected phrases.

As I ran up the stairs, I heard the sound of singing. When I reached the white doors Adolphe flung them open. 'Hold on!'

The sound of Callas was so loud in the candlelit red room that I thought the walls would dissolve.

'What's she singing?'

'"Vissi d'arte, vissi d'amore." What else? I have lived for art, I have lived for love.'

I spread my arms and tilted my head back as I had seen Callas do in a film.

'Open the mouth more,' Adolphe said. 'She had a mouth like the Grand Canyon. Tilt the head back farther. Sometimes she flung her head back so far I thought it would roll off. If only you could sing, Charles. All your problems would be solved. Since opera is the greatest lie you wouldn't have to invent minor ones, and even your ego would be assuaged by all that applause. There's a little place in Casablanca . . .' Adolphe didn't finish his fantasy. '"Vissi d'arte,"' he began, '"vissi d'amore."' He stopped abruptly with a kind of gargling sound

37

as Callas ascended to one of her wild high notes. 'What a scream!' Adolphe clapped. 'La Scotto thinks she can scream but she can only yell. There's a world of difference ... You haven't said a word about how I look.'

He was dressed entirely in a white silk evening-gown.

'Elsa made it for me.'

'Schiaparelli?'

'Who else? The ugliest genius of the twentieth century – except for Charles Laughton – but what a genius!'

I told him of the American friend who had rung me earlier, whose dithyrambs about Schiaparelli had made me late.

'Everything is connected. Look at this gown. It's the exact copy of Elsa's classical masterpiece for Mrs Reginald Fellowes ... Who am I tonight?'

'God knows.'

'It is not every night that one hears oneself in a novel.' Adolphe paused dramatically.

'I have dressed as Iphigenia being led to the sacrifice.'

'Isn't that a little extreme? You're a hero in my novel – an impresario of survival.'

'You I suppose are the suffering-sacrificed. How predictable.'

'Wait and see.'

'You know, I don't even care that you are late. I was trying to whip up one of my rages but it just wouldn't come. I'm too thrilled. Choose a Buddha and go and stand by it – the candlelight isn't too flickery I hope ... I haven't appeared in a novel since I was in my thirties.' Adolphe started to spin round and round the sofa that he had covered tonight with a piece of 'bloodstained' Japanese white silk. 'And what an appearance it was. I played the lover – perpetually in bathing shorts – of an ageing film star. When not in bathing shorts I was lounging in silk pyjamas on sofas and reading Russian novels and drinking and being insulted. The ageing star was a woman. The novel was written by one of my houseboys (I use the word in the Malayan sense). It did me a lot of good. Convinced a lot of people who should have known better that I was heterosexual,

38

and protected me from blackmail. The ways of our Lord are strange.'

Adolphe sat down and folded the Japanese silk around him. His face changed and became hieratic. 'Now read to me.'

'The very next scene begins with you, you know.'

'All the best scenes should begin with me. Do I say something brilliant?'

'"I heard you were living with a woman," you say. "Wonders never cease."'

'Oh Charles, did I really say that?'

'You did.'

'I apologise. Oh, if we could only erase what we said! But Time will do that for us anyway, scrub everything out with its lavatory brush.'

'Do you want to hear about you or do you want to go on doing you?'

'Both, darling. Why should an old empress choose?'

I had arrived at Adolphe's party, drunk, and late.

'I heard you were living with a woman. Wonders never cease.'

Adolphe stood before me, swathed in black leather, with three purple scarves round his thick but scrawny neck. A young man with greasy blond hair done à la Rasta and a purple and green painted hairpin through his left ear was leaning against him, nibbling his right ear, making what sounded like imitation bird-noises.

'Pas ce soir, chou-chou. Go and find someone even more famous,' Adolphe said, giving him a squeeze with his black gloves that had gold fingernails painted on them. The young man pouted, did a last little bird-call, turned in the doorway hung with vine leaves and lit by Christmas lights in the shape of cucumbers to eye me coldly, stick out his tongue, and walk out.

'Wonders never cease,' Adolphe repeated.

'It wasn't that wonderful, as I am sure Anna told you.'

'Some of my best young friends have been ruined by women. Women don't have the resignation of us vieilles folles. They want

39

everything. No manners! You loved her, no doubt. I've heard it before. When am I going to convince you that you can't just go around loving people?'

'I said that, did I?' chuckled Adolphe. 'The truth will out.'

Adolphe paused, eyed me.
'You're looking peaky. How do I look?'
'Dazzling. Whom do you eat to keep that slim?'
'He's Arab. The only word he can say in French is out, but he says it in so many different ways. I light a candle for him in gratitude every Sunday in Notre-Dame.'
His row of flawless Manhattan-gold teeth glittered in the lamplight.

'Harley Street,' Adolphe whispered, 'but what is accuracy?'

'Come into the next room,' Adolphe took my arm, 'and cheer yourself up. There are members of Holy Mother Church disporting themselves in a fashion you have to see.'
One of Adolphe's chief remaining pleasures was organising the seduction of cardinals.
'I've seen them before. If they are the same ones that were here last time.'
'My, we are blasé. Doesn't human depravity interest you any more? When one's lost interest in that one's lost everything.'
Adolphe stroked my cheek. 'I'm going to amuse you. I'm going to dazzle you. At my age that is what a man has to do with the young. Not that I fancy you. My feeling for you is of an altogether different, more starry, order.'
'I'm so grateful.'
'You're not. Gratitude is not one of your charms, but that's all right. Tell me about this woman of yours. You're much too lugubrious tonight, to take any interest in anything but your own misery.'
Two men dressed as clowns came in and took off their shirts to reveal two tanned Opera-Bath torsos.
'Really,' said Adolphe, raising his voice, 'I do think you should remember what your dear mothers would say if they saw you. Go on about yourself, Charles.'

I was about to begin when Adolphe put a soft hand smelling of lavender soap across my mouth.

'No. I'll tell you. Madame L'Italienne — she was Italian, wasn't she? Anna wasn't making that up?'

I nodded.

'Madame L'Italienne, a woman of a certain age, told you after a month or two of trying to give you an erection, that you had no talent, that you would be fat and past it at thirty-five. Right? Don't answer. Just stare in astonishment. Were you baffled, shrewd, all-forgiving till one day you'd had enough of the taunts on various continents and said everything? You don't have to answer.'

'Who could?'

'Don't be cheeky,' I said, taking away his hand. What a scenario you've lived! Ageing Circe meets queer social-climbing Ulysses. Because she cannot keep him in her ruin she sees to it — how expertly — that she puts the first twist of real terror into his eyes.'

'You're slipping. I had wrinkles already. Terror too.'

'You're a writer,' Adolphe said mockingly, rolling the 'r'. 'Your profession is humiliation.'

'Those who want to be happy are always humiliated.'

'Did you write that? I hope not. All this talk of happiness, happiness,' Adolphe spread his hands in the air. 'At my age it just sounds silly, not moving, not even interesting. I was thirty-one — your age — when I gave up the idea of happiness. Just gave it up, one day, sipping a mango juice on location in Sri Lanka, overlooking the Bay of Colombo. Just gave it up, threw it away, heaving a great, great sigh of relief. I can't tell you how much better I've felt since. Expecting nothing is good for the complexion. Tomorrow I will take you to the Georges-Cinq for cocktails. And show you a gaggle of the richest women in the world. It's not just face-lifts and sperm of hippopotami that give them that perfect scrubbed look, you know. It is well-heeled, well-accepted despair. The desire for happiness is a harpy with fat hands and claws like razors.'

'You've been reading too much Baudelaire.'

'I never read these days. An ageing film director can't afford to read too much. Too depressing. One must keep up one's belief in make-believe.'

Two black men passed us holding hands. One had green hair and the other had red circles painted round his nipples.

'Adolphe, we love you,' they said, in high giggly voices. 'We love you and we love your lovely party.'

'I know,' said Adolphe, 'it's lovely to feel surrounded by so much love. Now go away and let me talk to this skeleton here. Dancers,' he turned to me, 'so sincere.'

'You'll never lose your belief in make-believe,' I said.

'One can lose everything. Corruption is a taste like any other and has to be cultivated and protected. What do you think of my party?'

We were now in the big red oblong room that was his living-room. Great winding sheets had been put over the Buddhas in the corners. The black marble tear — four foot tall — that adorns the centre of the room was arrayed with rows and rows of plastic phalluses.

'I've seen it before, Adolphe.'

'What you mean is, you hate it.'

'All right, I hate it.'

'Look, my lovely,' Adolphe said, stroking the tip of the black tear, 'I know these people are vulgar and hopeless. That is why I love them. They wear their greeds openly. Most of them, as you know, would fuck anything that moved for a film part, or a month of free meals at an expensive restaurant, or an introduction to some fifth-rate publisher's fifth-rate friend of a friend. So what? They are honest about it. They are not looking for happiness, like some dreary romantics I know; they are looking for what they imagine — poor fools! — is power. How much more nearly truthful that makes people.'

Adolphe paused and pointed to a youth on the other side of the room in a pyjama suit, leaning against a television actor with a toupee.

'After all, Charles, if anyone assumed that that little tart over there in the pyjamas — and I happen to know whom he stole them from — was anything more than a tart in purple pyjamas, it would be their fault, wouldn't it? He has a tight arse, green eyes that go with the suit, a line in flattering chat; he knows how to order a wine — I taught him, I should know — he knows where to get his clothes — when someone else is paying — There is nothing noble about him, but nothing too that demands or expects happiness — except the kind of happiness that comes from owning a big fast car or going to dinner with the sort of duchess who likes the criminal fringe, and which doesn't? In a way, he is a sort of master of life; he has simplified it. You should be jealous of him. You and Anna are both still spoiled romantics without a single truthful thought in your heads.'

'And you, Adolphe,' I said, rattled, 'are you a master of life?'

Adolphe smiled. 'Of course not. I was born sixty-seven years ago. I was reared on Rimbaud and Hugo. I had a possessive, frustrated mother who wanted me to be what she had never been — a great singer. What chance did I have of real cynicism? You may have noticed how bad my films are.'

'Many people have.'

'Not the dear old public, however, bless them. Shall I tell you why they are bad? Because I do not dislike my people enough. "Morality is hot but art is icy" — Henry James. Well, I'm not icy. I withdraw from the final thing, whatever it is, because I want my idiotic girl to get her idiotic man and settle down in some idiotic cottage. Everything I know tells me they haven't a chance. Have I ever had the courage to show that? I always have my characters forgive each other. I have more scenes of forgiveness than any other modern director. Forgiveness in trains, in the Boule Miche, once even in the lift going up the Eiffel Tower. One of my three cardinals said that I was the most Christian of film-makers. He was being rimmed by a black man at the time, so I took what he said with a pinch of salt. I need a drink.'

'So do I.'

Adolphe's voice softened. 'You know, I'm almost happy. I know I have never really been loved — how many people are? I have wasted what little talent I had — but that is not such a dreadful thing as you imagine — what else is talent for?'

'You frighten me.'

'I don't frighten you enough. Something in you will never be frightened enough, and that is not a compliment. And on that note . . .' Adolphe waved to the purple pyjama boy, who waved back. 'I must go and see that my cardinals are not being murdered. Even if they want to be.'


'Bravo,' said Adolphe, stroking the 'bloodstained' silk cover.

'Do I detect a certain colère?'

'Not at all. You've done what no one else has ever done. You've made me almost fall in love with me. I had no idea I was so wise . . . I did have an idea, actually, but it was hovering and ethereal. You've Rock Hudsoned it, given it flesh.'

'Don't be a bitch.'

'You're the bitch, stealing all my best lines. Is this to be my final role in life — playing Bodhisattva Jones, ladling out worldly wisdom to the hungry in great soup-spoons? It's a good part. One quibble though, and one question.'

'Go on.'

'Not until you've got into the red dress you wore yesterday.'

'No.'

'Yes.'

Adolphe ran out into the bedroom and brought back the red dress. I put it on gingerly, as he watched, rolling his eyes.

'The quibble first,' he said. 'You make me seem as if I care about my films. While it is true I ruined them by sentimentality, it is not true I cared. I never cared about my films. I've cared about people, not art.'

'And the question?'

He motioned me to sit by him on the sofa.

'The question is,' his eyes narrowed and sparkled, 'Do I frighten you?'

He smiled. I was silent.

'Silence? Is that a confession? Answer me.'

'I think you did frighten me. At the time I was writing about, you were a little ... appalling to me.'

'Appalling? With my suggestions of Roman decadence?'

'Yes.'

'With my bitter, many-faceted wisdom?'

'Sort of.'

'With my Zen-like changeable violence of mood and tone?'

We were laughing now.

'With my vanity that rivalled and out-smarted yours?'

'Do we have to go on?'

'And now? Do I frighten you now?'

'No,' I said. 'And it is not because you are at all familiar to me. In many ways you are stranger. But now I trust you.'

'Did I hear Charles aright? Did I hear the most suspicious man I know, using the word "trust"?'

'Yes. I trust you.'

'You trust me. So you are growing up, after all.'

'Don't be so smug.'

He held my hand and stroked it gently. 'Don't be so defensive!'

We sat for a moment in silence.

'Look,' said Adolphe suddenly, clearing his throat, 'why

didn't you describe the party more? What a party that was! One of my most seedy, and all we had were a few clowns and a nancy in purple pyjamas. Where is the Duchess of T being brought in like Heliogabalus in a wheelbarrow by five naked barrow-boys? Where is Cardinal R with his long green wig? And, the boys! What a bevy of brutes there were that night. Tonio with his razor-blade earrings, Arthur the English queen with those weirdly rotating eyeballs ... To have used me as a symbol of the Worldly Corruption your soul was trying to fly from and then to have missed the most gorgeously corrupt details which would have had them squirming with delight in Tulsa, tut tut! One can be too subtle for Tulsa, you know.'

'You know, I'm sure.'

'We'll let that pass. No, on second thoughts, it's quite depressing enough, your version of my party. By now we are all suffering for you, in you, through you.'

'Go fuck ...'

'No armed forces slang around here, thank you. Read on. Where are you?'

'I am alone. You have gone off to rescue the cardinals.'

'I must come back.'

'You do.'

'More wisdom?'

'Would you call it wisdom?'


I was leaning against the door. Adolphe returned.

'My dear, I could see you talking to yourself. Very poetic. Who was the audience?'

'Anna'.

'I love Anna. A pity she will never come to anything.'

'She has already come to something. She has made herself.'

'She has made herself,' Adolphe said, swaying slightly. 'Marvellous old Anna. That is what I mean. Anna will scare away everyone whom she wants because they'll see she cannot be tamed or perfected. What man wants a woman who is already herself? What well-upholstered hetero wants to be tested? And she doesn't have art.'

'She loves her work.'

'In a way. She doesn't believe in it. It's a stopgap for her, an

45

entr'acte between disasters.' He smiled at me. 'Of course, to believe in art is only another kind of disaster. Like the desire for happiness . . . Are you writing?'

'No.'

'You used to scribble away.'

'I've lost interest.'

'You want to live. That is what always happens to my writer friends. They spend months producing some unreadable novel and then they wake up to the fact that they haven't lived. I can see it written all over your face. You want to live. You have come to Babylon to find truth again, to be given back life.'

Adolphe started to giggle. The same blond boy who had been nibbling his ear and making bird-noises when I arrived now came and stood by him, so drunk he could hardly stand.

'What, little sparrow? Find no one famous to fuck tonight? Don't worry. We all fail sometimes. Go away now and play somewhere else.'

The blond boy stuck out his tongue again before shambling off.

'Such sweetness that boy has. Comes of living all your youth in provincial Borstals.' Adolphe put both his hands on my shoulder. 'I am often cynical about art around you, partly because you have such a fey nineteenth-century belief in it and partly because you might one day make it and I know I never have.'

'Yes you . . .'

'Don't flatter me. I don't need it. I know exactly what I have done and what I haven't. Let me give you some advice. Get back into your room at Anna's. Shut the door. Bolt it if necessary. There is nothing out there, nothing for you. You will find nothing in the streets of Paris but good food and syphilis.'

'What have you been reading?'

'Don't be smart. Listen. I'm telling you the truth and because I'm slightly drunk and because it is the truth it sounds hollow. Get back to your unimportant stuck-up art. Why live when you can write, why live when you can write away like a mad thing from morning to night, scribbling all over life's ugly face.'

I started to laugh. 'I never thought I'd hear you extolling the ascetic life.'

'Perhaps I understand and love you more than you understand and love yourself.'

'You've never been alone for a second. There's a bum-boy behind every Buddha.'

'Cheap, Charles. Look, have another big drink. Go into the dark-room to the right of the toilet and find some chunky Breton or a little Marseilles acrobat with green eyes. Do anything you want

46

to. Only don't stay too long. Go home. There is nothing for you in this world here. Go home. Have a coffee and read something sober and brilliant before you sleep.'

'Being alone is as bad as being here.'

'Well, no one would ever say you were nice,' Adolphe suddenly hugged me. 'You're ridiculous and you're still thin.'

'Thin? I've put on weight.'

'Darling, feel this.' He put my hands on his backside and wobbled it. 'Too much Toblerone. Not all the masseurs in Tangiers could get me into my old pants. The shape is over. From now on I'm going to eat as much as I like. No nose-jobs, no bottom-jobs, no chin-lifts. Nothing. I'm just going to crumble. Let the rouge run. I'm going to be myself, on several continents, like Shirley Maclaine.'

'And then?'

'And then? I'm going to die. That's what usually happens "then". Somewhere in Switzerland. Near a lake. It's very important to die by a nice view ... You know what you should do, Charles.'

'What?'

'Take a long holiday from all of us.'

'Suicide?'

'Too long. Why not Morocco?'

'You're always giving me advice.'

'There's something so helpless in you, I can't help it. It's like telling a child patiently, over and over, "Don't cross the road in traffic without looking to left and right or you'll get run over".'

'I've been run over.'

'So far, the ambulance has arrived in time. One day you'll just bleed to death in a side-street. Don't, for God's sake, choose a Paris side-street. Too cold in every sense of the word and at every time of the year. Now Morocco ...'

The blond boy had returned. This time he dragged Adolphe away like one of the stage-hands at the end of a modern production of *Don Giovanni*. Adolphe turned and looked at me, momentarily quite sober.

'"Sois sage, ma douleur ... et quittez ce pays funeste."'


Adolphe smiled. 'Aren't you mixing up your quotations at the end there?'

'You did.'

47

'And did I really exhort you to return to your room and try for Parnassus?'

'You did.'

'My Lord, you must have looked shaky. Quite impressive, my speech, though. Shows the seriousness underlying the comedy, and all that stuff. Tulsa will love it as much as I do.' Adolphe snorted. 'One thing . . .'

'A quibble?'

'A demand. Tristan must appear now. There has to be a sexy little illusion soon, Charles, or we'll all go white. Of course, I can't afford illusion at my age but you've got at least one more decade, if you do your exercises. I can't have illusion in my life but I can bloody well have it in literature and that is what I thought you were going to give me. After the wit, I want love! Out there on the page where I can savour it and leave it when I like for a sandwich or a snatch of Callas. I know what Garbo meant when she said, "I don't remember any of their names. All I remember is that they always said the same thing." But one can still press some joy from the farce, at a distance. You're not going to deny me a little wrinkle-room pleasure, are you? Where is Tristan? Can't you hear them in Tulsa on the football field, linking arms and shouting, "Where is . . .""

'There is no Tristan in this book.'

'But there is Love, isn't there? It isn't all bitter wisdom and boys with purple pyjamas? It isn't all me?'

I laughed. 'There is Love, dear Adolphe. Amor makes his appearance next.'

'Next? So there is going to be a plot in this novel after all? I'm so relieved. Love always brings a plot with it . . . But I can't take Amor this evening. Don't sulk. It is two. I don't think anyone could be expected to bear on one evening both their appearance in a novel and the Birth of Love. I'd have a seizure and the last time I did that I didn't enjoy it, although it did happen at dinner with the most boring people and livened things up a bit. At my age, I need to prepare for Love. I need to forget everything I've ever experienced about Love to try and hear the word again without giggling or throwing rotten

48

aubergines. And presumably in the next stretch I say almost nothing. Well then, I need time to compose myself. One should never be careless about one's disappearances.'

'But Adolphe . . .'

'We're on a train, darling. You can't get off now. Come tomorrow and we'll feast in honour of love. If you say no I'll never do my Callas imitation for you again. Be warned, and obey. Even for someone as self-preoccupied as you, there will be a certain piquant pleasure in reading a love story to a queen long past her reign.'

'I don't think . . .'

'Don't think. It wrinkles one. Anyway, I don't mind. The pleasure is piquant for me too, in a different way. Until tomorrow.'

Adolphe stood up and walked over to the gramophone. He put on Callas again.

'"Vissi d'arte . . ." The later recording. Note how much more desperate the voice is.' Adolphe turned the music down. 'Maria did live for Art and Love. Very grand. Look where it got her. One should live neither for Art nor for Love. One should live for life itself. Less grand, but kinder to oneself and others. Take that down. Of course it takes a lifetime to do that. Take that down too. Go now, before I dazzle myself into glossolalia.'

This time he went to the gramophone and put on a foxtrot.

# ·THREE·

I n fact I didn't see Adolphe the next evening. He rang in the morning maliciously early and said 'something too bizarre' had turned up: a Sicilian princess friend of his ('she keeps the title but there's nothing left') had been arrested – yet again – for smuggling drugs at Orly airport and needed him (him!) as a character witness. Could I bear to do without him that evening, and come the next, when he could have the red dress pressed and get hold of a rare recording of Maria singing 'Convien Partir' from *La Fille du Régiment*, and in every other way prepare himself for the 'passions ahead'? He realised what renunciation he was imposing on me, but it was good for me, in small doses.

So Anna and I spent the evening together at her flat. We emptied the contents of her tiny refrigerator on to chipped blue china plates, and ate them with some Monbazillac on the floor of her sitting-room. Anna turned off all the lights, lit the large spiral red and green candles in her bronze candlesticks, and we lay on the floor, as it dissolved into the shadows of a Parisian summer night, listening to the sounds from the street and talking.

'I'm so proud of myself,' Anna said.

'That's unusual. Keep up the good work.'

'I wrote three cheerful songs today without wanting to commit suicide. Corruption is becoming easier. And were they cheerful! "You make me feel wild, you make me feel a child." Absolute rubbish.'

We were silent.

'I've been writing about you and Hans,' I said. 'What did he look like?'

'He had the body of a lanky acrobat, and the eyes of a Siamese cat. Pale eyes that suddenly flared with cruelty or danger, just like a cat's ... Did my voice shake once as I said that? Did you see me reach for my Monbazillac with a trembling wrist? You did not. Progress. And you, what are you up to with Adolphe?'

'Anna ...'

'Don't be lazy. I want the whole thing.'

I acted out for Anna, as far as I could, everything that had happened on the first two evenings with Adolphe.

'Is the old leprechaun trying to seduce you?'

'No.'

'Are you sure?'

'Adolphe has never for one moment ...'

'You're very vehement. What does it matter whether he is or not?'

'It matters a lot. What is happening seems beyond all that.'

'You're sounding like an American girl. You must stop teaching in America. It's making you seven years old again.' Anna smiled. 'Don't worry, I do know what you mean. The old fox is parading himself, all his selves, for you. He realises what a perfect audience he has. You and your emotional gerontophilia. All anyone has to be is old and you imagine they are Lao Tse. Usually, of course, it's women. You and your galère of sibyls. Adolphe is a kind of ancient glittering woman, of course, a cross between Edna Everage and the last Manchu empress.'

'You're jealous.'

'Of course.'

'But you love him.'

'I introduced you to him, didn't I? With the idea of "marrying" you. Why, when I am so wise with other people's lives, am I so stupid with my own? Is there some law by which we can only help others by remaining helpless ourselves? Doesn't sound right, does it?' Then Anna began to laugh quietly, her laugh that begins right at the back of her throat and

54

slowly spirals forward through every sound of malice and amusement.

'Oh, Charles, there you are, reading to Adolphe the story of the most passionate love of your life . . .'

'We haven't got there yet.'

'There you will be, reading to him the story of your love . . .' Anna was laughing so much she had to stop. Then she said flatly,

'You are in love with him.'

'With whom? Whom am I in love with?'

'Adolphe . . .'

'Good God, Anna, what on earth . . .'

'I wish you could have heard the way you said that. It was like David Niven in one of those early Hollywood comedies. You have met your match in Adolphe. Someone cleverer, sharper, sadder, wiser, madder than yourself. Your alter ego, your true Mum-and-Dad in one.'

'Your attempts at psychoanalysis are always feeble, at best.'

'And at worst?'

I couldn't think of a satisfyingly sharp reply.

'Perhaps I've put it all badly,' Anna said, 'in my usual exaggerated way. There must be things in your and Adolphe's meeting that I know nothing about, but you'll find out what I've been groping to say, and when you do . . .'

'Any prophecies?' I asked acidly. (Anna is famous for her prophecies.)

'With you two, anything could happen.'

'Anna, you are . . .'

'Grow up, Charles. Pass me the rest of that wine. You don't deserve it.'

Someone began playing a cello in the place Furstenberg, a long slow winding melody I did not recognise.

'Do you know what that is?' Anna asked.

'No.'

'"D'amour l'ardente flamme."' She drained her glass triumphantly. '"The fiery flame of love" from Berlioz's *Damnation of Faust*.'

It was going to be difficult to read anything, I could see. Adolphe was dressed as a Franciscan monk, in a long brown robe. Instead of a cowl he was wearing a long Schiaparelli headscarf with green and red insects on it – beetles with beady eyes, several strands of ants. All the Buddhas had been covered with white cloth. The saffron sashes that usually swing from the chandelier had been taken down and the chandelier switched off. The room was unlit except for one dim lamp near the sofa.

'Did you miss me?'

'Of course.'

'What depths of emotion you can demonstrate when necessary. I don't suppose you are at all interested in what happened between me and the Sicilian princess yesterday in a variety of locales (and with the most divine policemen – it's only Paris and Rome for policemen, although New York has some heavenly Poles). I won't bore you with me. Let me just say I saved her from everything, especially herself.' He got up from the sofa, did three small hops, and then said solemnly, as if in Latin, rolling his consonants, 'Charles, before you read answer me this – is life a voyage at sea, a journey through mountain passes, a battle, or an opera?'

I groaned.

Adolphe went on, 'Well, of course, it's an opera.'

'Why?'

I was smiling.

'If you are going to smile, remember to clean your teeth.'

'Why is it an opera?'

'It just is. Why is Niagara Niagara? Life is an opera. God is the poet. The music is by Satan. God wrote a libretto when he was young and Satan stole it and ran off with it to hell. There he sat for ages composing music for it. He brought the opera back to God, who refused to listen to it. Eventually God got bored with Satan's pleas and gave permission for it to be performed outside the walls of heaven. Are you listening?'

'You fraud, you've stolen this from somewhere.'

'Yes. From Machado de Assis. And whom did he steal it from? Answer me that.'

'I don't know.'

'You don't know! So you don't know he didn't steal it? How do you know he didn't meet a little old lady with a mantilla and one remaining black tooth on the top of a mountain, who told it to him? Be grateful I steal from the best places. Only the unoriginal are obsessed with originality. So, as I was saying, God consented to have the opera performed outside the walls of heaven. In fact, he designed the earth as an ideal theatre for it. Satan begged God to come to rehearsals. God refused but did insist, however, on sharing the royalties. I'm not going to go on with this opera analogy much longer, Carlo mio – but you will note, please, that God's refusal even to attend rehearsals of the opera is one reason why the performance has abounded with incongruities, lapses, sudden departures from any known text.' Adolphe laughed and rubbed his hands. 'And that of course is why it is a grand opera. These hiatuses keep the opera from being predictable. They also ensure the right amount of farce. And God's libretto, though marvellous, is rather relentlessly sublime. Not much humour. That is Satan's contribution. How I love his bassoons and jazzy clarinets! Now for you. For one of your versions of the opera. Enter Love, singing.' Adolphe adjusted his headscarf. 'One's head must be properly covered when one talks – sings – about love. Sing to me! I don't mind if you miss a few notes in the middle register, but you must hit the top notes squarely. My eyes may be snaky but my ears still enjoy the top notes, the kind that set the candelabra rattling and have all the old Zsa-Zsas in the stalls reaching mistily for their binoculars.'

'Don't frighten me.'

'Don't play Little Red Riding Hood. I know you're made of tungsten. I used to stand in the wings with Maria. Before she went on she would cling to me – all eyes and scrabbly fingers – and say in a little-girl whisper, "I can't! I can't! I haven't got any voice left." Then her music would sound, and in less time than it took me to wipe her stage lipstick off my lapels, she was out there, arms wide, throat wobbling, Medea or Norma to the last staring eyeball. Sing! By the way, how did you look on The Night?'

'Don't remember.'

'If you don't remember make it up. Tulsa expects every writer to set the scene. That black shirt you have with the frayed cuffs, your bell-bottom black trousers with that silver Indian thing you used to wear round your neck that year — Wear them. Them and bright red socks. Red as the lips of Venus.'

'Adolphe . . .'

'No arguments. Go and stand over there by the potted geranium, and sing. I've poured out a vodka for you.'

'You think of everything.'

'The function of the old. Only they have time! Or no time. So there you are at my dreadful party, ungratefully not noticing the corrupt beauties I have assembled. Were you planning suicide, leaning against the door? No. You are the murderous, not the suicidal type. Which is why I feel close to you. "My life is over," you are singing, sotto voce. Your life, Charles, will only be over when you shut your mouth.'

'I haven't said a thing.'

'You've been chattering away inwardly. Don't think I haven't heard you. Adolphe leapt on to the sofa, tucking his legs neatly under him. 'Don't I do a good imitation of a gazelle?'

I was staring meaningfully into space.

'Don't worry, dear, I'm subsiding. No more athletics, I promise you.'


'I was leaning against the door. Adolphe had just left. I had closed my eyes . . .'


'A perfect moment for Satan to improvise. Hear that clarinet.'


'"What are you doing here?" a voice said.'

58

It was an English voice, low and serious and warm. I opened my eyes. At first I did not recognise him. The idea that he could be here, at this absurd party in Paris, in these days ...

'Look,' Adolphe interrupted, 'it's precisely at absurd parties ... Parties are one of Satan's favourite devices. To get the soprano and tenor together ...'

'Mark,' I almost shouted. 'Mark! What the hell are you doing here?' I grabbed his shoulders and shook him. He was smiling, baffled, saying nothing.

'Darling,' Adolphe laughed. 'Don't change a line. Why is it that when we meet Wonderboy we always speak like Rita Hayworth? Can it be the banality of the movies enshrines a great truth?'

Mark stood smiling, baffled, saying nothing. The same stocky, firm build, the same short tawny-blond hair, the same blue eyes with their passing glints of wildness.

'Stop,' said Adolphe. He was laughing. 'Oh, my darling here you are, standing in front of one of the sexiest men in the Western hemisphere – I would love to say that he had a mole the size of a testicle on his left cheek or that his buttocks were too Ugandan for perfection – but I can't. He was gorgeous. Here you are before him, preparing aria after aria, and you ...' Adolphe's laughter grew raucous, 'Don't you see what you are doing?'
'You'll tell me.'
'You are denying him. You are pretending to celebrate him while evading him. Bring out the stardust for him, boy, bring on the violins. Give Tulsa a hard-on.'
'Adolphe!'

'Of course I know that's not your kind of stuff. All very noble and psychological. But can't we have a little sweat under the armpits? Look. I'll help you. I'll ask you questions: what was it that you found particularly sexy about Mark?' Adolphe smacked his lips. 'I and Tulsa want each detail. Each minute, steamy, haunting detail. If they do not joggle my brain and nuts how will I follow you down the labyrinths of pain to follow?'

'How do you know what's going to follow?'

'Darling, be sensible. How many plots are there?'

'His mouth,' I said suddenly.

'Put it in. Put in the mouth. What was it like?'

'Full like the mouth of Michelangelo's Brutus – rather sensual and hurt. A luscious mouth. As much a woman's mouth as a man's. A mouth that could . . .'

'Get carried away! I'm not shockable.'

'A mouth that could kiss violently, that wanted sex, without admitting it. A debauched mouth, but dignified at the same time, restrained and wild. Mark used to keep it slightly open while he talked, like Brando in *Streetcar*.'

'Probably got it from there. Never underestimate the vanity of the male. And the teeth?'

'Small. Even. Brilliant.'

'Teeth are too much. I used to go wild over teeth and no one ever talks about them, do they? But they're so thrilling. Well, that's the mouth and teeth done. I am so excited I want to go and lie down in a quiet place.'

'His neck!' I said wildly.

'Once started there's no stopping you. I love necks. How I loved necks when I loved bodies. Springy necks on thin but muscled shoulders. I devoted one summer I remember just to those . . .'

'Mark's neck was rounded, lush; a neck that seemed to flow upwards fully and fiercely from the shoulders, that were not thin at all, but glowing and rounded.'

'A neck like a large golden swollen phallus,' said Adolphe.

'Is that decent? Is that even English?'

60

'Put it in,' Adolphe ordered. "Neck like a swollen golden phallus." That will sell three hundred copies in Tulsa alone. That's exactly what Mark's neck was like and why you couldn't take your hands off it. Now for the eyes, pondsnipe. Oh, the eyes I have looked into! The foxy ones, the foggy ones, the proud Roman Emperor ones, the ones like Giacometti's buttons for Elsa S, opaque with green dots ... To Mark's eyes. "Blue and piercing" will not do. If you could describe those eyes, Charles, the reader will understand everything. Mark's eyes now. No, don't you do them. I'll do them.'

'Look, Adolphe,' I said, 'Mark was not trade. He was beautiful, but what moved me in him ...'

'Leave the soul stuff for later,' Adolphe interrupted. 'Now we want the Body. If he had had the same soul in a different body, would so extended an opera have been composed?' He lay back on the sofa, putting his feet into the air. 'It had always been Mark's eyes,' he began, mimicking my 'poetic' voice, 'that moved me most. They were of a blue that shifted with every light and every emotion. Sometimes when I looked at them they were the transparent flying-fish blue of the Caribbean. Sometimes when they looked at me they were the thick opaque blue of Tibetan amulets ...'

'Cut.'

'We need purple, you prude. You were crazy about this man for years. Didn't you lie awake thinking of similes for his eyes? Or was it only my exquisite doomed generation that loved in that way? You may scrap the Bahamas and Tibet, but you have to say something electric.'

'His eyes were dark blue, piercing, electric.'

'No'.

'Yes.'

'We mustn't quarrel like Italians. We have the mouth and neck at least. Was he unshaven? I used to love them unshaven. Won't you make him unshaven, just for me? So I can imagine stroking the golden stubble, running my knuckles gently ...' Adolphe continued in a hushed voice, 'He was unshaven, which gave him a Dostoevskyan look, the kind of look that sets off rude health so well. Yes?'

'I'll think about it.'

'Ungrateful swine.'

I read on.


Mark had a frayed blue denim jacket on and a darker blue shirt underneath it, open to the waist. How often he had worn just those colours in the years I had known him! I wanted to reach out and button up his shirt. He is drunk, I thought. But there was nothing drunk in his steady look.

'What are you trying to do?' I said. 'Kill me with joy?'


'You fishwife,' Adolphe interrupted. 'That's vulgar even for you. I would have said something similar at your age. Survivor's cruelty. Vivent les survivistes.'


Still Mark said nothing. He stood there, staring at me, smiling . . .


'What sort of smile? Superior? Serene? Satanic? A mix of the lot?'

I ignored Adolphe. I repeated:


. . . staring at me, smiling.


'Sorry, Charles,' Adolphe said flatly. 'I insist on knowing what kind of smile it was. Surely the smile is still with you, hovering in front of you. After all, when Fate smiles one does not forget it. Think of what Henry James would have made of that smile. Fifteen pages without a full stop. The masters are never afraid, dear Charles, of lingering over one of Fate's masterpieces.'

'Adolphe . . .'

'I am from the era of slow long novels. The era when one wouldn't have dreamed of flying to Venice, but always took the long slow Oriental Express. That way the beauty is deeper ... Mark has several smiles. I saw some of them. You must have seen the whole repertoire. That kind of dashing, sexy, clever, confused man always had a whole quiver of smiles to charm others and protect himself. The English I'm-a-good-boy-underneath smile. The it-hurts-me-more-than-it-hurts-you smile. The Brutus smile, the smile they, in the last freezing circle of hell, have to go on smiling for ever, chomping away at each other as they do so. Good God, what sharky waters are we in? Keep it light. What was Mark's smile?'

Adolphe closed his eyes.

'It was a quiet smile,' I found myself saying. 'Not embarrassed or hostile. Not even very surprised. As if he half-expected to see me there. His smile seemed to say, "So here you are at last, I have wanted this for so long, and so here you are!"'

'Does he exist, this man? Give me his telephone number immediately!'

I realised that I was still grabbing his shoulders ... I took my hands away. We stood gawkily for a moment.

'Looking into each other's eyes silently at last?'

Looking into each other's eyes silently at last. We stood gawkily...

'Were you sweating?' Adolphe asked excitedly. 'Did you see the way he fingered the edges of his jacket edgily? I want everything.'

'You weren't there.'

'Not in this version. I have been in others. Satan's plots tend to be the same, you know. It's the variations that fascinate the connoisseur. You were the first to speak, I bet.'

63

I said, 'Hardly the scene for you, this, I'd have thought,' pointing to two leather-jacketed boys touching each other up slowly in the doorway opposite and making small slurping noises.

'That must have been René and Giorgio,' Adolphe cried. 'They do that at all my parties. It's the only thing they know how to do. I wish they'd learn mime, or something.'

'The last I heard of you,' I went on, 'you were living in some bijou village in Suffolk with an orchard swept by sea-breezes.'

'An orchard swept by sea-breezes!' Adolphe clapped. 'You can't be serious!'

'I am. I was. It was a phrase from one of his rare letters. He would remember his little attempt at poetry – at conveying to me his marital bliss.'

'I'm loving this part. How were you saying this? The would-be regal drawl? The head tilted back?'

'Naturally.' I read on.

'Yes,' I said, 'I thought you were working in some rural Eden and commuting to work for a publisher's. The sweet old bourgeois life. How is Kate?'

'Enter Kate, the suffering wife.'

'How is Kate?' I repeated, hoping to see him wince. 'I have so many questions to ask you,' I went on acidly. The two leather boys stopped twining in the doorway and came closer to stare at us lushly and tongue-kiss. 'So many questions. After all, it has been eight years.'

'Seven and a half,' Mark said.

'How precise you can be,' I said, 'when it suits you.'

My voice, even as I tried to make it harsh, sounded shaky and febrile. I was talking so as not to look at him. I felt weakened by his health, endangered by the light spilling on his neck, down his chest.

'Are you drunk?' Mark said. 'You look drunk.'


'I can hear his voice now,' Adolphe cried, 'that correct but rich voice. Don't look at me like that. I'll be quiet until the end of the scene, when you leave the party.'

'How do you know we will leave the party?'

'Of course you are going to leave the party together. I gave it, remember? You'll forget your own novel,' Adolphe said, wagging his finger, 'and then where will you be, lost in the world without your novel . . . Why are you smiling?'

'The next line I say is, "How do you come to know Adolphe?"'

'I was,' said Adolphe, 'getting restive for my next appearance.'


'How do you come to know Adolphe?'

Mark smiled. 'You were always good at interrogations.'

'And you were always good at smiling and wriggling out of them and saying, "Why must you know everything?" What else am I supposed to do? Stand here and gaze at you? I thought we might try and have a little conversation.'

'Why not? How do I come to be here? I was a publisher for a bit. Now I've become the next worst thing. A journalist. Freelance. It's not going too badly. The *Observer*, no less!' Mark lifted his right hand in the air and raised his eyes to the ceiling. 'The great *Observer* has sent me on probation to do a piece — two thousand words and not a comma more — on Adolphe. "Get as much elegant dirt as you can." What do you imagine they meant by elegant dirt?'

'Only the *Observer* knows what the *Observer* means.'

Mark cleared his throat, nervously. 'I met Adolphe for the first time yesterday. He invited me to the party. He put both his hands on my right knee, squeezed it, and said, "My dear, you are too straight for your own good. Come to my orgy. It'll bring out the colour in your cheeks."'

'He doesn't know you very well, does he?'

'Thank you.'

'Will you be going back soon?'

'Not a gracious question.'

'Old women are gracious. I am not yet an old woman.'

'I'm staying,' said Mark deliberately steadily. 'I'm staying for ten days.'

'A little wife-trouble perhaps? Needing to get away from the kids?'

'I'm staying for ten days to do the piece here and then maybe I will get an interview with Truffaut.'

'Truffaut? I hate Truffaut. French without tears, Adolphe says, and so not French at all. But I can imagine you liking Truffaut. The English do. All that evasive humour, and trickiness.'

The first Truffaut film I saw was with you. *Shoot the Pianist*. You loved it.'

'You remember everything. It's touching.'

Mark put his hand on my neck and lowered his head.

'Don't,' he said. 'It debases you.'

'Take your hand off my neck.'

'No.'

'You could have written,' I said. 'You could have phoned.'

He smiled. He had won.

'Written? Where to? Whoever knows where you are? Someone said you had gone to live in a monastery in India; someone else said you were in Venice. How can you blame anyone for not keeping in touch when you take such pains not to be anywhere long?'

'I move,' I said, 'so as not to have to face the disappointment of not being wanted anywhere.'

I had not meant to be so dully self-pitying.

'I did telephone, but you were always out or away.'

'Don't give me that. Don't spoil our ecstatic reunion by clichés. It's a big enough cliché already.'

'I could have written or phoned but Kate was jealous. She was jealous of everything you were to me; she even hid the books you sent.'

'I don't believe you. Kate likes me.'

'She likes you. But she is afraid of you and she is afraid of liking you.'

'I don't give a fuck for any of your dreary suburban reasons. I had forgotten you.' I said it as brutally as I could; what right had he to stand there with his open shirt and his hand on my neck, and so close I could smell his sweat? It was ridiculous, this scene. I wanted it over. The warm strong smell of his body hurt me.

'I don't believe you.' Something in his voice, something sad and warm, unsettled me.

'I had forgotten you,' I repeated. 'These days I live in a state of

66

amnesia. It is enjoyable. Or not wholly unenjoyable. Preferable to memory, on the whole. I recommend it.'

'You are bitter. It . . .'

'Doesn't suit me. Is that what you were going to say? When once I had such a glow in my eyes?'

'You put it well. Better than I could have done. It doesn't suit you, because it isn't you.'

'And you, I suppose, know exactly who I am.'

'Yes, I think I do.'

'Presumably that is why you neither rang nor wrote.'

Mark threw back his head and laughed.

'What the hell are you laughing at?'

'At us. At you. At this gaggle of freaks and cocaine addicts. At us meeting here of all places. We're going to have to leave, you know, and go and talk.'

'How masculine of you! How decisive!'

He brought his other hand to my shoulder.

'We're going now.'

'OK,' I said, 'but take your hands off me.'

'You don't like it?'

'If I didn't know you I'd like it.'

Two men stood in the doorway. They removed their jackets and shirts. They were both beautiful, muscled and tanned. I felt scrawny. They started to dance.

'Yes,' I said to Mark. 'Let's go. Why not?'

As we passed the dancers in the doorway, one of them put out a hand and tickled the back of my neck.


'Giorgio, I bet,' said Adolphe. 'He'd tickle anything.'

'Thanks.'

'I didn't mean it like that! Charles?'

'Yes?'

'I love you being vile. I'm not surprised. I always imagined that being loved by you would be like being loved by Anna Magnani on grappa.'

'You flatter me.'

'Not really. Think about it.'

'Mark is not frightened of me, if that's what you mean. He never was. That's the point.'

'I *had* got it. But of course he is frightened. He's just brave.

67

For now, he's brave. Besides, you're frightened. That's nice. Not that it makes you nicer. That's nice too. Back to the two amanti going out into the snow?'

'So you remember it was snowing that night?'

'How could I forget? By the time I got to bed when everyone had gone I leaned out of the window to get some fresh air and my wig froze.'

'You weren't wearing a wig.'

'At the end of the night I was. I had to wear something.'


Mark and I walked silently down Adolphe's spiral stairs into the square of Saint-Sulpice. The raw night air startled us both. A light snow had fallen on everything, transforming even the rows of cars into mythical creatures, waiting only for some secret signal to be startled into life.

Pointing to the towers of Saint-Sulpice, I said nervously, 'Adolphe knows all there is to be known about that monstrosity. He says it's like the ego — all sorts of unlikely styles flung together. He says that once a year if you stand under a certain window there is a long penis of light that lights up the Heliogabalus by Delacroix. It starts at the thighs.'

'I don't want to talk about Adolphe or Heliogabalus. Or the bloody ego. I want to talk with you. I'm here for ten days.'

I turned to face him. He stopped in the freezing starlit air, pulling his coat around his ears. He looked smaller down here, older, more fragile.

'What else have we ever done but talk? Talk by the fire, talk by the river. I've got a whole world of talkers to talk to. I've got Anna. I've got Adolphe who is a hell of a talker. I've got all my London and New York and Paris friends. I can talk my way around the world and not draw breath. You're here for ten days. How do you know that I am not doing something during those days? I could be going south in a Maserati with Alain Delon. I might be leaving tomorrow on the night train to Venice. You know what an exotic life I lead. You know how difficult it is to reach me, or phone me, or write to me. Now Brando is in Paris and so I must drop whatever it is I am doing and talk. So we will repeat in Paris what we did in Oxford. We will talk. But I was young then, Mark. I was prepared to take nothing and to ask for nothing and to expect nothing but talk. I've changed.'

Mark started clapping slowly. 'This time leave out Alain Delon

and the Maserati. I have it on the best authority that now he's
married again he's very straight.'

'How straight is very straight? I never know. You might be able
to help me.'

Mark whistled, and shook me by the shoulders.

'Don't be a bastard. You're good at it but it really doesn't suit
you.'

'You keep saying that. If you'd had such a vision of my real self,
why the silences? I am not going to be generous and humorous
with you. You've hurt me too much and I'm too angry.'

'Charles. Listen. You talk so much you don't listen. Look at me.
That is all I ask.'

'That's easy enough.'

I stared at him. 'I'm looking at you. What's supposed to happen?
I'm supposed to melt, am I, seeing this big blond baby out in the
snow, dressed like an extra for *Dr Zhivago*, remembering ...
Sorry, Mark, I'm amnesiac and I'm freezing.'

I turned and walked away. I was trembling. Mark came up
behind me and held me to him.

'I'm not going to let you go like this, without hearing me out. I
have hurt you and I have been a coward, but you can't dismiss me.
You can't just wipe me out, and go home. I want to understand
you. I need to. Why don't we meet in silence if you're so fed up
with talking?' He started to laugh. 'Silence by the fire, silence by
the river. What more can I do?'

'You could kneel in the snow. Without your coat.'

I disentangled myself from his arms.

'OK. Pax,' I said. 'You don't deserve it.'

I felt exhausted and leant against the back of a car.

'Yes, I do,' said Mark. 'I do deserve it. I've stood here and taken
your shit and not walked away. If I was the bastard you were taking
such pleasure in inventing, do you think I'd still be here?'

'You saw me before I saw you at Adolphe's. Why didn't you just
walk out of the party, and then we'd both have been spared this
scene?'

'I wanted to see how you were.'

I reached for some snow from the car's back window and pressed
it against my cheeks and eyelids.

'No. You wanted to stand there with your Kouros aftershave
and your shirt open, and watch me tremble, see that old doggy look
in my eyes. That doggy look has drained away. Sorry about that.
Look, Mark, if you wanted a return trip to Sodom — to revive a few
schoolboy memories, or convince yourself that you are still free —
go back up Adolphe's stairs and find a boy who'd be delighted to

delight you. For a fee, of course. A meal, say, in the good part of Lipp. Cheap at the price, I'd have thought. Nothing a rising journalist cannot afford. I never pay, myself. But I gather a lot of married men do. Keeps it all kosher, no nonsense.'

'Woooooa,' Adolphe said. 'One really can't treat Marrieds like that. They need careful, sweet handling if they are going to deliver. How vulgar of me! This was a Great Love. And you were having far too good a time being brutal to care whether he delivered or not.'

When I had finished Mark said nothing. He skimmed the top of the snow on the car with the flat of his hand. Then, he said, calmly, 'Did you listen to yourself?'

'You don't get those rising periods without listening to yourself.'

'Did you hear how you sounded?'

'You can assume my effects are calculated.'

'Look, Charles,' Mark's voice was tired and slow. 'I'm not going to fight you. I'm not going to try and match you. I would lose. I'm not as witty or sharp as you. I don't want any power over you. I don't want to see you tremble. But I won't let you say it was only you who suffered, only you who chose a truthful life. Not just because it is not true — you know it isn't — but because I remember you so much finer than that, so much more generous.' He stopped and rubbed his eyes. 'Don't hide in bitterness. It's too easy.'

Mark held out his right hand. I looked at it, its big open palm streaked with snow.

'It was a good speech.' I took his hand.

'I meant every word.'

Mark came and leant his head on my shoulder, for a moment.

'You hurt me,' he said. 'You meant to and you did.'

'If I mean to hurt I usually do. It's a gift I have. I'm glad I hurt you.'

'You don't mean that.'

'Not entirely. Seeing you was a shock. It is a bad time. I'm hopeless to everyone these days. Myself especially.'

I noticed for the first time that Mark had not done up his shirt.

'Do it up,' I said. 'We'll be arrested. You'll die of cold.' I did it up for him. 'We can meet tomorrow if you like.'

'Why not?'

Suddenly, we were laughing.

'It is so good to see you I can't . . .'
'Don't,' I said.

'Oh my God,' said Adolphe, standing up and swishing his Franciscan robe about him. 'Was he really as nice as that? I thought he was nice. But that nice?'

'That nice.'

'So sincere? Not the slightest bit wormy?'

'Not the slightest bit wormy.'

'You don't have a prayer. Those eyes, those shoulders, that half-goodness.'

'I didn't have a prayer.'

'It's dreadful when they are beautiful *and* good. One has no defence.'

'One has thousands of defences. Always.'

'You sound sad.'

'Reading it all over makes me sad. Mark was brave that night.'

'I am brave with you every night.'

'Yes.'

'But then I don't look like Brando. Ah well, I have my own charms. Count your blessings, before I count them for you.'

I had forgotten to close one of the windows in Anna's sitting-room and when I returned I found that the wind had blown snow along the sofa, in tiny surreal patterns. The window creaked and flapped on its unoiled hinges. I couldn't sleep. I drank two brandies and listened to a tape Anna had insisted I hear. 'The real thing', she'd said. It was by a blonde singer whose name I've forgotten. On the cover, I remember, the woman sprawled on a pile of dirty clothes, all bright vulgar colours, puces and budgerigar-yellow.

> If I told you tonight
> That I loved you
> Would you say all the lies
> I need to hear . . .

Enough of that. As I stood up to take the tape off, I knocked the bottle of brandy off the table. Across the rue Furstenberg, an old woman drew her curtains, looking out at the grey of the early dawn. She caught me looking at her and stared back, expressionlessly.

'Well, this *is* something.' Anna on the phone, at noon.

'Trust Anna,' said Adolphe. 'Always there when the blood's flowing.'

I told her about Adolphe's party. Then I mentioned Mark.

'I don't want to talk about it,' I said shaky from too little sleep and a hangover. 'I want to hear about Hans.'

'I'm not going to let you off that lightly.' Anna's voice was crackly, conspiratorial. 'Is he the Married you used to go on about? Such lyrical raptures you used to indulge in. Your voice would acquire a kind of shake and you'd lean forward and say without a trace of irony, "Our love was pure, you know." That's after telling me for an hour how beautiful Married was, like a mix between a Breughel peasant and a . . .'

'Anna, please.'

'Fall down on your knees and bless that woman.'

Anna laughed. 'I'm just paying you back for hours of envy. You made him sound so mouth-watering. And I was struggling with that Italian princeling at the time. Remember the one, with the paunch and the one wall eye, who kept promising me palazzi, palazzi? And all we got was paparazzi. Not quite the same thing. How did you meet Married first? For the second I've forgotten. Was he the one in the storm at sea, when you stood like Norsemen on the poop, while everyone else was sensibly puking in the restaurant?'

'Mark and I met in a library,' I said with dignity.

'Now I remember. You stared at each other for months over Webster and Tourneur. From *The White Devil* to *The Duchess of Malfi* back and forth, back and forth. In that terrible Upper Reading Room in the Bodleian. First there and then at Adolphe's party. One freak-show to another. You do choose the strangest places to meet. Is life trying to tell you something?'

'You're jealous.'

'Jealous! Cooped up in this cheap hotel for a rainy weekend with an increasingly impotent Buddhist? Jealous? Married came over

72

and sat next to you, clearing his throat and stroking his blue-jeaned thighs and you saw the address on his file and then you wrote to him. What did you write, by the way?' Anna was laughing so hard she started to cough.

'I hope you choke!' I said. 'I wrote a calm note: "We know each other by sight and I would like to meet you." Manly. He wrote back, "I don't quite know who you are but I'd be delighted to meet you." '

'The perfect male note. Cool, killing . . .'

'We met. I wore my reddest red shirt. We talked for hours in a little coffee-shop in Turl Street, in the back, in the half-dark.'

'I bet you talked about the Shakespeare sonnets. Englishmen of a certain genre when they are picking each other up always talk about the Shakespeare sonnets.'

'How would you know?'

'You told me.'

'No, we talked about George Herbert.'

'That old prune. "Love bade me welcome but my soul drew back . . ." I should think it did; very sensible of it.'

'Mark loves Herbert and so do I.' My voice sounded ridiculous, and I started to laugh.

'You used to meet at the coffee-shop regularly,' Anna went on. 'Then, one day, he told you he was married. You were very George Herbert about it all, took it squarely on the chin. Because, although married, he was interested. He was at the gazing-into-the-eyes stage, which as every would-be adulterer knows, is agreeable. You let him gaze. You felt as if your body were singing. You actually said that. God, the things you've allowed yourself to say to me! You talked about everything – Death, George Herbert, Plato, homosexuality, George Herbert . . . And one fine winter morning he leant forward and said, "I think when two men love each other (I hope he said 'men' and not 'chaps') they should express it completely," and you felt fiery all over. You were wearing your blue sweater with holes in it.'

'Please.'

Anna had no intention of stopping. 'You wrote poems. Most of them incomprehensible. It was a High Love, you see, Achilles and Patroclus, and one day towards the end you saw how much he loved you. He was standing in a doorway in his house . . . And you stood with him in the doorway, two Greeks together, gazing into each other's souls.'

'Did I tell you that too?'

'In virtually those words, I'm sorry to say. One thing I bet you don't remember.'

'You'll remind me.'

'I saw him once. You took me to see him in the library. I was visiting from London. You leaped up and down and said, "You have to see him." And we went up into that grim library room and you pointed him out to me from behind one of those shelf-ladders. Do you remember what I said? "He looks just like the others." More beautiful, but in the same mould. Same build, same profile. He was, I saw, the composite Perfect Man you'd been looking for. All the others had been plastic models for him. You were furious. You said that I was trying to destroy your life. It was one of our best quarrels.'

'And were you?'

'I was trying to preserve it. He was so much what you had always wanted. In fairy stories, as I'm sure you know, it's when you get what you want that the real trouble starts.'

'Thanks for that thought. But why should it always end in disaster?'

'Because the dream is mad. Because life does not allow too much happiness. I'm sounding like one of your early poems. Because Dreamboy does not exist and the penalty you pay for making love to ghosts is death of one kind or another.'

'I'm going to be sensible. A few drinks, a meal, a sober chat or two. And that's that.'

'Rubbish.'

'And what are *you* going to do?' I asked.

'I'm going to take Hans to Venice, as I said. If that doesn't kill his sutra business, nothing can. Venice is my last card, my last hope that he will choose the things of this world, which include me . . . I'll ring you when I get back to France. Even I can't afford to ring international.'

'No final words of wisdom?'

'Take the vitamins I bought for you. They're on the top of the fridge. I'll ring in a week.'


I stopped.

Adolphe looked at me. 'What's up?'

'I've suddenly remembered something Anna said that I didn't put in.'

'Something naughty?'

I paused. 'She said, "Mark looks exactly like your older brother."'

'A little harmless substitute incest. Put it in.'

I thought for a long moment and then said, 'When I was seven, my older brother molested me.'

Adolphe paused, briefly. 'Anna knew?'

'Yes.'

'Wicked little stirrer. And does Mark?'

'Yes.'

'Well, then, shove it in. Let the whole truth be known. "The truth shall set you free." Besides, the search for the perfect brother is one of the main themes of homosexual love-literature,' Adolphe was saying in his German-professor voice. "And if the lost, infinitely-to-be-longed-for brother was, in reality, a molester. Well! That *is* interesting. It sickens the plot deliciously. What happened?" If you tell me yours I'll tell you mine.'

'A molesting story?'

'Darling, nearly everyone has their molesting stories. It's one of the things you discover as you grow older, and memories become less moralistically opaque. Perhaps we'll create a new genre and it'll take Paris by storm. Pardon the frivolity. Some things must be serious, though I can't at the moment think what?'

I looked at Adolphe; he was smiling gleefully.

'Nothing much happened. I was seven. He was sixteen, very beautiful and warm. I remember him being warm. I remember not having much idea about what was going on, except that it was forbidden and pleasurable. He was everything I wasn't. I felt scrawny, elongated somehow. I was elongated as a child – all hands and funny faces. He was broad-shouldered, athletic, blond, while I had brown hair that everyone called rat's fur.'

'Rat's fur! I'm going to call you it from now on.'

'Don't you dare.'

'Rat's fur! Rat's fur!'

'Do you want the dirt or don't you?'

'Of course I want it.'

'The sexual part was not disturbing. What came afterwards was what I remember. He insisted when it was over that he scrub me all over in the shower. He scrubbed me so hard that he made me cry. Then he hit me hard about the mouth.'

I was trying to tell the whole thing insouciantly, but the memory winded me. 'And so I suppose I was condemned for a long time to try and find him again, the beautiful brother, both fascinated and terrified that he would turn out to be brutal, so afraid of his own feelings that he would have to humiliate mine.'

'God, how dreary these childhood patterns are! If God exists, why did he make children so helpless? Was Anna right about the brother and you and Mark?'

'Only partly.'

'In what sense?'

'First tell me your story. Keep the bargain.'

'My story's over in a flash. Sorry. It was my father who did it, your honour.'

'Your father?'

'Don't sound so surprised. Happens all the time in Sicily and Upper New York State. It went on for years. Started in the bath when I was about six and went on until I had to try and fight him off in my adolescence. He used to get drunk and follow me round the house, wheedling and begging, in his woollen plus-fours.' Adolphe laughed. 'It was those plus-fours that saved me, probably. They were really droopy – the kind you see only in the basement of costume museums. They saved me by making him seem ridiculous. If he had worn his banker's suit, or his father's Prussian military uniform, I might be dead.' He turned to me. 'I often bless the old pervert, you know.'

'Bless him?'

'What does Nietzsche say? The things that don't actually kill us can sometimes make us stronger. He doesn't say "can", of course. Nietzsche doesn't quibble like that. If I hadn't been idolised by my mother – which ruined me in a different, perhaps more damaging way – I mightn't have been able to be amused at this world-famous banker with thousands of lives in his well-manicured hands chasing his son around, in plus-

76

fours. Every time I have seen a banker since, or a politician, or any homme d'affaires, or any so-called "distinguished" man at all, then I think two things: what would you look like in plus-fours? And when did you last molest your daughter or son or both? A slightly extreme position, you may say, but liberating from respect for this world. And to lose respect for the things of this world, dear Charles, is a good stepping-stone for the next. It taught me one other thing that I don't regret learning, although I wish I had learnt it in a more conventional way.' Adolphe paused to take off his scarf and run it through his hands. 'I learnt one could rely on almost no one. You can love people – yes, that is allowed – but should ask nothing from them. They are very fragile hysterical things, lost and bewildered themselves and unable to do much more, most of them, than spread their fear and confusion. And they are – whether they know it or not – nearly all liars. My father when sober believed himself to be a pillar of the community, a beacon of liberal ideas, a loving husband, and all the rest of it. God knows what he thought of his plus-fours activities in his heart. I rather suspect he didn't think about them. Just as one afternoon he could decide on a move that would bankrupt some pathetic tin-pot South American republic and in the evening weep at *Fidelio*, so at night he could chase me round in plus-fours and next morning go to early Mass. A monster? Not really. I don't know what the word "monster" means. Or if my father was a monster, we are surrounded by them.'

Adolphe suddenly, although he was smiling, seemed very fragile. I hugged him.

'Thank you for sharing that.'

'Don't be so American. We should share everything with the few people we do trust. That way, before it is too late, we will understand something.'

'And help each other. Is that too "American" as well?'

'Yes. I don't think I am helping you. I'm just being myself with you. That's the most I can manage. I would hate myself if I thought I was helping you. It would mean there was some kind of barrier between us. Tell me, now, why you think Anna was half-wrong about you and Mark.'

I got up and walked around the room.

'Ask the Buddhas for help,' Adolphe called out to me. 'That's what they're there for.'

'Anna was right in so far as most of the men I loved and Mark himself looked like my brother. Anna was also right that the relationships I had had were mostly brutish and short. She was wrong in that she did not know how largely free of cruelty Mark was.'

'He had not written or rung.'

'That was cowardice but it wasn't an active desire to make me suffer. He was afraid of what we had been. I see that. And there is something else I saw even then.'

'That he was, with all his imperfections and fears, the Good Brother who wanted to see you and find you?'

'Yes.'

'That of course makes everything much more painful and complicated. What was it that Anna said about fairy stories, about the worst happening when the best arrives?'

'That's not quite true either.'

'Why?'

'Wait until tomorrow, or the day after that.'

'You're tormenting me.'

'Just playing your own game back at you.'

'You learn fast.'

'You teach well.'

'I nearly forgot,' Adolphe said, 'I got hold of that record of Maria singing "Convien Partir" from *La Fille du Régiment*. Could you stand it?'

'No.'

But he had run to the gramophone and put it on already. Over the billowing waves of Callas I shouted, 'Tomorrow? Same time?'

'At last,' he shouted back.

'At last what?'

'*You* are asking *me*. We're getting somewhere!'

I saluted Adolphe. In his Schiaparelli cowl and swaying

Franciscan gown, he saluted back. As I was leaving, Adolphe switched out all the lights. I turned back to see him taking the white cloth off the Buddha from Burma and throwing it around his shoulders like a fur.

·FOUR·

The day after my third meeting with Adolphe, I met Anna for lunch at Le Bilboquet. She had woken up early, stumbled over me stretched out on her drawing-room floor, flung down three cups of instant coffee, and announced that she was off to wander Paris in the summer sunshine to finish off two new songs.

She wandered into the restaurant late, haggard but exuberant.

'Isn't Le Bilboquet heaven? I love all these dreadful imitation Gauguins, and that one over there – Princess Grace ascending into the arms of Christ – must be the worst painting in the world. Thank God for kitsch! There are days when that painting saves my life, it makes me laugh so much.'

'How are the new songs?'

'They're black, they're terrible, they're mine, and I don't care if Michael Jackson won't sing them – I'll sing them.'

'You can't sing.'

'I can hear Michael's little baby voice, "Oh but Anna, these are too saaad." Bet your bottom million dollars they are. They're so sad I feel like getting up on this table and doing the cancan. Sad is right! Sad is true! Order something cheap for both of us. I'm going to pretend on Expenses that you're a visiting Brazilian night-club owner, but just in case . . .'

I knew perfectly well we were having lunch to talk over the previous night with Adolphe, so I told her everything I could remember.

'The plus-fours story. I love it. I hope it's true.'

'Of course it's true.'

'You are so besotted with Adolphe you believe everything

that comes out of his mouth. Doesn't it occur to you that he has a rather low truth level, as they say in Minnesota?'

Anna was smiling.

'Out with it, Anna, you're cooking up something.'

She opened her black leather handbag and pulled out a biography of Tennessee Williams from it, flourishing it in the air as if she were a lawyer producing evidence at a trial.

'Read what it says here.' She put on her glasses and a Southern drawl. 'I'll read it: "I was having at the time exciting conversations with Adolphe about the possibility of turning my latest play into a film. He was enthusiastic about everything, and I was taken in until I realised that he was playing with me. A mutual friend told me that he considered me a pathetic has-been and was only being 'kind' to me for old times' sake," et cetera.'

'So?' I said.

'So? Adolphe is a wicked old queen. He may be living in a sort of mystic daze at the moment but he's been around.'

'Perhaps that's why he's in a mystic daze.'

'How do you think he became so famous? By being the Buddha? Come off it.'

'By the usual mix of talent, toughness and opportunism.'

'Oh how worldly you sound.'

'Look, Adolphe is old. He has undoubtedly been ruthless in his time, like almost anyone else. Probably more than most ... But there is something amazing about him now.'

'Oh well,' sighed Anne, 'you're hooked. It's to the end of the play, come what may, I can see that '

'You don't think it's going to have a bad ending?'

'How do I know? I'm just a no-good near-forty-year-old trying to write bad songs and failing. Eat your Grande Jatte, there's a good boy. And now could we please turn to me? I saw the divinest young man in the park, just like the young Nureyev ...'

After lunch Anna went home to work and I walked alone to the garden of the Palais Royal. It was a high, clear, cloudless afternoon. In that light, the full summer light of Paris, in which each thing, each person, is wirily, buoyantly solid, everything delighted me – the two dark skinny boys playing tennis in the colonnaded forecourt, their red shirts flashing like tropical birds against the ochre of the pillars; the old Spanish-looking woman with the moustache and turquoise bandanna, snoring under a tree while sparrows frisked around her. Behind the fans of the fountains lucidly, endlessly opening against the whitish blue of the sky, I could see the fountains of my childhood in Delhi, as if through a gauze of slightly less transparent light which at any moment could be drawn back. Lutyens designed them for the approaches to the Viceroy's palace; every evening I had seen them lit up red and green. Along with the peacocks that danced in the park behind our house, I thought them the most exotic things in the world.

These thoughts led me to Adolphe. I longed for him to be there so I could share each detail with him and enjoy him gesturing and laughing beside the fountains. Anna's warnings about him seemed comic in this light, warnings from another life altogether from the one he and I seemed to move in so simply. I thought of the photograph I had seen in my dream a fortnight before: myself as a clown being led by this fat man with Adolphe's face, dressed half as a maharaja, half as a brahmin; what struck me now was the strength of the fat man's arms, the solidity of the way he enfolded my hands in his.

I did not, I realised, feel afraid of Adolphe. As a child, the peacocks in the park behind the house had never seemed afraid of me; I had wandered peacefully amongst them and they had danced for me, willing to open the full fan of their splendour. Was that the role Adolphe saw me in – the child whose love allowed him the liberty to dance without shame in all his colours? Just as I had always remembered the dance of those peacocks and tried to bring its sumptuousness into everything I wrote and did, so now, witnessing Adolphe's dance . . .

My thoughts stopped there, as if on the edge of laughter. Really, I thought, I have no idea what is happening. I would have to abandon myself to the game Adolphe was playing with me or be left with nothing but a handful of useless phrases and half-intelligent guesses. Abandon myself? For a moment I panicked that I would not be able to. Then I thought, Adolphe will help me, he will make it easier for me than I have any right for it to be.

I turned to walk home. It was then that I saw, two benches behind me, the old man with the pigeons. He was long and thin and mischievous-eyed, like an old tinker, with a comic-opera prop of a nose, bright-red like Adolphe's shrine-room, and hooked like the Edwardian door knobs of my childhood. He was smiling and sitting completely still in his worn-out floppy three-piece black suit. His thin hands rested, palm-open, on his knees. All over him, pigeons were clambering, dozens of them, in milling clusters, their beaks dipping frenziedly, their wings partly outstretched. He had, I saw, scattered bread-crumbs all over his body, made himself one long impromptu dining-table. He caught me staring at him, and winked. He has only to give the signal, I thought, and his birds will ascend with him into heaven.

'Little red-toed monkey,' began the note that Adolphe had pinned to the white door, 'when the door opens you will not see me. If you want me, you have to clap three times.'

The doors flung open. I clapped three times. From the back of the room I heard Adolphe's voice.

'My gowns were gorgeous. I wore hardly any make-up. I needed no lights. No introduction. Just a spot. A spot would come on . . .' Adolphe rose from behind the sofa in a long white late-forties dress with a fox-fur stole, a five-stringed necklace of pearls, two large pearl earrings in the shape of shells, and a blonde wig.

'Who am I tonight?' He began to sing:

Though he's as mean as can be
And never buys me no whisky
He's the kind of man
Who needs the kind of woman like me.

'Too easy. Gay Dawn from *Key Largo*. The bar-room scene, when she sings so badly for Rocco the Mafioso he refuses to give her a drink.'

'Miss Gay Dawn, sir, at your service. It's almost the best name in films. I'd kick and claw to get the part in a re-make. Yes, tonight, I am Gay Dawn. I wanted to be something appropriate for the reading of the Meeting and the Memories. Or will it be the Memories and then the Meeting? I want to be the Gay Dawn of Love, and gay at the dawn of gay love. These pathetic puns are my tribute to Eros, wrecker of grammar and friendships, in whose hot breath the world sizzles.'

'Are you drunk?'

'I gave up drink two years ago, the same year I gave up all working-class boys who did not come from Third World countries.'

Adolphe stood with his hands on his hips. 'What happens in a hurricane?' he asked.

'The wind blows so hard the ocean gets up on its hind legs and walks across the land.'

'I should have guessed you'd remember the jokes about destruction ... You're going to wear that red tonight if I have to hire some Yugoslavs to force you into it.'

'Do I have to?'

He threw me the red dress that was lying across the sofa. 'Bow to the Buddhas in the four corners, hummingbird, before you change selves. One must ask their permission. Our changes must be good, or else we are changed in ways we do not understand to things we do not want. All this wisdom is giving me migraine.' He put his head in his hands, and then walked over to me, taking me to him by the red collar of the dress. His voice changed, became menacing. 'It's my turn now to play at Memory. You're not the only one with Memories, kid.' He threw up his hands and ran into his bedroom, returning a second later with a crumpled green and red striped football jersey.

He circled me several times, muttering and whooping like an Apache in an early cowboy film, then went back to the middle of the room and, winding the football jersey round his middle, began to sing, brokenly this time:

Though he's as mean as can be
He's the kind of man
Who needs the kind of woman like me.

His voice rose. He broke on the high notes, biting at them with what seemed a savage bitterness. I had never seen Adolphe in such a state. Suddenly, he broke off. I heard the sound of stifled sobs.

'Do you know whose jersey this was? Do you care? Do you know who once ran in the Bois de Boulogne with this jersey outlined by the wind against his perfect body? Do you know why I have kept this jersey thirty-two years five months and fourteen days? Do you know why sometimes in the middle of the night I stagger up from my cauchemars and run to the drawer where . . .'

I was frozen. I had no idea what was going on. I walked towards Adolphe and for a moment, as he lifted his head, I thought he was going to run towards me and embrace me in tears.

Then he screamed with laughter. 'Oh Charles! You idiot!'

Adolphe fell to the floor, and rolled over and over clutching his sides. He gasped, as I stood hovering and dazed above him, 'This is more fun than I can bear. I will have a heart attack. My hair might even grow again.'

He stumbled to his feet and tottered towards me, tearing off his blonde wig. 'Charles, will you ever forgive me? Listening to you yesterday, I made up a plan. I was going to bring out this football jersey and invent some story about it to make you cry. I was going to tell you how it belonged to the love of my life, how he had been shot down in Normandy in the last days of the war, how I kept it all these years. Actually, I bought the jersey last week for a godson. Your face, darling!'

'What's wrong with my face?'

'It's showing coarse amazement. Never show coarse amazement in Paris again, or you'll be invited nowhere.' He started to
chuckle. 'I came across an old letter the other day. It was
tear-stained (or perhaps it had been left out in the rain). It said,
among other nothings, "I will always love you." I hadn't the
slightest idea whom it was from. I read it again and again. Even
the style didn't seem familiar. Then I remembered. It was from
Pierre. He was the love of my thirties, or so I seem to
remember. I suffered five years for him, got him, lived with
him for five years and then he died in a car accident. The whole
epic in one sentence. And now I have forgotten his hand-
writing.' Adolphe laughed. 'How furious Pierre would have
been. He was such a child. Or am I thinking of Bertrand?
Don't look so shocked. One gets them wildly mixed up, you
know. Their aftershaves, their socks, their letters, their little
bed-noises. Sometimes I think they all were just one actor –
like Alec Guinness in *Kind Hearts and Coronets* – with a varied
wardrobe of clothes and a gift for accents. Proust says that the
saddest thing is we forget even the saddest things. What
nonsense. How marvellous that we forget it all. Memory is very
overrated. I've never felt freer from it. From all the names and
situations, all the décors. You've seen what happens to old
films? How they wear thin, how in scene after scene the sound
trails off, how streaks of washed-out white appear, obliterating
the hands, faces, shoes, chairs. You've seen how the film itself,
as it plays, reveals holes and scrappy edges, seems suddenly
transparent. That's how I feel. Is this happiness, or heartless-
ness? I'm not sure, and I'm not sure I care. Tell me about you.'

'About me? My décors and situations?'

'Don't be petulant. Just because I'm wise doesn't mean all
my friends have to be. One can't afford to be too wise too
young. It wrecks one's chances of a career. Take what you
need, swivel-hips, and postpone nirvana until your hair starts
to fall out and you have a nice fat bank-balance.'

'You don't mean that.'

'No. But I *am* interested in the unravelling of your amour.
Where are we now? You are in Anna's flat. Memories are

arriving like camels at an oasis, loaded with old gold. With what regal slowness they come. What funny noses they have. We need music. The desert air should ring with music.' He stood up. 'We need Maria. "Tu che le vanita" from *Don Carlos*. "You, Virgin, who know the vanity of the world." Vanity, vanity, all is vanity. As a child I did not know what the word meant but knew from the ring of it it must be exciting. Listen to that part where Elisabetta remembers the one beautiful day she and Carlos were granted in the forest of Fontainebleau . . .'

He walked to the gramophone. Callas began:

*Tu che le vanita conoscesti del mondo . . .*

'Start!' shouted Adolphe, 'while we have that voice of flame and tears boiling around us!'

'I prefer to wait until the aria is finished.'

'Afraid of the competition, are we? But then, who wouldn't be?'

The aria ended. Adolphe spread his hands and closed his eyes.

'Come on, hummingbird, break my heart . . . And what season is this Memory set in?'

'Autumn, in Oxford. Ten years ago. Mark and I have been walking by the river. I am wirier, thinner. Mark has three fewer lines on his forehead, is in a blue suit and shirt with a red scarf. On the other side of the river a gardener is burning leaves. The smell drifts across the water.'

'I am there,' Adolphe whispered. 'I am hiding in the bushes like a drunken old classics don, training my binoculars on you both.'

'Mark is standing, saying nothing, leaning against a wall.'

'The god of summer is leaning against a wall? Isn't he frightened his suit will be dirtied? No. He is on fire. He is

90

closing his eyes, drinking in, as they say, the afternoon and you. He is smiling as if you were in bed together.'

'Whose memory is this?'

Adolphe flung up his hands. 'Don't be possessive. Don't stop me. Mark's hand is on your shoulder. How Greek! His thumb is rubbing up against your neck. My binoculars mist for a moment. I am aware I am participating in a moment of tenderness. I lose myself in your moment. My head is as clear as Mark's green eyes.'

'His eyes are blue,' I said drily.

'One can't be completely clairvoyant. Continue.'

'Mark is standing, saying nothing, leaning against a wall.'

'How high is the wall?'

'Adolphe.'

'Is his whole body against the wall? Does the wall stretch far above him and overshadow him? The image is more ominous if . . .'

'The wall is about seven metres high. A pile of leaves is being burnt to the right of us. The smoke is being blown in our direction. It is so wild, that smell . . .'

'Ah! The smell of smoke! The smell of locker-rooms! The smell of the scorched grass in the armpits of young men! I've read about it. My binoculars are misting.'

I made a determined effort to go on.

'Mark is standing with his mouth slightly open . . .'

'The repressed Victorian sex in all this is too much for my old heart.'

'Mark is standing with his mouth slightly open, as if he wanted to swallow the smoke, to take into himself all the brilliance of that air. It is frightening to see him so naked for a moment. It was the moment I saw him most clearly.'

'No,' Adolphe screamed. 'No.' He leapt up from where he was sitting. 'Everything else I can take – the leaves, the mouth slightly open, but not that. It was not the moment when you saw him most clearly. It was the moment when you saw what you needed in him. It was the moment when you saw in him the Beloved you needed, the One you'd been waiting for. You did not see Mark: you saw Tristan, you saw Mark Antony. The lover and the Beloved are not the same person. To love the lover you have to see him as he is: *human, guilty and imperfect*. To love is to see, and to bear what you see. But when the Beloved, the 'Tristan' is about, you don't see much but flame. I see the Beloved sometimes even now in a young man drinking coffee alone in a café, in a boy running in red shorts in the Tuileries. I see Him: I raise my hands in prayer; I thank all the gods there are I do not need Him any more; I go home content. A vision livens up the day, after all. Nothing like a little contained ecstasy, preferably around cocktail time. Don't look at me like a bruised pear, it doesn't suit you.'

'You are a sad old queen.'

'If that's your version for tonight, enjoy it. Sad old queen, for purposes sad and mean – and possibly obscene – decides to demean ... You can play six years old with your London friends, but this is Paris, un cirque de miroirs with Yours Truly at the centre. It's an adult city with no illusions. Just like me, though I do say it myself. But then, Paris says it itself too with its colonnades, its sweeping, calculated gestures. I tell you what I know and what I am. You are young. You are enjoying your opera. I am old. I am enjoying mine, and I am enjoying yours, although not always with the reverence that you require. That doesn't mean I don't think your opera good. I've been known to giggle in the last act of *Rigoletto*, even with the tears pouring down my face. Maria, you know, was a prig with absolutely no humour. One of the reasons she died young. I want you to last. Back to Brando and the wall. But don't fool yourself you were seeing *him*. Or if you do, do it only for the purpose of the work. For the work's sake, a few radiant lies are permissible.'

'Thank you.'

'You'd better thank me because you won't find another one like me. They don't make them like me any more. It took a lot of privilege, humiliation and joie de survivre to create me. Listen and thank me while you can. Thus speaks Carlotta the Last.'

'Not for the last time.'

'You'll be so bored when I'm dead.'

'You're never going to die.'

'The saddest thing about dying is missing one's own funeral. What will Greta wear for my cortège? And do you think I will get Notre-Dame? Imagine them all in there, eyeing each other up in the stalls. I won't be there to laugh: Laugh for me. Promise me. And now, no more death. To Mark, the wall, life . . .'

'The light fell on Mark's hands as he stood there silently against the wall.'

Adolphe giggled. 'It would. Light is like that. 'And the light fell on his hands . . . And the light fell on his brown/black/blond/purple hair." Delete where necessary.'

'Look, if you . . .'

'Don't threaten me. Flatter me. That's the way to get me to do anything. So. The light ten years ago is falling on Wonderboy's hands. The violins are soaring, the leaves are burning, both tenors are clearing their throats before the dust begins. Wonderboy's hands are large. Large but sensitive. Half butcher-boy, half Polish pianist. They are glowing, as if on fire. They are glowing like the red heart of Jesus glows in those nineteenth-century paintings.'

'That's going too far,' I laughed.

'I always see how far I can go by going too far. Good God, Charles, are you in love with these hands or not?'

'Yes.'

'Then put some Tosca into the hands please.'

We were both laughing now. Adolphe extended his hands in the air.

'And for these hands. The things that were done for and with and to these sweet, sweet hands. Does he say anything, the Beloved, with light on his hands and the tang of burning smoke in his nostrils? Does he say a thing?'

'He does.'

'And do you store the words over the words – what a slip – I mean, over the years?'

'I do.'

'I thought so.'

'I do, not knowing I do.'

'The words we do not remember we remember are the ones we cannot remember to forget. And do these words return to you that afternoon, to hurt and haunt you?'

'They do.'

'And are they – Charles, don't hate me – are they – don't loathe me – are they rather banal, as all such words stored in the poacher's pocket of the heart are? Are they, when repeated, even in your voice (flattery!) . . . hollow?'

'It has been perfect today,' Mark said. 'We must never forget this.'

Adolphe groaned. 'With that low intense voice of his?'

'Exactly.'

'The line is cheap but the effect . . . My dear, it's a wonder you survived. Did he mean it?'

'He meant it. You can tell.'

'I never could. It's amazing what people were thinking when you thought they were thinking of you. We will never know whether he meant them or not. Nor perhaps will he. Nor does it matter. What matters is that those trite words burnt themselves on your memory.

When so I ponder, here apart
What shallow boons suffice my heart

94

What dust-bound trivia capture me
I marvel at my normalcy.


'Dorothy Parker. And what did you say back to those words as they winged their way to you over the words – I mean years?'

'"I do not want this," I said out loud.'

'Perfect! How badly you knew yourself! Were you so afraid?'

'Yes.'

'Poor little chipmunk.'

'Anna was saying that afternoon in my brain, "Look to your right. The ivory elephants are laughing at you."'

'Just what Anna would say. Not that she wouldn't do exactly the same thing. And what did you feel, after all this mémoire?'

'Angry at being opened. Angry at being peeled.'

'Angry at being merely human. Admit it. You had been bamboozling yourself for years that you were beyond illusion. And now those hands, those words and Wonderboy were there. You must have been livid with life for refusing you the self-mastery you were planning. I can see you stamping those military feet of yours. That you should fall again where you fell before, in the same place, against the same wall, even. Those ivory elephants must have been laughing! Twenty-nine *is* a teeny bit young to be giving up the world, especially when you still want to be a success in it, and look in every mirror as you pass. Why can't you love your contradictions? I do.'

'You've had such practice with your own ... Guess what happens next.'

'Mark burst naked through the window. Diana Vreeland writes and asks you to marry her.'

'You ring up.'

'Liar! I never rang! After that party I went off to Africa to try and make a film. How much can a famous old queen stand? Answer: Anything. Continue. I shall put on my Mater Dolorosa expression.'

The phone rings. It is Adolphe. He was ringing to find out what had happened after his party.

'Darling, I had to know. Seeing you there with that delicious journalist. It was touching. You were radiating.'

'Don't be disgusting.'

'Love is so important, as dear Gloria says. What she means, of course, is expensive.'

'Mark and I are old friends.'

'The lines you come up with! They'd make a Hollywood starlet blush. Can those green eyes of his . . .'

'They are blue.'

'Can those greeny-blue eyes of his be as innocent as they look?'

'I don't know and I don't care.'

'Are you going to see him again?'

'What are you up to? What on earth is it to you what I do?'

'Good. When you get evasive something is always up. He's got *it*. Brawn, a touch, not too much brain.'

'You make him sound like a steak.'

'He's married, he told me. A bit too quickly. Three children. It's always best with married men, you know. That's what Jean always said. At one time in my life I wouldn't look at anyone who wasn't respectably married. Set hours, set emotions, plenty of guilty rough sex.'

'It's not that simple.'

'You must learn that banalities will not defend you from the still more banal truth. It is that simple.'

'It can't be.'

'It's the responsibility of the shrewd to make it so.'

'I'm not shrewd.'

'Well that's true.'

'You didn't ring me just to gossip?'

'What more serious pleasure is there? But you're right. I'm off to Italy tomorrow to rest.'

'Everyone's going to Italy, except me. Anna's going to be in Italy.'

'We're abandoning our little boy to Paris. Will he be all right on his own?'

'He will be happier on his own than he has any right to be.'

'Something rather stiff in that tone of yours. God, I hope I don't meet Anna. She loves lecturing almost as much as I do and she'll lecture me on how my films are getting worse. I know they are, but must I be told? All this honesty about these days. I blame it on the Americans. They really believe Honesty is Truth. Think what would have happened to Culture if that had ever been the case!

Where's Anna going to be?'

'Venice.'

'Perhaps she won't see me on the Zattere slinking between contessas in my toupee and dark glasses. Never mind, Anna, I can cope. It's you who scare me. Don't get too crazy about Married. Keep these things in their proper boudoir.'

'For God's sake!'

'Listen. I'm the wisest as well as the richest person you know. I had a Married once. An Italian. A tiger. He used to like it in the open air. When I say open I mean open. I nearly died of pneumonia.'

'Earlier you said . . .'

'So I contradict myself? So what? When I come back from Venice we'll have dinner. And you'll tell me everything?'


'Well,' Adolphe said, skipping from the window to the sofa, 'You've made me give you cynical advice and packed me off to Venice. Think you can get rid of me as easily as that? So that your passion can unfold without the voice of the world interrupting and laughing? At least it's Venice. You could have sent me somewhere dreary, like Genoa.'

'Would I do a thing like that?'

'The young can do anything and not even notice . . . Read on. More Memory?'

'Yes.'

'How did I guess?'


After Mark left Oxford I wrote a bad television play, collected the cash, and left England. I lived in Greece for a while, trying to write a novel that I eventually threw into the sea off Spetses; I wandered Turkey, trying to avoid being raped by policemen and truck-drivers, and writing in the long evenings poems as elaborate as they were empty. I returned to England to take up a temporary teaching job. I lectured in a windowless room with squeaky plastic chairs about Jacobean tragedy. One girl wrote at the end of her last paper, 'Why do you never look at the class when you speak? Do you hate us?' I withdrew from my friends, who did not seem to mind. I took to walking the streets for hours at night, not from curiosity and not to pick anyone up, but to be doing something. I wrote short stories that always ended with deaths or gory accidents.

Late one night in that period I met a man at a party in London. We took cocaine together lying on the burnt grass in the yard, and he did a long and boring imitation of Mick Jagger with a dustbin lid. Partly to stop him and partly because I was feeling lonely, I invited him back to the tiny flat in Earl's Court I was living in. The only half-good thing about the flat was that it was near a male massage parlour and I had made friends with the masseurs and listened late into the night to their fantasies of finishing with their London life for good and setting up hotels in Sri Lanka or scuba-diving clubs in the Seychelles. One sad-eyed, lanky Swede and I tried to have an affair, but gave up out of disbelief.

I took the man from the party back to my flat. I gave him the remains of a bottle of Dubonnet the Swede had left for me. The man knocked it back ... When he was asleep and snoring beside me I found myself moved in a way I could not define. I was angry with myself. It seemed absurd to find anything moving in what had just happened. The man turned and lay on his back, almost knocking over the glass on the bedside table. Then I understood: the man had Mark's back and Mark's shoulders, almost exactly. The joy I had been feeling was that of sleeping with Mark for the first, only, time. I woke the man up, and threw him out.

'I thought so,' Adolphe said, smacking his lips.

'Thought what?'

'That you had never ... You know ...'

'Bravo.'

'If only you and Mark on one of those walks had actually ... you might have got over him. If only when he was leaning against the wall you had said, "This is absurd. We can't go on posing for a Greek catalogue like this," and reached à la Magnani ... Don't look at me like that. I'm not at all sorry you didn't. I like the highfalutin' tone of the whole affair. What would have happened if Beatrice had given Dante the come-on? Pas de Paradiso — No, that's not true. The Dantes of this world find their Beatrices, come hell or aqua alta. They ransack reality until they get exactly the kind of elevated torture they need. All is for the best in this best of all possible opera-houses.'

'How do you know that if Mark and I had been lovers we might not have ...'

'Reached Olympus between lunch and tea when Kate came back from work? I don't. Anything is possible. But do you know the story of Violette Leduc and the dress-shop?'

'You know bloody well I don't.'

'Aggression prevents learning. Violette was in Schiaparelli's. She was feeling heavenly, French and elegant and happy. She turned and saw the sweetest little girl and thought, "How heavenly to be here with this sweet little girl in this wonderful shop feeling heavenly." The girl then said to her Mama, pointing at Violette, "If I had a face like that I'd drown myself." Often it's better to imagine the dress-shop than be in it.' Adolphe smiled. His face softened.

'In those years you did not see Mark, did you catch glimpses of people who looked like him on buses, in railway stations? Did you see his walk, his hands in people in the street?'

'Yes.'

'A real true-blue obsession. I had one of those when young, I think. Or did I read about it?'

'I was in Turkey once,' I said, 'sitting in a café in the docks in Izmir. There was a man loading a boat about thirty yards away. He had Mark's body. When he stood wiping the sweat from his forehead he stood as Mark would, his legs slightly apart. I stayed an extra day to see him again.'

'Why didn't you give him a fiver and take him back to your hotel?'

'Sometimes . . .'

'I am too disgusting for words? Sorry, I just can't help asking the most basic questions. Why don't you admit that you loved your obsession, that you would do anything in those days rather than lose it? Its odd light could fall on the world from any angle at any time. Better to preserve that light than live in a lightless world. How eloquent I'm being. You had a grim choice – how awful to be young – and you chose poetry and Mark and illusion rather than bleakness and truth. I don't blame you. I would have done the same. I often did.'

'It was not an illusion entirely.'

'Are you sure?'

'No.'

'Good. There is hope for you.' Adolphe patted my knee. 'That's enough half-truth for now. Isn't it time to meet Mark again?'

'You like him, don't you?'

'I like you liking him. It makes you almost human. It must be time to see you two together again.'

'We are meeting, at Lipp, for dinner.'

'How cruel of you!'

'Cruel?'

'Don't be faux-naïf with me. No one goes to Lipp to talk. They go to be stared at. Lipp is the place the rich take their wives to make them feel ugly. The noise the swing-door makes! The people that keep making their entrance through it! Television producers in too-tight hand-me-down Saint Laurent suits; cultivatedly starved-looking young men with patent-leather shoes. Taking Mark there was like taking Aladdin to the mineshaft.'

'I wasn't . . .'

'Never mind. It is seven-thirty. The curtain rises on Brown-Eyes and Green-Eyes staring at each other in Lipp. The swing-door is creaking. The waiters are wandering about in their white aprons. And on the other side of Paris – cut – Adolphe prior to his departure for Venice is sitting down to a bit of lettuce and Callas.'

'You are not in this scene.'

'I am! I am sitting at the table across the way from you and Mark. I am in disguise. I am doing my Vicomtesse de Ribes imitation – costume-jewellery and a tight waist – so tight I can only eat shrimps.'

'Liar!'

'Think what colour I would lend to the scene if I were in it.'

'There must be some scenes where you don't appear.'

'I know what you mean. One can't give the public the star all the time. Read, my piranha. I accept my detachment with detachment.'

'Piranha?'

'Think of all that gold dust on their sides, if you don't like the teeth . . .'


In the acrid light of Lipp Mark looked older. I saw, with a sour half-pleasure, that the years had puckered a few small lines around his eyes and made his skin more leathery. Yet his face, as I had feared at Adolphe's party, was more handsome than when I had first known it. It had become more decided, clearer-boned. His eyes had deepened in colour; they seemed shadowed, too, in a way I had not remembered.

'You looked at me so strangely when I came in,' Mark said hesitantly, taking off his leather coat and throwing it across the chair opposite.

'It's hard to believe you are here.'

'Touch me,' he said ironically, his eyes narrowing.

'With all these waiters watching? Certainly not. I have my solitary reputation here to uphold.'

'How can you be a regular here? I hate the place. It unnerves me.'

Mark hunched his shoulders slightly.

'Yes,' I said. 'I like to sit here surrounded by these mirrors, eat oeufs au jambon, and watch.'

'Habits die hard.'

'You should know that.'

He was still wearing the blue shirt of the night before, grimier now around the collar. He was unshaven.

'Yes,' he said. 'I should know that.' He sat down, challenging me to hold his gaze.

I avoided it. 'How was Adolphe?' I said.


'So I do come into this scene; how lovely!'


'Adolphe was word-perfect. Every epigram polished and presented on a silver platter. What are you going to have?'

'I don't feel like eating anything.' His hands were unsteady. He is miserable, I thought to myself, not without satisfaction. He's unhappy. I leant across and put my hand on his. He started. 'Do you think,' he said, 'we are the first people to touch each other in Lipp for a decade?'

Mark took his hand away and said flatly, 'You were brutal last night.' I said nothing but smiled slightly.

**101**

'I know that smile. I've seen it before. It's your superior I-slip-away-and-leave-you-to-do-it smile. I have it. Your effects last night were calculated, as you said. They worked. I suffered.'

'There is a letter of Charlotte Brontë's I recommend to you. In it she is writing to a married man whom she loved. She says, "I do not want revenge. I want you to feel for one week what I have felt for years." You suffered. I am sorry! It'll go away. Kate will comfort you.'

'God, you're stupid,' Mark said quietly.

'Not stupid. Hard. I've had to become hard. There was no other way I found to survive.'

'Charles Agonistes. Don't you ever change your part?' He paused. 'Look, I know nothing about you. I knew that last night. I have thought of you every day, but I know that I know nothing. But you seem to think you know all about me. That is what I find hard to bear in you. Your omniscience, your quotations, the belief you know what has happened.' Mark paused and reached for my hand that was still on the table. 'We do not have much time. There never is much time. How often will we be in Paris together?'

'A plea for Socratic ignorance, a show of humility, followed by seduction . . . The years have not made you subtler.'

Mark shook his head angrily. I trained my eyes on the small tufts of dark hair about his ears, determined not to be reached by him.

'Everything I say,' he said, 'will sound corrupt to you. You don't think I know that? You can twist everything I say. You can make it all sound stupid.'

'Why should I play the part you want me to just to make you more comfortable? If you think I will play "worthy" you are going to be very shocked. I'd rather fall on the floor and scream. Less worthy, more truthful.'

'I wouldn't scream here. You'll frighten the waiters.'

'One more homosexual hysteric will not ruffle them. The only reason for not screaming is that no one is ever moved. Besides, when you go I want to come back. Lovers come and go but the oeufs au jambon at Lipp stay for ever.'

'God,' Mark said, 'do you ever listen to yourself?'

'Of course. For long stretches it's all I have to listen to. Now isn't it time for the photographs?' I sat back, to out-stare him.

'What photographs?'

'What photographs? Why, the Family Photographs. Don't forget I've not been privy to your triumph as a heterosexual. I want to see all the photographs. Surely you carry them? Even journalists carry photographs of their families. Comes in handy sometimes to soften up a client. Kate and Mark. Kate under the blossoming cherry tree, Mark and X and Y (what *are* their names?) with Kate by the Rover 2000 . . .'

'Oh, those? You want to see those?' His tone unnerved me.

'Not really.'

Mark grabbed my hand. 'What do you mean, not really? It is essential you see them. I want you to get them right.'

'Mark . . .'

'I'm going to give you what you want.'

He reached into his jacket pocket for his wallet and drew two photographs from it. One was of Kate in a blue dress standing in a doorway with her face in shadow. The other was of Kate standing in a garden with her children clustered round her, holding on to her skirts. She was not smiling.

'In the first photograph,' Mark said, thrusting it towards me, 'you can see my wife Kate, short for Katherine, with second names Cecilia and Helen — after her grandmothers, — just pregnant, twenty-eight years and seven months old. You are a writer. You appreciate accuracy. She is a strong, blonde, clever woman with a slight squint in her left eye, large hands, an acid tongue — when she needs it — and a great capacity for loyalty, sex, and good humour. She is, you will notice, although her face is in shadow, staring out at me, her husband. Do you see how she is looking out at me?'

'Mark . . .'

'Shall I characterise that look for you in words? Shall I put it into words? You love words. It is a look — I say this first — that I deserve. It is a quizzical, sad, puzzled, angry look. She understands, you see, my wife, that I find it hard to love; that I am evasive, a kind coward, a nice shit. It is not only you who knows me, you see. It is a look that says "I love you but I fear you. I fear your silences, I fear your reserve. I fear all parts of you that fear to love me." It is a moving look. Well-caught, too, wouldn't you say? It takes almost genius to get a look like that out of a sitter. Genius or cruelty. But then it is so hard to tell the difference, isn't it?'

Mark had clenched both his fists. 'Damn you,' he said. 'I tried to reach you. I tried hard. I failed. I'm no good at it. I failed now as I failed before. But damn you for not seeing I was trying.'

'What good places we choose to have our scenes in. Adolphe's party, Saint-Sulpice, this sea of rich fat women . . .'

'Savour the incongruity. Write it all down. Don't forget that girl by the door with the long blonde hair and the sapphire necklace.' Mark put his photographs back into his wallet.

'I am sorry,' I said, looking away from him. Mark leant forward.

'Do you realise you have not asked me one serious question

103

about what I am doing, or what I feel about my life? Not one.'

A waiter had come and stood by us. It seemed so incongruous — the waiter's red face and bushy grey-tipped moustache, the way he stood with his feet firmly, solidly, apart, like a butcher. Mark and I smiled at each other, our first unguarded smile.

'He at least,' I said, 'could be a part of no one's fantasy! Let's get out of here. Let's walk.'

'Let's walk.' Mark's voice was exhausted. 'But let's walk in peace.'

'Walk in peace. It sounds like one of the slogans of the moral majority. I can't promise to walk in peace.'

'Let's walk anyway.' Mark stood up. The waiter looked at us, rolled his eyes, shrugged his shoulders. Mark looked frail, almost ill, beside him. Then Mark laughed. 'You've got fluff all over the back of your coat. Just as you used to. It's a more expensive coat but you are as careless as you were.' He brushed my shoulders and back a little too hard. The girl with the blonde hair and sapphire necklace sitting by the door was looking at us both and smiling. It was a conspiratorial smile, and I, without meaning to, smiled back.

'Happy?' Mark asked ironically.

He put both hands on my neck and stood behind me to steer me forward through the swing-door into the street, as if I were a child or too drunk to see straight.


I smiled across at Adolphe. 'Had enough?'

'I never have enough bitchery, violence, and suppressed sex. Whoever does?'


The night was so cold, the breath of the passers-by wreathed them in brief mist. We walked, shoulders hunching, our hands bunched tight in our pockets, down the rue de Seine to the river. I felt, leaning against the freezing night wind, as if my face were being burnt away, layer by layer . . .

'You have no gloves on,' Mark said.

He took both my hands into his gloved ones and rubbed them.

'I feel like one of your children.'

'My children never go out without gloves.'

'Glad to hear it. I think I'm drunk.'

'You're not drunk,' Mark said. 'You're exhausted.'

'So are you. It suits you. Brings out all those new lines around your eyes.'

We were standing by a closed bookstall, whistling at the cold, looking down at the river. Mark kicked a pile of gold leaves at his feet.

'You, I suppose, don't feel guilty,' he said. 'Martyrs don't have to — that's why they choose to be martyrs.'

I turned to him. The stark yellow light of the streetlamp fell across the bottom part of his face. His eyes were in darkness.

'I can't talk to you if your eyes are in the dark.'

Mark stepped forward. 'Is that better? Are the conditions for intimacy now perfect?'

Two cars screeched to a halt on our left and their drivers leant out of the windows to swear at each other and drive on. Mark and I exchanged looks and smiled. 'There are tears in your eyes,' I said.

'It's the night wind. Don't build your hopes . . .'

I started to walk down the steps to the river. 'Guilty?' I said. 'Of course. The moment I start to love anyone I feel guilty that I am about to bore or use or disappoint them, and one isn't often wrong.'

'Sometimes one is,' Mark said softly behind me, emphasising the *one*, mockingly.

'Sometimes one is . . . I began to feel guilty, I think, when I was in the womb. Too pleasant — I couldn't imagine how I deserved it.'

We had reached the bottom of the steps and faced the river. 'It helps to know you don't despise me,' Mark spoke haltingly, looking away.

'If I despised you, would I be here?'

The words surprised me but I could not retract them. I watched them hang in the air, white, like cigarette smoke, uncurling towards him.

'You could despise me and still be here,' he said. 'For curiosity's sake. From boredom. For revenge.'

I turned to walk down-river.

'I always remember you walking. Walking fiercely, stopping fiercely. Waving your arms about and walking and stopping and talking.'

'You make me sound like an Italian policeman.'

'You always used to say that if you had been a dramatic soprano, that would have solved everything.'

'And you used to say you should have been a Russian violinist. We did too much walking, Mark. It was our way of making love. If we'd been Americans we'd have bought two identical track-suits and jogged together.'

'You destroy everything.'

'"The truth is my only friend," as the song goes. "I have nothing else to hold on to / Although it's brutal and cold too."'

'One of Anna's songs?'

'Yes.'

'Not much good.'

We were standing at the river's edge. That night, it was sluggish and ice-black.

'Must truth always be like that?' Mark asked. 'Or is that how you want it? Do you have no memories of us that ...' His voice trailed away.

'Tell me one that I should resuscitate. I'd be grateful.'

'That afternoon when we stood by the river ...'

'Another bloody river.'

'And all the leaves of the trees on the bank opposite suddenly fell in one burst of gold ...'

'You're very poetic.'

'Do you remember what you said?'

'No.'

'You said, "How shall we hold so much gold?"'

'Hold and gold in one sentence like that? How dare you remember such a banality? Stick to the leaves falling. "In one burst of gold." Leave our bad poetry out of it.'

'You were talking about us. You were talking about our love.'

'I was oracular in those days, ...'

'You were talking about how much joy we had been given,' (Mark turned to face me) 'how much love we had been given and how you were afraid neither of us could bear it.'

'All in that one banal sentence. You are my only good reader, the only one who fills out my bad lines with truths that aren't there.'

'They were there,' said Mark. 'Don't be childish.'

'Do you blame me?' I said coldly. 'Some things, especially pure and beautiful things, should be beyond recall. Since I saw you yesterday ...'

'You've become considerably less amnesiac?

'I have started to remember things I would rather not remember.'

'So have I.'

'I want to be calm, Mark. Calm, dull and free.'

'Liar. You want everything. That is why I love you, and why you scare me.'

'Very moving. What do *you* want?'

'The same. In my fashion.'

'In your fashion. Does the hard gem flame business really attract you or are you scared as hell?'

'I am scared as hell and it attracts me because it scares me to hell. Why do you ask questions to which you know the answer?'

'It passes the time.'

'I do not have your bitterness, or your work, to protect me,' Mark said suddenly drawing his coat around him.

'I'll teach you, if you like. You wouldn't make a good pupil. You have faith in life. You glow with it.

'You say "glow" as if it were some kind of disease.'

'Sometimes I have thought it was.'

'I don't have as much faith as you believe. But it suits you . . .'

'How's Kate? What about her?' I said, cutting him short, as we walked into the shadow of a bridge. 'Doesn't she protect your faith, help you go on glowing? Doesn't that red bicycle in the hall glow away most demons?'

Mark looked away. 'I want to tell you about Kate,' he began. 'She was so generous. When I left publishing because I couldn't stand it, she didn't complain, although we had no money and she was pregnant with Sebastian. She stuck by me. She even managed to be encouraging without patronising me as most women would have done. In the next ten months when I was crawling around London trying to get someone to let me write articles, Kate . . .'

'Kept your chin up, did she? For better or for worse . . .'

Mark closed his eyes. 'You're making it hard.'

'Deliberately.'

'I deserve more from you, and so does she. Kate is good. She is beyond anything I can do to her . . .'

'Men always have that fantasy about women. It allows them to torture them serenely.'

I watched his face.

'You have all the answers. I tell you what I know. You can listen or not. Kate is strong. She always was, and as she has grown and had children she has become even stronger. You do not know her now and are unable to judge. She is so gentle with our children.'

'Ah, brave new world. I knew there would be children in this act.'

'Charles . . .'

'Go on. I'm sorry. I want to hear.' I moved closer to him.

'Before we had Paul I was afraid. Kate can be hard sometimes. But Paul — his beauty — softened her. She used to sit on the stairs crying at his loveliness. It was strange. I had never imagined she could be so moved by anything. She'd have nightmares in which she'd leave him in the park by mistake and he'd starve to death, or dream that in her sleep she'd rolled on him and crushed him . . . Each of our children has brought her a new warmth. I feel jealous sometimes, and excluded, as if I only existed to give her these children, so that she could love them and herself through them . . .

107

Does any of this interest you?' He said the word 'interest' drily.

'Yes, despite myself . . . And what is Kate to you now?' I spoke more harshly than I intended; Mark winced.

'I have a right to know.'

Mark put his hands against the dark crumbling stone of the underbelly of the bridge and leaned against it.

'Kate knows I love her and have drifted away from her. She knows I feel remote from her and helpless at feeling so remote.'

'She bores you. Why don't you say it?'

'She doesn't bore me. I have known her since she was eighteen and I still find subtleties in her. The truth is, she looks to me for some quite ordinary affirmation of herself and I cannot give it, or cannot give it for long at a time.'

Mark turned away from the stone and faced the river, his hands in his pockets. 'We love each other but we do not fit. It is as simple as that.'

'Simple?' I asked. 'It doesn't sound simple.'

He stood, saying nothing, his face bowed and set in sadness. I put my right arm through his left. 'Come,' I said, 'let's walk.'

'That's all we ever did — walk and talk, walk and talk.'

'Don't quote me. It doesn't suit you.'

'Who are you to tell me what suits me or not?'

We smiled and leaned together lightly, walked on in the night wind.

'We are like two old women,' I said, 'strolling arm in arm after their tisane.'

'And what's wrong with that?'

As Mark had been talking about Kate, I had been remembering the first time I had met her. Mark had said, after months of our talking together, 'I have spoken to Kate about you. You should know each other.' I dreaded that first meeting as, years later, she told me she had dreaded it. I dreaded her beauty and her power and her long knowledge of Mark; I dreaded being shown up as a fantasist. What actually happened was stranger and more confusing: we liked each other. I had arrived early; Mark was out shopping; Kate came to the door. We stood looking at each other, discovering, as we looked, not rancour, but a kind of friendship, a surprising, unspoken recognition of the other's love for Mark. That this was not my invention Kate confirmed later by many words and actions. I had thought Kate beautiful the first time I saw her with her athlete's body, her hair, a darker, tawnier gold than Mark's, cut back from her face, her large vividly-lashed brown eyes, her hands, large but fragile-boned and bare except for her marriage-ring. How much easier my love for Mark would have been if I could have dismissed Kate, but there came to be ways in which I respected her more than him — for her courage, for her capacity for suffering, for a clear vigour which neither Mark nor I had. I found increasingly I shared her grief also. We loved, and were loved and betrayed by the same man. Mark evaded us both with the other, and the more deeply Kate and I knew that — although we never talked about it — the greater our awareness of each other became.

'You always liked Kate,' Mark said.

'It was very inconvenient.'

'And she liked you.'

'Why not? She knew I was no threat.'

'I was almost jealous of the way she talked about you. She knew I loved you and wanted to love you also, so she would not be cut off from the part of me that loves you. I resented that in her. It was as if she wanted to experience even my love for you ... There was only one thing Kate ever said against you. "Charles is in love with death and everyone who loves him will have to be dragged into his suffering or leave him."'

Mark looked at me to reply. I smiled and said nothing.

'She wanted to frighten me, I suppose,' Mark said.

'She succeeded ...' I felt exhausted. 'And she may have been right. Perhaps we would have destroyed each other. Perhaps the kind of life I lead would have unhinged you. Once when you were upstairs, Kate said to me, "Mark loves us both but he cannot choose. We must not make him choose or we will break him." Since if you did not choose, you would stay with her, she was being clever as well as accurate. She was trying to protect you. Perhaps she was trying to protect me — from destroying her and you, or trying to ... I wouldn't put it past her, trying to protect me. She is generous enough for that. That's what made me despair ... Kate's largesse.'

A barge glided on the river. It had only one light on and seemed without a pilot.

'You're cold,' Mark said, pulling the flaps of my coat round my neck. 'What happened to the scarves you used to wear?'

'I gave up scarves at about the time your letters stopped. The severe look from now on, I thought. No more camp. It's the eighties, after all ...'

'I'm happy we are here together.'

'Not scared?'

'Yes, a little. Aren't you?'

'Yes. And scared of you being scared, as usual.'

Mark smiled. 'Shall we see each other tomorrow?' He asked with an odd childish lilt that angered me.

'Why should I see you?' I said. 'You just bring pain – take your hands off my shoulders!'

'No,' he said, pressing them down harder. 'If our love brought pain, we shared it, just as we shared the joy. You know that as far as I could I gave myself to you. You knew it all the years we were apart.'

I wanted to say something wounding, but his courage shook me.

'I was lying,' I said. 'There were many times in these last years when the thought of your love gave me courage.'

I had said it. If his sincerity had been a game, or an unconscious lie, I was lost.

'You have been brave with me,' I said. 'Thank you. I will try and be brave with you.'

'You used not to find it so hard.'

I started to speak but no words came. I looked up at him. He nodded, as if to encourage me, and put his hands against my chest. We were both trembling a little. I covered his hands with my hands. When my voice came it sounded at a distance from me, younger and clearer.

'Four years ago, I was travelling in Yugoslavia. I was visiting the monasteries there with an older woman friend, and I went one morning to Mileseva to see its great painting, the angel with an impassive face, in white, sitting on the tomb of Christ. Something in the angel's face – its cheekbones, its eyes, its strong jaw – reminded me of your face. I started to feel ill, so ill that I went outside and lay by the stream that flows past the monastery. I tried not to think of you; I slowly emptied my mind; the water seemed to be passing through me. I felt that if I had the strength to roll over into the stream I would dissolve in it. All the time I was in that state I saw the face of the angel. This time it had your neck, your eyes, your hair. My friend drove me along winding bumpy roads to another monastery, Sopocani, where we were going to spend the night. She realised I was going through something and we did not speak. I was both in pain and unnaturally calm and clear. Everything I saw in the landscape around me seemed on fire – the stooks of wheat, the swallows above the fields, the faces of the peasants as they worked. The fields themselves were rivers of fire . . .

'That night I lay in the monastery guest-house, sleepless and still in pain. The window was open on to the night, a clear star-lit summer night, with all the scents of summer in the air, pine and hay and breathing water. I felt you come into the room and lie on top of me. I had my eyes closed but I knew it was you. You had not lain on me to make love to me, but to cover me, as a mother might cover the body of her ill son, to pour her strength into his flesh. Your body was very light; but I could feel all the tender and odd contours of it, your shoulders, the muscles in your thighs and hips, the bristles on your chin. I fell asleep, or perhaps I had always been asleep, I do not know which. In the morning I was well.'

I looked at Mark. His face was impassive and in shadow. He moved forward into the half-light and held me to him.


It was dawn in Adolphe's apartment. He had been silently curled up on the sofa, listening with his head bent. He looked up. 'Darling, you look like Lillian Gish in *Way Down East*. Extinguished. All we need is an ice floe for you to throw yourself down on . . .'

'And someone handsome to rescue me. Just before the floe goes over the edge. Don't forget that.'

'I couldn't forget that.'

I was grateful to hear his high, wild voice. As he spoke the objects in the room seemed to become real again.

'You have surprised me, peewee.'

'Peewee?'

'Remember one day to get me to tell you the story of Peewee, the black Casanova of Chicago. It's an epic. I've left it to Saul Bellow in my will.'

'I thought you were far beyond surprise.'

'Don't be arch. I thought you would play it safer. I didn't expect the visions yet. I know there must be visions. You'd warned me. I thought we'd have a lot more bitchery.'

'I didn't expect the visions either.'

'And Mark has surprised me. What these English bisexuals keep hidden! They're all latent Russians. I never guessed.'

'I'm sure you did.'

'Of course I did, but flattery is flattery. Take it while you can. We're all latent Russians, of course, longing for a whiff of God and truth to set us raving and seeing things in Technicolor. I, of course, have been out of that closet for years. And Kate, this English rose, smelling sweetly through your prose . . . I had no idea there would be a Sieglinde lurking in the wings – and what a Sieglinde – noble, virtuous, the works. How very inconvenient to know the wife when one wants to commit adultery. Even the kind of holy-copulation you seem to be after ...'

I looked away.

'You think I'm being heartless,' Adolphe sighed. 'Sorry. No more heartless than life. Was it Chekhov who said, "Nothing is as cynical as reality." If he didn't he should have done. Are you going to go on looking like Lillian Gish or are you going to have a good stiff drink and read on?'

'It's dawn, Adolphe ...'

'You young people these days are so weak. The first whiff of daylight and you fall to the floor like extras in a Kung Fu movie. Where has all the stamina gone? Errol Flynn, my dear, could have an erection for eight days without stopping. Enough of that. Mustn't lower the tone. Keep your eyes on that angel, Adolphe. Keep your thoughts celestial. I'm hooked, can't you see? There are more noble visionary latent Russians in your book than I've met for years.'

'Adolphe!'

'You think I'm being bitchy? Well, I am in a way, but only in a way. Besides, illusions about virtue are preferable to illusions about evil. A lie that elevates, peewee, is dearer than a host of low truths. Anyway, I'm tired of those works in which everyone is a latent child-molester. What is opera if not the clash of radiances? Your opera is fun. I love the bit about the fields being rivers of fire. For the peasants hacking away on them of course they were just fields. But such is life. One man weeps; another man wins the Lottery. You have your visions; and dear old Greta goes on staring at an imaginary spider in an imaginary cup. The Whole Caboodle is without meaning and contains every meaning one can imagine. That is what differentiates us: what meanings we can imagine. Don't look so sulky. Your visions are your visions; mine are mine. What do I have to say to get you to read on? That you make Yukio Mishima look like Pearl S. Buck? I was young once; I know the young need flattery, as vampires need blood. You need praise, chicklet?

112

You'll get praise . . .' He stood up and poured champagne into a long thin red glass. 'This is for you. Pure, expensive praise. What's next?'

'Anna rings.'

'Anna rings? Our stormy petrel, our skinny whippet. Do her voice, remember, or no more Ribena.'

Anna rang the next day, unexpectedly, early, and collect.

'Hello, Charles . . .'

'Where are you speaking from?' Her voice sounded distant. 'You're not in America, are you? You haven't decided to take Buddha to California? Remember, no cash lasts for ever . . . Why aren't you saying anything?'

'I'm so depressed I can hardly speak.'

'Where are you?'

'Venice. Good old rotten Venice. The Danieli'.

'And the Dalai?'

'He's in his blue marble bath upstairs. He says blue is the colour of emptiness. He's hardly talking to me. He fills the bath with my bath-salts and then lies in it for hours, contemplating – or so he says. Why am I in Venice with a religious freak where it's pouring with rain and all the cafés are closed when I could be in Paris?'

'Where it's pouring with rain.'

'But with you.'

' "The rain that raineth every day . . ." '

'Charles, don't quote. It's too early in the morning. I haven't even had a drink yet and I've got the worst hangover. I could only just see straight to dial the numbers. I'm not ringing to gossip. I'm worried about you.'

'Worried? I'm as right as rain. Sorry . . .'

'I had a dream last night about you.'

'All these visions and dreams,' Adolphe said. 'It's like medieval Germany! It's like Joan of Arc!'

'In the dream I was sitting at the pontoon outside the Calcina. I was alone. It was a grey day. There was no one at any of the tables. A waiter shambled up to me. He had a note on a tray, from you: "Catch the next boat that passes." I looked up and saw a vaporetto approaching, slowly, the stop beyond the Gesuati. I got up and ran

113

towards it. It was empty. The boat was going towards the
Redentore and as it went mist gathered round it, a black mist. At
the end of the boat there was a black box.' Anna paused and sucked
in her breath. 'You were in it. You weren't dead. You were lying
there . . . I stood by you. It was all I could do. Once I tried to hold
your hand but you looked at me angrily. Charles, what is happening?'

'Nothing.'

'Don't lie. What's happening with Mark?'

'We talk, we walk, we go over ancient ground.'

'You're not going to tell me, are you?'

'No.'

'Let me say this one thing, then. That ghost is dangerous. It is
the ones that shine that are the most dangerous; hold them to you,
and they burn your skin away. Venice is full of haggard succubi
talking to themselves — shall I dump the Dalai and come back?'

'No. I feel you have something to learn from him.'

'You know perfectly well I have nothing to learn from him. He
can't even put the top back on the bath-salts bottle. Charles . . . Are
you going to last? That black box . . .'

'I am going to last. This is the year in which I decide to live as
long as Sophocles.'

'Don't fall into the dark river. Remember that line from one of
my songs. You see I know what I don't do. Don't fall into the dark
river. And remember the moon.'

'What do you mean?'

'That's for you to figure out. If I had a bass voice I'd sing
"Remember the moon" with a tremolo as wide as the place
Concorde. The Dalai has come down the stairs. How he grins! He
thinks the grin is seductive. If only he knew. Charles?'

'Yes?'

'Remember the moon.' She hung up.

Remember the moon. Anna was talking about the last time I had
seen Mark and Kate, eight years before. I had returned from a long
journey in India. They were living then in a cottage outside
Maidstone. It had been a tense, uneasy evening, Mark largely
silent, Kate confessional but barbed. When it was time to leave,
Kate had said, 'We bored you. I'm sorry. Our lives are very
ordinary compared with yours.' I had felt wretched.

Mark drove me to where I was staying in the country about
fifteen miles away. In a month I was going to be teaching in
America; I knew I would not see him for a long time; I knew he
would not write. I looked away from him across the bare midnight

114

fields, trying to find in their silence some strength for the months ahead. The night was a heavy one, louring, overcast, the kind of night I remembered well from my schooldays in Dorset and which brought back memories of the loneliness of public school. Just when I felt most alone, the dark clouds that were hiding the moon above the fields parted. A full moon emerged. The fields that had been sullen suddenly were soaked with moonlight, as if by a fall of dew; the clouds themselves, that a moment before had been bars of darkness, solid-seeming, seemingly impenetrable, glowed now as if lit from within.

I described that evening to Anna, and my astonishment at that moon. Anna had listened as if attending to something behind my words. She wandered restlessly round the flat, hugging her stomach, opening book after book on her shelves. Then, she stopped in the middle of the room. 'Give me a piece of paper and a pen,' she said. 'Any scrap will do.'

I gave her an old envelope. She wrote out this poem by Basho:

My house
Burnt down

I own
A better view

Of the rising moon.

'I found it last week,' she had said, 'in a book of my late unlamented husband's. It helped me. Now I give it to you.'


'Stop,' said Adolphe.

He was standing and staring at me. He began to laugh, a low soft chuckle. 'Oh pondsnipe, pondsnipe . . .' He was shaking his head from side to side. 'If you knew, if you only knew.'

'Tell me.'

'Tell me,' Adolphe mimicked. 'Isn't there some English folk-saying about what happens to those who ask to be told things? I'll tell you.' He came and took my hands in his. 'I too was once given that Basho poem.'

'By Anna?'

'Long before I knew Anna. Long before I knew you. At the beginning of my new life . . .'

He was enjoying himself, watching my confusion with delight.

'Your new life?' I repeated stupidly.

'You think I've always been Adolphe, don't you? Always whirling about this apartment. The young see the old as fixed. They never imagine that they too have "experiences". We are linked, Charles, linked in ways ... No, you'll see. Mustn't help you too much. I'm so happy.' He clapped his hands.

'Will you please ...'

'Patience, pondsnipe, I'm going to tell you. Don't I tell you everything? About fifteen years ago – long before you, little watervole, nosed into my life – I felt at the end of everything. What, I thought, did I have to look forward to? More bad films, more paid boys, more parties. I was full of self-pity and used to spend evenings thinking of easy ways to kill myself. I'm a coward, so the Japanese way – which I thought the most noble – was hors de pensée. Besides, if you're going to do seppuku you have to get someone else to chop your head off, and who of my friends could I have relied on to do that? Can you imagine Delphine waving one of those things about? Greta would enjoy the idea but get bored half-way through. One evening I decided it had to be pills, small pills because I didn't want to choke, white pills because I liked the symbolism, very poisonous pills because I wanted it to be all over fast. I rang the right doctors – if you think film people have no morals, they are yogis compared to doctors – and got a whole fistful of things that looked like silkworms in a tasteful black box. I decided I would do it after lunch. It was the end of May and the light in this room is beautiful around three. So why not be Japanese in this at least and die in spring sunshine? I wrote four letters to close friends, as witty as I could make them. There was one thing I wanted to do in the morning before – not what you're thinking, pondsnipe. If Jimmy Dean himself had come through my door in a see-through kimono, I'd have given him a drink and gone to bed alone. I was that bad. Not that Jimmy was best in kimonos, actually ... I wanted to have one last

116

coffee at the Deux Magots. I had lived years in that place. I wanted one last bad coffee. You don't believe me?'

'I believe anything.'

'Liar. But, believe me, if you can't believe that you won't believe a word of what is to follow. What do the Jesuits say, start by believing little things and build up to the great big things? Wise old snakes. I'm the other way round – I've always somewhere believed the great big things. It's the little things I find crazy. Anyhow, picture me, fifteen years younger, soberly dressed, with dark glasses (so that Mary McCarthy wouldn't recognise me) sitting alone at a table right at the junction of the pavement and the boulevard Saint-Germain.

I drank the first coffee fast, the second slowly, the third very slowly. I felt suddenly cheerful, expansive. No one around me had the slightest idea that this old balding man in a grey suit with glasses was contemplating his own death. They probably thought I was a tourist. There was some street-theatre going on. All my life I have hated street-theatre in Paris – those desperate calculating faces, the clothes that walk straight out of Colette's music-hall stories. But this time it was different. For one thing it was performed by an Indian, about fifty years old, long and thin like a fakir. I have never seen him since. Perhaps that was his one performance in Paris. He was dressed like Charlie Chaplin, except for a turquoise bandanna, but he was not doing any Chaplin routines, walking funnily or dancing or laying his head sadly on one side. He was fire-eating. Most fire-eaters have terrified eyes and a fixed smile and something drawn about the cheeks. His eyes were dancing; every time he plunged the fire into his mouth he spun round on his heels in a jig, like a child who has just been given a sweet.

He lit six two-foot torches and began to juggle with them. I have watched jugglers in God knows how many shows and circuses, but he was the greatest I have ever seen, flinging the torches up, catching them with his hands behind his back, in his teeth. He did not merely fling them up, he made them dance together in all sorts of patterns – squares, mountains, circles. I went into a trance watching him. I remembered, over

117

and over again, words I had read once in a Zen sermon: "The world is like a firebrand which, when swung round in the hand, resembles a wheel of solid flame." We are all fire-people, Charles, all fire-eaters. But unlike that Indian we are not masters of the transformations we create; we whirl the flame around and frighten ourselves with what we have done, like children who begin drawing a face in the dust, and run in terror from it; we throw the torches up and they fall from the sky burning others, or ourselves . . .' Adolphe paused. 'Do you believe me when I say I'd rather break all my Callas records than lie seriously to you?'

'I believe you.'

'Louder!'

'I believe you!'

'Take that edge out of your voice. Belief should be gracious and flowing, like Maria in "Casta Diva".'

'I believe you.'

'You don't know what you've let yourself in for.' Adolphe spun round on his heels, as he had described the fire-eater doing. 'As I watched the fire-eater, I felt myself being watched. I looked around. There, at the edge of the crowd, practically in the street itself, were the eyes that I had been searching for. They belonged to a young, tall, oriental man in a red robe. It took me a few second to realise that he must be a Tibetan and a priest. There, near the Deux Magots, in the middle of a packed, steamy May morning, surrounded by young men with the escaped-convict look that Paris specialises in, and old women with handbags like clubs. The Tibetan was staring at me and grinning. He nodded. I nodded back, as if we were old friends recognising each other. Then . . .'

'Let me guess. He turned into a dog. He vanished in a puff of Arpège.'

'Your attempts at vulgarity are always successful. I wonder why you repeat them . . . No, he did not vanish or change into a dog. He raised his right hand and beckoned me. When I say beckoned I mean summoned. There was no arguing with the look in his eyes then, or the command.'

'And you got up.'

'I got up. The priest summoned a taxi, got into it, and left the door open for me to get in too.'

'And you got in.'

'You see, you know everything. It's marvellous what a narrative sense you have. I got into the taxi and the priest and I sat in silence. He held my hand, leant forward to the taxi driver, and said, "Musée Guimet, vite s'il vous plaît." I remember looking at the taxi driver – a fat man in his late fifties, who was sweating so hard he kept his left hand free to mop his brow – to see if he noticed anything strange about us. But taxi drivers have seen everything, they are the weary-lidded Magi of our civilisation. It did not seem at all strange to him that a bald man with glasses, unshaven and shaky, should be sitting in the back of his cab, holding hands with a Tibetan priest. Ça, c'est normal ... perhaps he was right. Muttering and swearing at the traffic, with the radio on full blast, he got us to the Guimet in under ten minutes.'

'What did the Tibetan priest look like?'

'All my life as a film-maker I have looked at faces, from every angle, from every viewpoint, imagining them in shadow, in light, lit from above, below. But whenever I try to remember that man's face it changes. Now, for instance, I see a thin, elongated mountain-peasant kind of face with high cheek-bones but a broad forehead. Last week, I remember, he had a different face, rather like the Dalai Lama's only coarser, with bushier eyebrows. I long ago gave up trying to remember how he looked. What a joke! To have spent your life filming faces and then not to be able to "film" the face of the man who saved your life. I do, though, remember the colour of his eyes.'

'Which was?'

'Brown. At least I think so – unless ...' Adolphe was laughing. 'You really don't believe me but je m'en fiche. We arrived at the Musée Guimet. We walked up the stairs. I thought he was going to take me to the Tibetan room and kept thinking idiotic thoughts like "God, I hope he isn't going to ask me questions about Tibetan philosophy." We passed through

119

the Tibetan room quickly. He walked very fast, as if we had an appointment that had to be kept at an exact time, or else. I remember feeling rather piqued at how fast he walked. Can you imagine? Perhaps the man at Bethesda whom Christ made walk again was annoyed that he still had the same thin legs, and Jairus thought, after the initial euphoria of his daughter's resurrection, "He could at least have got rid of her buck teeth." There we were, anyhow, practically running through the Guimet, past pimply students in blue jeans and old ladies dozing on their feet, none of whom seemed to notice us. Then we came to the Indian Department, and the Tibetan, clasping my hand tight, stood me in front of the great dancing Shiva at the centre of the Bronze room. There was no one in the room but us. Adolphe spread his hands in the air and smiled in a way I had never seen him smile before – delightedly, without a trace of irony or knowingness, a dazzling, childlike smile. If only I could say what happened then. I will try. For you, I will try. God knows you don't deserve it! But then I didn't deserve it either. How can one deserve anything so . . .'

'Stick to the point!'

'Can't you see I'm nervous? If I had hair it would be standing on end. Imagine me with hair, snowy like Larry Olivier's, all harripilated.'

'Harri . . . what?'

'Look it up. The Tibetan priest stood me in front of the statue. From behind he leant his whole body against me. Without any warning, with a cry like nothing I have ever heard, he hit me tremendously, straight, bang-wham, between the shoulders.' Adolphe closed his eyes. He was trembling. 'I'm going to come and sit next to you,' he said, 'and I am going to take your hand. You must help me to tell the rest.' He spoke in a very soft childlike singing voice, one that I had never heard from him. He came to where I was sitting on the sofa and sat down by me. Our legs touched. His was very warm under his dress. He took my hand in both his hands and turned it over and over, squeezing it as if trying to make it suppler.

'When the Tibetan hit me between the shoulders I was

looking up into the face of the dancing Shiva. I saw what anyone would see, a broad calm South Indian face of refined beauty, cast in bronze. When he hit me, the face exploded. The face exploded and I exploded with it, into a million fragments, images, sounds, feelings. I saw the fire-eater, dancing on an empty white beach; I saw scenes from my childhood as if from a great height, through binoculars; I heard the music my mother used to play for me in the evenings, fragments of Chopin and Chaminade; I heard garbled stretches of the Masses I had participated in as a schoolboy, with the same light falling on my hands as had fallen then through the stained-glass windows; I saw my lovers leaving rooms with nothing on but a white towel, laughing at me or beckoning me to follow; I saw the Tibetan himself as I had seen him at the edge of the crowd outside Les Deux Magots, but this time wearing a crown of flames.

And behind all these apparitions I saw the Face itself, reassembled but immense now, covering the sky, its vast calm eyes two pits of fire. Around it, playing in the sky as if in water, I saw huge animals with different heads, always of flame, great disembodied jaws of flame, sometimes chomping and howling, Shiva's animals, that as I looked at them in terror changed and became tender, docile, and took on the faces of my mother and grandmother, of Callas, of lovers who had been good to me. I saw, Charles, the whole cosmos was God dancing, that everything that happens is His dance, even the most terrible things, that He is dancing for ever, in massacre as in harvest, in every energy, however sinister, mocking, destructive, cynical, contemptuous, blasphemous; that there is nowhere which is not His dance, no destruction which is not a message from Him.

I saw, I understood, I knew that everything that exists in dancing in Him and in everything else, dancing in God and dancing in and through every other thing, transforming and being transformed, that there are no final barriers between anything or anyone, but that all is flimsy, provisional, sandals He wears for a second and then throws away. I saw that all the things I hated myself for and detested in others were part of His

121

dance also, and that I could not turn away from them in disgust.

To know that nothing but God exists, that everything that exists is only and for ever God, the misery as well as the exaltation, the small snails on the stones by the river as well as the yogis meditating by it, that is more than peace, more than acceptance. It is to be free to dance yourself. Nothing is created that cannot dance. Each of us has our own dance to give, our own unique steps which no one else can copy. If it is our own entirely then it will be entirely in Him and entirely fulfil His purpose in us. That is the paradox: that we are most Him when we are most ourselves, that we are most ourselves when we are lost and hilarious in Him. You and I and Maria and Jimmy and everyone else are only ever like the juggler of Notre-Dame, fools with tiny hopes and skills; but if we offer our foolishness, our hopes, our skills, if we offer them with humour and rapture, then they become holy, not walls that separate us from Him but dances within His dance. We become one of His billion limbs. The Hindus say that the name of God is SAT CHIT ANANDA – Law, Knowledge, Bliss – co-existing like the Trinity for ever, each feeding off the other, each exploding into being simultaneously. The greatest of these, pondsnipe, let me tell you, is Ananda, which is bliss. It is bliss that we came on to this earth to know; bliss we glimpse in love and in the highest friendship. A shadow of this bliss falls on us when we are moved by the light in a street or by a painting by Chardin or by the sudden wild leap in Callas's voice; these are our broken images of this eternal and indivisible bliss, broken, yes but each with a small hand-mirror in it that reflects an eyelid or cheek-bone of the Divine Face.'

Adolphe stopped dead, laughed, and then started leaping round the room, spanking himself. 'Take that, you goof-head! How could you dare to speak of Holy Things with such confidence, and at such length. Oh God, God, why did you give me such a power over words? Take this cup from me, Shiva darling! Give it to Charles here, who seems to want it!'

Adolphe sat down, buried his head in his hands and shook it

violently. Then, he looked up. 'It's all your fault, you wretch. Where were we? Don't worry. We do get to Basho in the end.' He stood up. 'Well then. I had my little old super-bash before Shiva. I leapt and leapt and was healed. I turned round to see if the Tibetan were there. He had gone. I should have realised he would be gone, but I felt sad. I wanted to thank him. Imagine wanting to thank someone for that. What would I have said? "Thank you for getting me to see God." Sublime gratitude is one of life's extreme problems . . .

'I left the Guimet, walked to the Seine, threw my costly little pills into the river, and then walked and walked all around Paris. Charles, the joy of seeing Paris with that pall of self-hatred that I had been carrying round for years, utterly lifted! The relish of it! Walking down the rue Mouffetard, watching the old women selling peaches; sitting in the rue de Buci, watching the tourists watching the tourists; stumbling round the Jardin du Luxembourg, where even the worms wriggling on the flowerbeds were marvellously witty creatures. Some flowerpots high on a window-sill in the rue des Grands Augustins seemed to me then the most beautiful things on earth. I often go to visit those flowerpots – no, I am not going to tell you the address . . . I walked and walked, and came at last to, of all places, the Shakespeare and Company Bookshop. I hadn't been there for years. It was nearly empty. The wiry old American who runs it was sitting by his desk reading. He didn't look up. It must have been about two in the afternoon. I walked to the table in the middle of the shop where new books are displayed. Two caught my eye. The first was a large new illustrated edition of Blake's *Songs of Innocence and Songs of Experience*. I opened it with my eyes shut, praying for a sign. When I opened my eyes I read the lines,

And we are put on earth a little space
That we may learn to bear the beams of love.

'They were lines I had known since I was a schoolboy, but then I read them for the first time, with my being, as you,

123

pondsnipe, would say. It took everything that I had not to fling my dark glasses in the air and shout them out loud. I realised what you would have told me in that English voice of yours, that "beams" refers both to the cross of Christ and to the burning light of love, the fire around Him. I realised that suffering, burning, rejoicing and giving light were the same thing when they were at an absolute pitch of truth. I realised that to live at that pitch was the only thing that mattered. Then I reached for the other book, and opening it read the Basho poem for the first time.' Adolphe paused and recited it slowly.

My house
Burnt down

I own
A better view

Of the rising moon.

'To burn down the old house of self and see the moon at last. To see those flowerpots, the faces of the old women, the little wriggly worms, you . . . I received the poem; I read it, there in the Shakespeare and Company Bookshop, with the tears running down my cheeks, then went home and slept for twelve hours. And here I am.'

'Saved?'

'If you like. Your word, not mine. Use whatever word suits you. Anna gave you the Basho poem; Life gave it to me.' Adolphe patted my hand. 'Do you know what I want now?'

'To sleep?'

'To hear Mark's voice again.'

'You can't. Not after all these sublimities.'

'I do not distinguish between sublimities. I'm like Shiva himself in that way, if not in many others. We must re-enter the world before I let you wander the streets of Paris again. Who knows what might happen to you if you left now with the flames of Shiva dancing round your forehead? I want to hear Mark's voice because I feel we need its sanity between us, and around us.'

124

'You're in love with him.'

'I love him. I love you. I love him in and through you. I love you through him. It's all very complex and very simple. Doesn't Mark at least ring you after all those revelations-by-the-river?'

'How did you guess?'

'Pumpernickel, I'm not nine thousand for nothing! Let's get back to reality, whatever that is. First reality, then breakfast.'


Mark rang next day at about five.

'I didn't know you knew my number,' I said.

'You gave it to me last night, you fool.'

'Where are you?'

'In the Trocadero. With Adolphe away, I've been talking to film critics about his work. They are all the same, these Parisian critics, the same blue-grey trousers, the same murderous asides. I'm exhausted.'

'Did you get anything for the Great Article?'

'Lots of malice of course. Stories about Adolphe having it off with all the electricians ...'


'Electricians? Must have been in my early period.'


'Lots of nonsense about how films should not mean, but be, or not be but mean, or both, or neither. You know what I mean. I feel lost in the French desert. I hate every empty sentence I write down.'

'Adolphe says if you don't hate your work you can't be any good. Hatred polishes. I don't believe him, but sometimes it's reassuring.'

Mark was silent.

'What did you do after we parted last night?' I asked him.

'I walked all night thinking about us, about what you had said.'

'I always think walking is the only way to see any city.'

'Bastard ... I had a letter from Kate this morning.'

'The radar third sight of women! Is she always so Victorian?'

'She loves to write letters.'

'What did she say?'

'The house is dead without you. Every moment ...'

'Kate is a poet. I've always known it.'

'Her honesty makes her a poet.'

'Honesty never made anyone a poet.'

'I shouldn't have fed you that one. I'll learn. I'm not as soft as you imagine.'

'You think I imagine you soft?' My voice sounded cheap, abrasive.

'Stop it,' Mark said. 'Let's both stop it. Last night was so wonderful, how can we be talking like this today?'

'This is reality. In reality people change, and protect their own. You know that.'

'I know that ... Am I going to see you tonight?'

'Have I ever missed a chance of seeing you?'

'You must see me clearly, or you will be lost.'

'You have no faith.'

'You're there at last. I have no faith.'

'But last night ...'

'I emoted. I gave out. I had a ball. I will store last night in my chest of memories and wrap it in damask and take it out every leap year. That is last night. Thank you for last night.'

'I'll be with you at seven-thirty. I don't have much time.'

'It was you who threw our time away.'

He had already hung up.


'Well,' Adolphe said, 'love isn't going to have an easy time getting you on its hook. There, with Mark bathing in his flea-pit in preparation for the rigours ahead, we must leave him. What after-shave does he use?'

'Kouros.'

'Well, there is the Kouros bottle, white and sleek on the shelf as he sits in the water, muttering.'

'Muttering?' I laughed. 'Mark doesn't mutter.'

'No one visits you without first practising their lines. One has to come armoured.' Adolphe stood up and stretched.

'This evening, I have to go and see my doctor.'

'Nothing serious?'

I was picking up the leaves of my manuscript that the changes of the long night had scattered.

'Nothing serious at all.'

I looked up. In the full morning light he looked small and white. 'I have tired you out. Forgive me.'

'This fagged look is one of my best. I do it when Greta's

126

here. She goes puce with jealousy. Pondsnipe?'

'Yes.'

'Walk with Basho.' He burst out laughing. 'Let's go around Paris saying to all our friends, "Walk with Basho." They'll think we've finally turned! And in fact if we meant it we'd be sane. Le beau monde understands nothing, bless it. That's why we live in it. One is certain of being misunderstood. There's a kind of peace in that.'

He started to laugh again. 'I'm thinking of you walking up and down the rue des Grands Augustins trying to find those flowerpots. When you find them they'll just sit there being very flowerpotty and not radiate anything at all. Find your own flowerpots. That's all I have to say to you. Now leave me. I feel sleep coming over me. Remind me to tell you the story of when I got the Argentinian Ambassador to dress up as Carmen Miranda. It goes on for ages and discredits half the crowned heads of Europe.'

# ·FIVE·

was so exhausted and elated when I left Adolphe's that morning that I could hardly walk. I kept telling myself that I needed rest, to sleep, but the morning was a brilliant one and I wanted to stay with Adolphe's presence longer, to carry it with me through Paris. I wanted to remember every nuance of what he had said. I found myself stopping on the corners of streets, sitting on stone benches by the Seine talking to myself in his voice, even, when no one was looking, practising his gestures, the way his hands clawed the air or fluttered upwards when he was talking, almost independently of the body, like two small doves released by a secret signal from his lap. I had a sudden hunger to ring up a friend and go over dressed as him. Charles as Adolphe as Saskia or Rembrandt's Jewish Bride, something lush and golden. Love had prompted me, like everyone else, to strange hungers, but never one so strange as this. I had kept lovers' clothes, small pieces of paper, scraps of drawings, all the normal fetishes of passion. I had never wanted to be someone else, or felt that a mere trick of make-up and intonation could transform me into him.

Thinking of Adolphe in this way, I remembered some stories of rites in Africa that an anthropologist lover had once told me – rites in which identities are exchanged between magicians, with a slaughtering of cockerels, circumcisions and sacred chanting. Was something like this happening in that apartment in Saint-Sulpice, surrounded by Buddhas and the bric-à-brac of Adolphe's contradictory yet unified life? Everything he and I had said and done in these last days seemed at once spontaneous and ritualistic in a way secret from both of us.

Was I inventing this? The thought did not perturb me.

Hadn't Adolphe said, 'It is we who invent the world.' What did the word 'invent' mean in such a context? As a child I had told long, exotic lies, but they had also always seemed far closer to the truth of my imagination than the versions I was forced to pretend to accept from the 'adults'; I had lied to keep my heart alive and magical. While thinking of Adolphe, I thought of Mark and of the book I was half-way through reading to Adolphe. I had written the book, I realised, partly to rid myself of Mark — to leave him in my past immured in my words, where he could no longer move me. Yet, reading in my own voice to Adolphe what Mark had said, re-living it all as I read, I felt as close to Mark as I ever had done. I smelt his body; I saw the way his hair fell. Adolphe had given me this gift too, among all the others. He had restored to me the 'present' of love, in which love is fresh, before words shape or pervert it. Adolphe had been a medium through which was restored to me my love for Mark, long after I had thought it over. Something stranger was happening also. There were times, I realised, when I was reading Mark's lines, that I changed myself — my voice, the way I stood — to mirror his. I held my back straighter. Once, for a moment, I felt my arms thicken, my face broaden . . .

'Guess whom I dreamed of last night?' Adolphe asked, as soon as I came through the white doors. 'Before you guess you have to admire my outfit.' He was dressed in a flaming gold caftan, with a head-dress of peacock feathers. 'The caftan is like the one Claudette wore for *The Sign of the Cross*. Just saying Claudette's name makes me feel holy all over. She has disproved for ever that dreary myth that one can't be rich, beautiful, brilliant, old, and happy. May you live for ever, Claudette! And the peacock feathers — they are in honour of Hedy Lamarr who lived that dreary myth Claudette disproved. A dance of opposites! As always — Hedy, the loveliest of them all, who ended up stealing stockings from Bloomingdales.'

'It wasn't Bloomingdales. It was some shop in Los Angeles,' I said. 'Anyway, you look fabulous. Luminous.'

'Darling, how sweet of you to say so, unsolicited. You have a line in chat. You should go into the movies. Now I know someone . . .'

'No, Adolphe, not the movies. Ever. Is that clear?'

'Not even for a million dollars?'

'Not even for two million dollars.'

'I always knew you were stupid. Think of it, boy, you and me, in the films. We'll show them.'

'Show them what?'

'Show them money. That's all they want to see, boy. One thing I did, Charles, I *made money*.' Adolphe began to laugh. 'I said that like a Texan. I *made money* . . . You still haven't guessed whom I dreamt of last night.' He parted his peacock head-dress to reveal, right at its heart, a small plastic red apple wobbling on a green plastic stem. 'Isn't it the best? To remind of sin and mortality. These days I'm so light-headed I might forget . . .' He shook his head from side to side, to make the apple wobble more. 'Guess, damn you. How can we play games if you won't play?'

'You dreamt about Mark.'

'You knew all along.'

'I think so . . . Adolphe, before we take flight – how was the doctor?'

'And I thought you were interested only in yourself – how sweet of you to remember.'

'How was he? First the doctor, then the dream.'

'I love you English. You still think you rule the world. First the doctor, then the dream. My doctor was divine. Of course, I dressed up for him. Sober, with just a hint of frou-frou about the neck in the purple silk scarf that Marlene gave me for consoling her one evening for being the most famous and beautiful woman in the world. And red socks tucked beneath black trousers – very long – to give me courage. I listened to Maria for an hour before I went – the early *Tosca* – to give my cheeks the right brave colour. I rushed into the office, brushing aside two countesses, and flung myself into one of the doctor's easy chairs. The easy chair is in grey and so was he. My doctor, by the way, looks exactly like a truffle-fed Omar Sharif. There I

133

am, flung in his chair, gazing from grey to grey, Grey Dead to Grey Living, with the most heavenly sexy smouldering grey-blue eyes. I gaze into these eyes as long as is decent, and then I say – remembering I am paying by the minute – "Well, doctor darling, you've done all the tests and whatnot. What is it? Is it curtains? Or is it just paralysis with slow loss of all mental faculties?" What did he say? He said, with a hint of regret, fluttering his divine lashes ... He said I would live another twenty years at least. I was almost disappointed. No Barium meals? No sojourn in Lausanne for the breezes and the canasta? No final trip to Sri Lanka to search for absolution in the rain-forests? "No," he said, smiling. (His teeth! Darling! Row on row of seed-pearls.) "No," he repeated. "Business as usual." What a revolting phrase! I nearly hit him with one of his Peruvian paperweights. I knew I was expected to be relieved, so I managed, with effort to squeeze two tears from my left eye. This had the desired effect. Omar Sharif patted my knee. "Doctor," I said, "I hope you don't mind my saying that to have you pat my knee in that solicitous fashion was worth both my illness and the enormous bill you will be sending me." He smiled sweetly, looking at his watch. So you see. Business as usual.'

'I'm thrilled.'

'You should be.'

'I'm so happy, I'm ...'

'In Paris one does not get sentimental before midnight. Now that we've got the small business of my mortal illness over ... to the dream. I remember my instructions. First the doctor, then the dream. They are connected. Why don't we drink some champagne?' Adolphe pointed to a silver bucket with three bottles poking out of it on the window-sill. 'Monty gave me that as a making-up present after trying to kill me on a balcony in Sorrento. I don't suppose you want to hear that story.'

'I've heard it.'

'OK, peewee. You win. Pour out two long cool glasses of champagne.'

I poured the glasses. Adolphe drank his in one go.

'Did you know that as Chekhov died he drank one last glass of champagne and threw it against the wall? No? What do they teach you in those sodomitic English schools?' He raised his glass as if about to throw it against the wall. 'No,' he said, lowering it. 'Splinters might get into one of the Buddhas' eyes and then where would we be? In one of those Buddhist hells with perpetually thirsty throats as thin as grassblades . . .'

I looked studiedly patient.

'You know,' Adolphe began, 'that I liked Mark and thought him beautiful. That warm body, that face, half shark and half child-Jesus. If I had been a hundred years younger I would have loved him like you. I was going to say, but probably much better. As it was, on the two occasions I met him, I watched him with delight, partly of course because I suspected that you and he . . . I thought him beautiful, but I never really thought about him until you started reading your novel, and I certainly never dreamed about him before, although my dreams are, as you can imagine, wildly populated.

In last night's dream, peewee, I returned to an old Turkish bath I used to frequent in Istanbul. Not what you are thinking, although I did sometimes let the hunchback masseur spank me because that gave him such pleasure (all masseurs in Turkey are retired torturers). Steam-baths are the only places I have found where I cannot think. Such a relief. Anyway, I was there again, in the centre's most vaulted room where the plaster is a rotten puce and there are sculptured birds on the ceiling. I was sitting there minding my own business, not thinking, when a young man in a long white robe came to me and told me that there was someone to see me, someone whom I had to see immediately. Oh God, I thought, it's some bloody journalist with one of those tiny Japanese cameras. White Robe took me by the hand and led me into a room where I had never been. I thought I knew every room in those baths.

'Mark was waiting there. The tiles on the ceiling were lapis lazuli, very fresh and glittering as on some of the Mughal tombs in India. There was no steam in the room and Mark was dressed – not in what he wore when I met him, brushed cords

135

and faded jacket, the usual journalist disguise – but in a long green and gold robe. It was gorgeous. He looked wonderful. I thought, is Mark dead and am I meeting him in his new heavenly identity? Not the sort of thought, you'll agree, I'm prone to think. "Adolphe," he said, "forgive me for taking up your time." "What is my time for?" I said. "I'm not here long," Mark said, "and I have something important to give you." "Darling," I said, "hand it over. I'm the most trustworthy person you know. And I've been hearing all about you. I feel . . ." Mark cut me short. "I know all that," he said, in a rather Peter Lorre tone, I have to say. But his face was shining, Charles. At times I thought it was lit from behind. I've done that in my time, you know, to impress people.' Adolphe poured himself another glass of champagne. 'Mark looked at me for a long time. Then, from beneath his green and gold robe, he brought . . . Guess!'

'Oh, for God's sake . . .'

'Guess!'

'A baby kangaroo. An ancestral Samurai sword. Three dead humming-birds on a string of seed-pearls.'

'Not very close. We're slipping. He brought a small leather-bound book, ornately and abstractly decorated à la perse. He handed it over to me. Guess what he said.'

'He said, "This is your life." He said, "These are the critiques of your films over a forty-year period. Read and despair!"'

'It's just as well I adore you unconditionally, as God is said – only said, mind you – to adore the world. By some of the wackier theologians, at least!'

'Adolphe!'

'Mark said, "Give this to Charles. It is one of the last copies in the world." He said it with the slightly shaky, rich voice of an Italian village priest saying the Mass. I was dying to ask him all sorts of questions, such as, "This is a dream, you fool; how the hell am I going to get this book to Charles?" and "What the hell is this book anyway?" and "Can I read it?", but being swept up into the fire of his blue eyes and green robe and all the lapis lazuli twinkling like Dietrich's sequins above, I said nothing and smiled. I did, however, I admit, begin to open the book. Mark reached out one of his arms and stopped me. "Only for Charles, Adolphe. Only Charles should read it." And then – don't be jealous – he came close to me and kissed me sweetly, and at length, on the lips. I haven't been kissed like that since Catholic prep school. It was heavenly! I noticed as he was kissing me that the room was filling with fragrance. It must have been oil of attar or something. Whatever it was, I can still smell it.' Adolphe closed his eyes and made little moaning noises. 'Well, that's it. Your divine messenger stands before you, awaiting instructions.'

'I have nothing to say,' I said slowly.

'No. It will take time to understand, but you will, little pondsnipe, you will.'

'You, of course, do understand?'

'Yes.'

'But are not going to tell me?'

'No. You have to find out for yourself. Of course, I might have to tell you later. You know what I'm like. But not now.'

I wandered round the room.

'Darling,' Adolphe laughed, 'you should see yourself! You look like Lillian Gish again, but this time in *The Wind*! I wish I had a camera!'

Then Adolphe began to smile mischievously. 'Wait here.'

'Where else would I go?'

'Where indeed?' Adolphe skipped into his bedroom, returning a moment later with his hands outstretched, pretending to be supporting something. 'It is heavier than I thought,' he said. 'This coming down into the sublunar world has given it gravitas. Take it from me, Charles. Take the book that Mark gave me for you. Go on.' Adolphe was now about three feet away from me. He was looking into my eyes calmly. 'Don't be scared,' he said softly. 'Everything is strange when you know it better.'

I was shaking slightly. 'I accept the book,' I said, holding out my hands.

'Well done. You are learning.'

We stood silently, Adolphe's eyes staring into mine, very large and lustrous.

'Put the "book" down on the sofa. We have so much to give each other,' Adolphe said, 'that we must give everything we can. Heavens, I'm soaring again. Cut my tongue out and stamp on it!'

'Adolphe, do you have any idea what is happening?'

'If I had an idea of what was happening, it wouldn't be.'

'Don't be smart.'

'I'm not. Why all this irritable reach after reason, peewee? And you a poet.'

'I wrote my novel . . .'

'So as to exorcise Mark. I know. It won't work because he has loved you and has a soul and loves your soul. Besides, what we create to escape our past returns to haunt our future. That is the law. Didn't they teach you anything at school? And now, enough of the Higher Rambling. I want the next scene! Let's dispel the heady fumes of this reality with another one! Though God knows they seem to be running in and out of each other these days, like rabbits in heat.' He paused. 'Mark is coming across Paris. Your armpits are fragrant with talc. You are poised, but vulnerable. Fate is coming to dinner. Not your dinner of course, since your cooking is worse than mine. You have been preparing your insults and sallies. You have put a line of kohl . . .'

'No make-up.'

'You don't have to wear make-up. You always have such naturally black rings under your eyes. It's indecent to look as if you've come from wild nights when you're as chaste as Saint Terese.'

'Not quite.'

'Not quite and not on purpose.'

'Bitch.'

'Good. You were getting a little solemn. It doesn't suit you . . . What were you wearing for the encounter? I must see it all.'

'Black shirt, black pants, black jacket.'

'When will you break yourself of the Savonarola look? If you want the pretty boys you have to look kind.'

'I don't want the pretty boys; I'm not kind. The pretty boys want someone who looks like a cross between a torturer and a butcher's assistant.'

'Well, we have been around. Were you wearing any jewelry?'

'I only have one piece of jewelry, that silver necklace you gave me. Can you imagine me wearing it to meet Mark? One must play the game, Adolphe. I looked clear, black, and masculine.'

'Can't have fooled him. I wish you'd put on that necklace, just for the hell of it. I used to meet my Marrieds looking like Theda Bara. But that was when a queen was a queen and no stinting the Cia Lenga. Now everything is so much more sotto voce, which is a jolly good thing, I suppose, though it does rather dampen the decor. Not this decor, mind you. Nothing, peewee, will every dampen my decor. My Marrieds liked the swinging censers and grass skirts. But then none of them was upper-middle-class English. That was a genre I avoided. Read. Stand over there by the phallic potted plants and read.'

'It is a long scene . . .'

'Of heart-rending pathos. I can imagine. But what you really mean is, will I shut up?'

'Right.'

'For you, peewee, I will remain . . .'

'Mum as the mice in *Maud*?'

'Mummer, if that's possible. What's the matter? You suddenly look very peaky. Not having second thoughts?'

'No.'

'What then? Seeing visions?'

'Yes, in a way.' I sat down on the sofa. 'It is strange, Adolphe. I see him again clearly as he was that evening, as he stood, in the doorway . . .'

'Oh, pondsnipe, hurts a bit, does it? The old heart aches, does it? That is what hearts are for. No weeping. Hold that head high.'

'It is as if . . .'

'He is there, I know. They are always there if you have loved them. Forget the sentiments flooding over you. It's art wot counts in the end. I don't believe that, but it's fun saying it. Cheering, even.'

'I feel as if I have betrayed him . . .'

'You have. Novelists are always selling someone out. Themselves as well as everyone else, if they are any good. It's betrayal, betrayal, all the purple and gold way to Parnassus. Betray with fervour and truth! Or go and teach Latin somewhere . . . Betrayal is the agent of almost any decent story. Think of the Crucifixion.'

'It's not so easy.'

'The higher betrayals never are. They take a lot of courage. Do you think Judas was a coward?'

'I'm going to give up writing.'

'You'll have to face you're a writer, as I had to face I was some kind of a film-director. Neither one an honourable profession. But even the juggler can attain salvation – remember that. If he offers up his pathetic juggling. Up to what? Find out . . . Besides, think how ghastly you'd be in life if you couldn't be ghastly in books. You'd probably be a rapist, or an actor. Think how awful it would be to be a bad actor – or an unsuccessful rapist.'

'You're not convincing, Adolphe.'

'I'm not trying to be convincing. I'm trying to be cheerful. Even more difficult.'

We smiled at each other.

'Mark gave you a book,' Adolphe said softly. 'Read it to me.'

'He gave me a book, yes, but was it this book?'

'Find out. And this time dare really to do his voice. You've been flirting with doing it. This time, let it appear, here, between and around us.'


Mark stood in Anna's doorway, leaning against the wall with his left hand. I opened the door, but he remained there, silently, studying me. I remembered a look he had given me years before, after we had picnicked in the grass by the river: I was leaving his house and turned to smile goodbye at him; he stood in his doorway, leaning as he leaned now, looking at me with the same sadness and the same longing. Then, as now, I turned away. It was instinctive, that slight turning away, a fear of falling into his need and never finding myself again. For a moment I thought I would close the door on him. Then I turned back. He was in faded blue jeans and a scrubbed loose white shirt.

'You never had those before,' I said, taking his hands, and pointing to the silver bangles he was wearing on his wrists. He raised his hands and placed them against my right cheek. The cold of the silver against my skin made me shiver.

'I bought them to remind me of you.'

'Liar. Come in, anyway.'

The hallway of Anna's flat is narrow. Mark's body and mine met briefly, tensely, in the corridor. I felt mine stiffen against him, against my will. He brushed past me, chuckling slightly as if at some admission we had both made. He walked to the sideboard and poured himself a gin.

'So you're becoming an alcoholic,' I said. 'Journalists always do.'

'I'm never going to be a drunk. Too many of them; one can't be imitative in everything.'

The lamplight fell on his head and shoulders. His beauty angered me.

'Why do you waste yourself,' I said, 'on pieces for mags people read only in the bath?'

Mark walked to the sofa and sat down. 'It's generous of you, to allow me time to relax.'

'It is you who keeps saying we haven't time.'

'Why do I waste myself? There are these things called a house, a car, children, a wife. You have read about them in novels. You probably despise them and think yourself above them, but they require money. You don't, of course, despise money, otherwise you wouldn't be here.' Mark waved at Anna's drawing-room. 'No, you don't despise money. You always seem to have enough of it. Or to find someone with enough of it to make you comfortable for a month here, a month there. You need quite a lot of money to keep three children in clothes.'

'I'm weeping.'

'It all sounds so banal to you, doesn't it? The travelling poet, the lonely yogi . . .'

'Where did you think that line up?'

'In the bath.'

'Not bad. I soaked my armpits, did you?'

Mark looked at me for a moment as if I were crazy. 'I'm not the sweet-smelling type. Outdoor sports, you know.' Then he said, 'Journalism bores me to death. I don't do it well enough not to feel soiled by it. But then what should I do? Teach English in a comprehensive? Put my family on the dole as I bash out a novel no one will buy because it won't be good enough either? Become a model?' He laughed at the last alternative, flexing his muscles. 'I'd be good at that.'

'How those queer photographers would love you, in your tight jeans and white shirt and your suggestion of thuggishness. Of course, you're getting a bit old now.'

Mark whistled. 'You were practising in the bath too. Yes, I am getting a bit old now.'

I walked to the window. An evening mist filled the rue Fursten-berg beneath me; the windows of the apartment opposite were blurred red squares.

'Poor Mark,' his voice began behind me. 'Bowed down with paternity, selling his shabby soul to a Sunday weekly. Not living the real life like Charles, the real artist's life.'

'Sarcasm doesn't suit you.'

'Not as much as contempt suits you.'

'Isn't eight-thirty a little early for home truths? Shouldn't we wait for the moon to be up?'

'In my family we start early . . .'

'Your family? Your beautiful pastoral no-nonsense bowling-on-the-green family? Your mother with her Sunday teas for the old age pensioners? Your silver-haired fox-terrier father? The nearest any of you get to emotion is when someone accidentally knocks over the Scrabble board.'

'My mother, dear Charles, is a drunk.' Mark's voice was cold. 'She has been since I was a child. A vicious drunk, too. The kind who says she hopes you will die one night and smiles at you sweetly the next morning as if nothing has happened. And my father, my silver-haired, fox-terrier father as you put it, is dying of Parkin-son's. Since he is an atheist and vain about his body he is also in great mental pain. Lost, and cruel to all of us.'

'I'm sorry. I didn't know.'

'There are so many things you don't know. Mostly because you never asked.'

'I know the place you went to school, your housemaster's name, the name of the first boy you fell in love with. I know the name of the make of violin you lost on Reading Station eleven years ago. God, the useless, embarrassing things I know . . .'

142

'You can produce the right details when you need to. It wasn't the details you got wrong. It was your vision of me. It took me a while to figure out your fantasy that I was sane and strong and rooted in England while you were a sort of Wandering Jew, condemned to wander the earth with a satchel full of travellers' cheques and books on oriental mysticism. When I found it out I was angry with you, a little contemptuous. It made me see you as less intelligent than I had imagined.'

'I don't . . .' I began.

'You are going to let me finish. I am not the things you thought I was. I ask you to understand that.' He smiled at me, hesitant, crooked. I saw from two thin lines on his forehead that he was sweating.

'I was young and scared when I met you,' I said. 'I was afraid of being homosexual. I needed someone to love whom I could idealise. I did make use of you. You are guilty too. You wanted a tame poet following you around . . . Let's stop this. We know it anyway. We have had all these years to think of the ways we invented and betrayed each other.'

'Yes,' Mark said gently, 'it's past; we are here. While I was talking I saw your face as it is now. I wanted to reach out my hand and touch it, as I did when we met in that café in Turl Street, and you stood in your old blue jumper. Then I wanted to touch it because it seemed so vulnerable, as if it couldn't last. Now I want to touch it because it has lasted, and will last. You have come into your real face, as I have come into mine.'

There was a silence. I saw the age-lines under his eyes.

Mark smiled. 'Shall I move you by reciting the first poem you ever wrote for me?'

'Certainly not. Was it very pure and noble?'

'I'm afraid so.'

'Does it have autumn leaves in it?'

'No.'

'That's a relief. Even though it doesn't have autumn leaves I don't think I could bear it. I can't bear anything I have written. And you? Are you happy to have fathered your children?' I smiled at the question, for its clumsiness, for what it showed of how many years and lives we had between us.

'Yes,' Mark said quietly. 'They are so funny. And they love with such abandon. I fail them, but I feel that they forgive me that. Perhaps they won't forgive me later, but now they do. It's comic, isn't it — children looking to their father to protect them, while he finds his only protection from himself in their need of him?'

I wondered, listening to Mark, if I would feel jealous of him, of them.

'I always wanted to lie naked with my father in the mornings,' I said. 'I wanted to begin the morning with the touch of his body.'

Mark smiled at me, startled. 'I cannot get up without touching them, without running my hands down their bodies. Kate is always asleep when they come in, and they come to me and lie wildly against me, as if trying to squeeze something from me. Paul loves me the most — he buries his head in my neck. He closes his eyes very tight and I hear him hold his breath as if he's drowning . . . I love that boy so much. Why did my father never tell me how much I would love my children? Mothers and daughters talk, but men have so few words for the passion they share. I will talk to Paul and tell him when the time is right and when I have the right words. I pray that the warmth in his body may not die out: I pray that it will stay as beautiful and free as it is now. If I had not loved you as much as I did I could not have loved him so much. How strange that is. Sometimes I imagine you and me in bed together with him between us, drawing from our love a different sweetness and power than those he draws from Kate's and mine, a lonelier power perhaps, something male that he will need. I have never said these things before. I have had no one to say them to.'

'You've had Kate.'

Mark smiled and shook his head. 'Kate and I are gentle with each other. But there are parts of my life she cannot and does not want to understand. My love of music, of poetry — she thinks them frivolous. She is jealous of them because she knows they take me away from her. I do flee from her sometimes, from the house, even from Paul.' Mark hesitated. 'I flee from her to the world I always saw as your world, the place where we met with such joy. You are the one person I share the whole of myself with . . .'

'We have never slept together, and Kate has given you the children you love. I could not have given you children nor could I have given you peace. Kate has given you peace.'

Mark said quietly, 'My soul stays with you. There is no other way I know of putting it.'

'What shall I do with your soul, Mark? How shall I be responsible for it? What are we? Lovers? Brothers? I don't know.'

'Why should there be words for what we are?'

'How will we decide what to do if we have no words for what we are? I'm tired of mystery.'

'You're impatient. That's different.'

'I am impatient. And why not?'

'Think of what we have. Think how hard it will always be to

understand it. Impatience is your great sin. Every mistake you have made with me and in your life has been because of your impatience. You hate the ambiguous; but the more extraordinary anything is, the more ambiguous it will often be. You know all this better than I do. You taught it to me.'

'When I wrote to you after you had left Oxford you did not reply for almost a year. Was that the "mystery" you mean? When you did write, you wrote a very un-mysterious description of painting the bathroom in your house. Painting the bathroom! Light green, wasn't it? I knew what you meant to convey to me through it: leave me alone, I belong to Kate, my family, the bathroom – don't talk to me now of mystery, of being the guardian of your soul. When I needed a few words from you – I could have lived on very little – you gave me the light green bathroom. Here you are now. I want to believe what you say. That may amaze you. I haven't wanted to believe anyone in years. I thought I had built a life in which I didn't need belief. Don't flatter me, Mark, help me.'

'I will help you,' he said. 'I think I now know how . . .' He walked to the sideboard and poured himself another drink, with the slowness of the already half-drunk. 'I will help you. At last I believe I can. Your sin is impatience. Mine is self-distrust, that English self-hatred we learn so early, which makes us treacherous. I have begun to see through it in me, to understand what havoc it makes. I always thought you purer and tougher, and that made me able to hurt you without too much conscience. I begin to see you as you are. You are so much weaker than I imagined. Thank God.'

He emptied his drink. 'I found a few school photographs the other day, in my parents' house. You never came to the house. It's old, surrounded by low hills. Although it has seen my mother's drunkennesss and my father's anger, it has always been peaceful, as if it holds a strength that cannot be stained by those who live in it. As a child, I used to stroke its walls as if it were a great silent animal that would protect me from anything. I found the photographs in an old trunk in the loft. They were a shock. I looked so cold in them, like a Gauleiter almost, with close-cropped hair, a smug smile. Head of the Sixth, of the orchestra, of the rugger team. Always the same cold, closed look. I realised for the first time, seeing them, how I had always adapted to what was expected of me. There was slyness in those eyes too behind their swagger, slyness, and cowardice. I saw I had been trained to be shrewd, ungiving, to use my mind and body to dominate those around me and to obtain from those above me the favours they reserve for those who play the game as cleverly as themselves. I was well trained and I was an excellent trainee – corrupted already by my

145

fear of my own desire, of solitude, of being called the names the solitary in England are always called. Kate changed me by demanding that I change; she had the courage to be harsh with me. But she did not change me enough, because I could hide from her in the worlds she did not want to understand.'

Mark walked across the room and stood over me.

'When I met you, Charles, everything in me was threatened. Because I could keep nothing hidden from you. I was amazed, and frightened. Not of homosexuality. I had accepted that I was bisexual. I was frightened of the intensity of our intimacy. In all my other relationships I had always known where I began and ended; I had always kept back a part that watched; with you I had the sense that we were each other. I felt myself drowning in you. Of course I did not write. Of course I wrote banalities. I hoped if I was cold to you I would find my coldness again, that you had taken from me. I hoped that if I hurt you enough − I knew how proud you were − you would leave me alone. The plan worked. My cruelties always work. I lost you as completely as any coward could have wished. All would have been well, except that by losing you I was also losing myself. We are each other, the best, the strangest part of each other . . . Nothing that happened to me − even my love for Kate or Paul − has been as rich as it could have been, because you were not there to share it.'

'It's cruel of you,' I said slowly, 'to have changed so much.'

'Cruel?'

'Yes. You leave me nowhere to stand. 'Don't think I didn't hide from you too. I hide from everything.'

'I've never thought of you as the hiding kind.'

'I've been running from everything for years − from sex, from money, from responsibility. From memory . . . I ran from you as you are into obsession for you, which I fed in solitude. I hardly needed you to be there at all. I hid from you in the poems I wrote for you. When you withdrew, I hid from your withdrawal. I hid in anger against you. I hid where I have always hidden − in my myth of myself as the victim. I should have rung you; I should have held you to our love. I did not, not from courage but from fear, from a need to be rid of you, because you made me feel too deeply. I have always made a parade of feeling so as not to have to feel, played passionate so as not to have to feel passion. Our disguises are different but the coldness and fear are the same. I have lacked the courage to be simple, and that in the end is the only courage: to be simple without myths or words or poses or beliefs to hide behind. All these years I hid in a contempt for you because I thought that I was living and growing and you were dead. Now I see you are the one that has grown.'

'The past can burn down,' Mark said passionately. 'It *is* burning down. We're in this room and I feel it is our first meeting, the first room in which we have met. I do not believe in the person I was; I do not believe in the person you were. What happened does not define or limit us. If we live these days well they will heal us.'

'Beautiful words.'

'But you do not believe them. You do not trust me and you do not trust yourself and you do not trust life.'

'You put it clearly.'

'You will have to trust me.'

'Is that a threat?'

'A demand. I cannot open everything I am to you if you do not trust me. You have to trust me, for my safety and yours. I'm going now. We have said everything we can say tonight. I'm exhausted.'

'Stay,' I found myself saying. 'Stay here.' I leant forward and kissed him on the mouth. Stepping back, I saw how sunken and bloodshot his eyes were.

'You are no longer afraid of me. How happy that makes me.'

My eyes filled with tears. Mark put his hand against my chest as if to steady me. 'You don't cry enough.'

'I had forgotten I could.'

'We used to cry a lot . . .'

'Those were young tears. These are not.'


Adolphe snivelled, 'Darling, it's *La Bohème*, Act VIII, set on Mars! The only bad thing, of course, is that I'm not in it! Couldn't you at least have put my photo on the mantelpiece, or paused half-way to show *A Long Way to Mexico*, that funniest of my films? Considering it was I who brought you together again, you don't talk about me nearly enough.'

'Don't be flighty. What do you think?'

'Being me, I adore all the grim comedy of human misunderstanding. So I loved the way you had to come to Paris and peel each other's eyeballs before you finally found out about Mark's mother, his background and your image of it. I had a black lover once who left me because I could never remember whether he came from Guadeloupe or Martinique. What's in three syllables? Only a world. I'm still not sure which he came from. And I thought I was madly in love with him, madly

147

enough to follow him around Paris with a broken milk-bottle under my coat.

Of course, if the ego wasn't so monstrous we wouldn't have all these super recognition scenes, with flashing lights, and soaring high notes, and then where would we be? Everyone would see each other immediately and float about smiling, avoiding each other like the plague. Very boring, though probably very healthy!' Adolphe paused and walked to a black box on the window-sill and drew out a cigarette and a long ebony holder. 'I feel like a Russian cigarette! I don't smoke often, as you know, but this is an occasion for a long cigarette holder. It's this Mark creature. Of course, thank God, I'm much too old to fall in love with anybody – but the beauty of him, the balls. I thought there was something wacky in those eyes. Very unlike any of my Marrieds, I must say, whose level of self-awareness was generally pre-neolithic. Though they did of course whisk off their clothes at the drop of a hatpin. That's about all they did do, if I remember. But Mark, my dear, Mark. Words fail me.'

'No they don't.'

'No, they don't, but I want them to at this second. I want a second's silence to drink to that man. What was he doing with you?'

'Thanks.'

'Actually I was proud of you. You do know yourself better than I thought. Of course you were enjoying yourself wildly in that aria about escape – I wanted to clap, or bring on the trombones – but you were not just enjoying yourself.'

'I wasn't enjoying myself at all.'

'Don't be pompous. There's hardly anything more enjoyable in life than a good self-excoriation in the presence of someone who's prepared to forgive one anything. And Mark, the divine Mark...'

'Don't mock him.'

'Mock him? I'm going to hire Delphine's houseboat and sail a silk banner with his name up and down the Seine! Have I made my point?'

'I have never known you not to. Do you know what was happening to me while I was reading to you?'

'I'm clairvoyant on occasions but not this one.'

'I was changing the book as I was reading it out loud. Not big changes, just small phrases here and there. They arrived, they seemed right, they seemed to be more truthful than the truth. God, that sounds banal!'

'Humans are allowed one banality every five minutes.'

'When Mark was talking about his son, I suddenly remembered the beauty and fervour of what he had said, and I elaborated on it, carried it further. And when I was speaking of how I had failed him and failed myself, I went further than I had meant to. You see what you do to me?'

'Make you honest? Don't be dishonest. I'm just an atmosphere in which you can be shameless. You have a long way to go, but you're trying. Two cheers.'

'It's stranger than that.'

'Of course it is.'

'It's the dream you had . . . the book . . . Mark giving you the book to . . .'

'Don't put it into words. Don't throw a net of words around it all. Let it breathe. Let us breathe. Let it and us dance together. Who knows where we might dance to? What's that song? "Let's Trip the Light Fantastic." What on earth is the Light Fantastic? Sounds like a Tunisian I knew once.' Adolphe, waving the remains of his Sobranie in the air, began to dance. 'Two steps forward, three swoops back, three great Russian strides forward, two hip-rumbas to the left — Our Light Fantastic. We've invented a dance! Don't stand there gawping at me! Come up and do it!' He grabbed me and forced me up, moving me back and forward, pressing my shoulders, my hips, my arms. 'I wish Mark was here,' he gasped. 'Oh, but he is! So is Anna! Bless all the dancers, however crooked their steps! Why isn't that one of the Beatitudes?'

We collapsed on the sofa with our arms around each other. Adolphe leant his head on my shoulder, and looked up at me, fluttering his eyelashes. 'Know who taught me to flutter like that? Dorothy Lamour, when we got stuck in a lift at the Waldorf Astoria. In an hour I got it down. Practise.'

'No.'

'I said practise.'

I practised.

'Not exactly geisha-perfect but not bad. You see, you can be human in spurts. It's fun, isn't it?' Adolphe paused, to catch his breath. 'You mean to say the book is changing as you read it out to me? How delicious! The power I feel!'

'Rubbish! And if so,' I said in his German officer voice, 'if so, you must give it up!'

'Darling, one should transcend not renounce. How easy it sounds put like that. The beauty of language: one can conquer evil and become the Buddha all within a one-comma sentence which doesn't even blush.'

We sat silently in the pale early morning light. Then I kissed Adolphe on the lips.

'What's that for?'

'Gratitude.'

'Never use that word to me! How could we be so free together if you weren't giving me something delicious? So why do we have to thank each other? It is, that's all. It is, as things should be. I want to tell you something. Are you sitting comfortably?'

'This sofa is for sprawling and displaying on, not sitting.'

'Don't be smart, or I'll cut your wings off.' Adolphe stroked my face and then stood up. 'Somehow I always need to stand up when I'm delivering. Maria Jeritza could sing "Vissi d'arte" lying flat on her back, but I need to be standing to do the big arias – this caused havoc, as you can imagine, in my now-defunct love-life. Can you imagine always having to leap out of bed to say anything? What I am trying to say, my dear Charles, through the whirligig, is that you came at the right time in my life. I love you but I'm not in love with you. I don't any more want to be in love with anyone. I know so many old queens that pay someone to pump away at their limp little you-know-whats or do odd things with them involving crowbars and ice-cream.

150

I've nothing against it, but why, I ask them, why not savour the silence, why not step out into the last freshness, instead of trying to recapture what didn't probably give you much happiness anyway? I get quite preachy, I can tell you. Why have we all been to the *Rosenkavalier* three hundred times, if not to learn in the end to play the Marschallin? Not that I'm playing her with you, pondsnipe. I'm playing myself. It is wonderful, this chatty silence at the end. So much becomes clear in it. I'm not scared any more of anything. I'm not miserable. I'm not, of course, "enlightened". I can't levitate or cure syphilis. I know what I have done and not done. And here you are now, to mock and cherish shamelessly. I'm lucky. It's a joy to know that I am able to love you without hurting you or being hurt myself, because it shows I'm no longer addicted to suffering. And also – please don't be offended – you bore me slightly, as all human beings who see each other clearly bore each other slightly, but in the gentlest way. You'll find out and you'll understand that this mild boredom is not the killer of invention but the mother of it. Understand?'

'I think I do.'

'I think you do, too.' Adolphe came up to me and held my face in his hands. 'And as for you, monkey-face, do you know that I have come into your life at exactly the right time?'

'I do.'

'Then tell me. I can stand a lot of celebrating.' He sat beside me.

'It's all right,' he said, 'you don't have to stand and walk around. You can sit. Say something just and tender. If you can't manage the just, the tender will do.'

'If I bore you, you infuriate me.'

'Well, that's the young and the old in a nutshell. Let's get on to the celebration.'

'You are finishing what I am beginning. You are everything I want to become – loving, flamboyant . . .'

'Pile it on!'

'You have learnt a style of survival that is not cold. You have created out of all the pain of your life a garden for others to picnic in.'

'The old queen with the heart of a Tupperware rose.'

I was laughing.

'And finally, I love you so much .. '

'No "finally" about it.'

'Because you are sweet, sad, and subversive.'

'All at once?'

'All at once.'

'Is that all?'

'No. I'm beginning to think, no, to know, there is something even further, even closer, between us.'

'Little banana, what is this something?'

'It's spiritual. You know damn well it is. There is no other word – and that doesn't help.'

'I know more than you know I know.'

'If you don't think I know that ... Will you tell me all one day?'

'We'll see. Depends on how you progress.'

'You make it sound like an exam.'

'It is, in a way. It is. It has to be. I adore sounding sibylline.'

'You sound about as sibylline as Carmen Miranda.'

'If you knew Carmen as I knew Carmen. I'm tired now. This empress has to retire to her boudoir to be ready for tomorrow. I think we should do something wonderful and special before you go. Do you know how they make love in Buddhist Heaven?'

'I didn't know they did.'

'How little you know! Heaven will be nothing but love-making of the most fine-flung, starry, musical sort! Heaven will be full of the most delectable sillinesses of every kind! I promise you. They make love, pondsnipe, by touching fingertips.' Adolphe stood up. 'Humming-bird, will you touch my fingertips?'

I stood up and opened both hands wide. Our fingertips touched. We swayed lightly.

'Well, did you have it?'

152

'Have what?'

'The Divine Whatnot.'

'No.'

'Neither did I. But we had something lovely, and I was pleased to see that your hands are so wiry and veined they look almost as old as mine.'

'Bitch.'

'No, darling. The clear, beady eye – la vraie tendresse.'

·SIX·

# ·SIX·

After leaving Adolphe, I sat on the rim of the large fountain at the centre of the place Saint-Sulpice. It is hard to sit on, because it is very smooth, and I kept nearly slipping into the water. Looking up at Adolphe's windows in the prosaic, clear June sunlight, I smiled to myself. How hard it was to imagine what had been going on behind those bland-looking ochre blinds on a morning such as this – Paris in its June bustle, old women passing with great plastic shopping bags, tourists coming down the steps of Saint-Sulpice itself, blinking into the sun and putting cream on their parched lips, workmen with pot-bellies on scaffolding, hammering without enthusiasm. Yet what had happened, and what was happening, did not seem foreign to all this ordinariness. Adolphe's world was fantastical, baroque; but so was this ordinariness, known in its real relations.

A young blond man came up to me, and we started talking. He rolled a joint and we smoked it together. He told me of his life: he had worked on railways; smuggled hashish in Turkey; he had been a male prostitute; nearly got married three times. What was he doing in Paris? Living with a young Moroccan girl he had met in Germany, waiting tables at Saint-Germain in the evening. 'C'est une vie,' he said, with some pride. 'Yes,' I said, 'c'est une vie.' 'Il faut danser avec la vie,' he said, putting an arm lightly on my shoulder and smiling. 'Yes,' I said, smiling at the echo of Adolphe and at the memory of our Light Fantastic. Three steps forward, three steps . . . As the man talked, all the different details of the square started to dance together – the two large drumhead towers of Saint-Sulpice, the glitter of the light on the fountain; the workmen scratching

157

behind their ears and waving to each other; the sign on the cinema: *'La Chambre de Musique* de Satyajit Ray'; the pampered little poodle by the trees, lifting one delicately shaved leg to pee. None of the details belonged to each other in any schema the mind alone could invent, or understand, and yet they could not exist without each other, for that moment or any moment.

A quoi tu penses?' the blond boy asked me. 'A la Musique,' I replied. He smiled. 'La musique . . . il n'y a que ça.' I asked him, if he had a knife and wanted to rob me, would that be 'la musique' too. 'Of course,' he replied, in English, 'but not good music.' He added, 'And I don't have a knife today,' showing me a scar above his left breast that he had got in a fight. 'That time,' he said, shrugging his shoulders boastfully, 'I nearly died.'


I'd arranged to meet Anna for lunch at La Cafetière. She was waiting for me, wearing a light blue cotton dress and gold sandals.

'Has the New Man declared himself?' I smiled.

'I know you think I'm hooked on Lerve, but there are days when I'm just happy because I am. And it's not because I've written a song about Death and Parting either. It's because I am Anna and it is June and you are paying for lunch. I'm going to eat like a horse, I promise you. They do the best gazpacho in the world here, and then there's côte d'agneau . . .'

'What's happened to you?'

'June has happened. It's happening everywhere, haven't you noticed? All the beautiful boys out with their white shirts flapping. Last night two girls with hooked noses, in flowery print dresses, played excerpts from the *Magic Flute* in the place Furstenberg. On flutes, too. Imagine! I was trying to work but gave up and flung open the windows, and just "let it all in", as Hans would have said. He wasn't entirely stupid, that one . . .'

'And you cried.'

'If you can't cry at Mozart, what can you cry at? First they did Pamina's "Ach ich fühl's", very sad and slow, and the Papageno and Papagena's aria: Pa pa pa-pa-pa-pa pa,' she began in her low hoarse voice. 'They'll throw me out if I sing any more. Did you know that on his deathbed Mozart talked on and on about Papageno? Mozart knew everything. I've decided I've been looking for a Papageno all my life.'

'Who wears Guerlain and drives a Maserati.'

'I'll surprise you yet. How's the Papageno of Saint-Sulpice? Tell him when you next see him that I'll never speak to him again unless he takes me out to dinner soon! Tell him that if he doesn't call me soon I'll come and take out all his feathers.'

'Adolphe's feathers are made of some unknown indestructible material. Platinum and asbestos . . .'

'I'm going to order for us both and then you are going to tell me everything.' Anna flashed her slim, braceleted wrist at a young waiter, who came running. She smiled at him, and he blushed. 'Gazpacho, Côte d'Agneau. You need a little meat, Charles. You look razzed.'

'No sleep.' I reconstructed as far as I could all the details of the last evening, the dream, the reading, Adolphe's Light Fantastic.

'Heavens,' Anna said, 'a spiritual orgy! What is it about Adolphe that gets everyone to take their mental clothes off and dance al fresco? He's a sort of psychic Messalina.'

'I'm in love with him.'

'At least you see it now. Why don't you go to bed with him?' Anna giggled. 'I know. There's no point for either of you. How lovely. One should either be free for it or free of it. Anna's first law of thermodynamics. She looked up, leant forward and kissed me. 'You look happier than you have for years. Since Mark . . .'


Adolphe opened the white doors himself, smiling.

'How did you know I was about to ring?' I said.

'Sheer genius', he replied.

He had a white chiffon ballroom dress on, a large paste tiara, and glitter in clusters of small stars all over his face.

'Who am I tonight?' He stepped back and crumpled his face. '"Now,"' he said in a small, erased voice, '"now I know I have a heart, because it's breaking."'

'That is the Tin Man in *The Wizard of Oz*.'

'Exactly.'

'You are not the Tin Man.'

'You noticed. No, tonight, peewee, I'm one of my all-time favourites, my ultimates. Ideally, I should appear and reappear in a large shining round pink bubble.'

'You're Glinda!' I cried, 'Glinda, the Good Witch of the North!'

'One day I'll do the pink bubble. I so love the moment when it sails over the green and golden hills.'

'You don't have the teeth for the part.'

'Darling,' Adolphe said, taking out his false teeth and waving them above his head, 'you have to suspend disbelief sometimes. It's only polite.'

'And I am Dorothy, I suppose?'

'You pose as Myra Gulch, but you're purest Dorothy underneath! Don't worry, it's not your most shaming role.' Adolphe skipped twice, took me by the hand, and dragged me into the room. The sofa was draped today by a long brilliant gold cloth, other sections of which were wound round the pedestals of the Buddhas. A circle of burning candles surrounded the sofa. At intervals between them were placed seven bowls of water. 'Seven bowls for the seven senses. That they may all be purified. Fire and water, mirror and shadow, and all around Glinda's Gold of Revelation. The gold comes from Liberty's. I was going to make it into a Harlow-type ball-gown, but thought it was more appropriate this way. And it is. And all manner of things are well!'

'What have you been taking?'

'It's the young who need to take things. All the old need to start to feel high is to look over their shoulder where Death is standing, with his legs apart like a San Francisco cop. My death of course looks like Jean Marais in *Orphée*, slipped into Casarés' black dress, with a shining silvery bicycle chain round his neck.' He dipped his beringed right hand into one of the bowls nearest us. 'Give me your face.'

'What for?'

'Too many questions make Good Witches angry. Give me your face.'

I leant forward. Adolphe, humming something, put water on my eyelids and lips. 'There you are. "And be not conformed to this world but be ye transformed by the renewing of your mind. For I reckon that the sufferings of this present time are not worthy to be compared with the glory that shall be revealed in us." Dear St Paul. For a tent-maker he had the most charming mind.' Adolphe went on, '"United souls are not satisfied with embraces; they desire each to be truly the other, which being impossible, their desires are infinite and must proceed without a possibility of satisfaction." Thomas Browne, *Religio Medici*. For a doctor . . .'

'He had the most charming mind?'

'Exactly, peewee. I suppose it was all that Death he dealt with – made his mind soar like a lark . . .'

'Like a lark? Really.'

'Remember that Glinda is a simple pastoral soul. That Thomas Browne, by the way, is all very beautiful, but it isn't true. Unified souls do desire truly to be each other and – this is Glinda's law and don't you ever forget it – they can be. Ha! They can be each other! Did you hear me?'

'Adolphe, the whole of Paris can hear you.'

'That's what I said to Renata Scotto after her Lady Macbeth. "Did you hear me?" she said in her little gin-soaked pixie voice. Enough of her. The mystery of compassion is that we can become each other. Practise believing that. Practise for a year without stopping, believing everything possible. Look, we can't go on like this all evening, or we'll end up like two Turks on a carpet, gazing sleepily at each other.'

'"United souls are not satisfied with embraces."'

'That's not entirely true either.' Adolphe kissed me lightly, then spread his arms wide in the air and sank on to the sofa beside me, flinging his chiffon train over my right leg.

161

'So,' he said, 'read to me. Mark and you have raved and sobbed . . .'

'Hardly sobbed.'

'I meant "sung". Sorry. You have raved and sung in Anna's apartment. He has left. It is three in the morning, someone is playing Chopin passionately on a piano in an attic.'

'No one is playing Chopin passionately in an attic.'

'Well, that's a relief. Chopin is too passionate to be played anything but coldly, like Bach. So, it's three o'clock. No one is playing Chopin or Debussy or Chaminade. Silence hangs over Saint-Germain. Your tiny hands and heart are anything but frozen.'

'Adolphe . . .'

'Silence hangs over Glinda too, the great chocolate star of silence. '

'I could not stay in the flat after Mark left.'

'I should think you couldn't. All those arias still throbbing off the walls.'

'I felt too over-wrought. All the objects in Anna's flat looked too heavy, too sad, too ornate.'

'And only twenty-two minutes before they had been burning with a secret light . . .'

'I'm warning you.'

'Warn away. Remember De Gaulle. A Frenchman always does his thing. Anyway, I understand. Mark was there; the objects burned away, sizzle, sizzle. Mark left; the objects, the elephants, the Ming whatnots, the candlesticks, they all, like sad animals at sunset, returned to their old gloom. That is how it is.' Adolphe shrugged.

'I needed the cold and silence of the night; I needed the river.'


'You're not going to jump in, are you? I thought no one tried suicide any more in modern novels.'

'Adolphe . . .'

He put both his hands over his mouth and rolled his eyes. I went on.


'The city was deserted; the quais of the Seine shone silently in the early morning light. I sat by the river and sang to it to keep me warm. I do not remember what I sang. I sang anything that came into my head — scraps of Cole Porter, of Mozart, louder and louder, listening to the sounds travelling under the bridges . . .'


'I wish I'd been there. I'd have giggled myself sick.

'*Adolphe!*'

'Sick with pleasure. Don't be paranoid. It makes you bug-eyed.'


'I was singing for Mark, trying to say with my voice what I had not been able to say when he was there. I thought that if I sang loud enough the sound would carry to him, would enter his dreams, bring him peace.'


'All those things at once? You were ambitious.'


'Mark did not want my singing . . .'


'No, he wanted you.'


'I stopped. It was dawn. I knew I had to choose to love him.'


'Amazing what a good sing can do for one. After a few songs, one's ready for anything.'

'I chose it lightly, as if I did not know it would cost us everything.'

'Nonsense,' Adolphe chortled. 'That is why you chose it. Anything less drastic you'd have turned your nose up at. You must have shivered with fatal delight, choosing to love him. At last. And about time. Paris at dawn is fatal to good sense of any kind. The people I have chosen to love at dawn, walking the Boule Miche or standing, like you, by the river ... The sun comes up; the bridges walk out of the night and stand sad and blue in widening pools of light. It is all a lot too much for any sensitive heart. It just has to go crazy. It's expected. I can't help wondering: which Cole Porter you were singing. Was it something specially for Mark?

> Where is the life that late I led?
> Where is it now? Totally dead?
> The marriage scene is quite all right
> Yes, during the day
> It's easy to play
> But what a bore at night.'

'You're wicked.'
'I'm not wicked. Cole was and knew almost everything. You know what he said when I visited him when he was dying in hospital? He was dying and depressed and said he was longing to go. "Won't you miss anything?" I asked him. "Won't you miss Broadway?" "Broadway?" Cole laughed. "Won't you miss les garçons?" "Les garçons? God no ... There is only one thing I will miss. Only one thing – my Queen Anne chairs ..."
Or were you singing:

> Paree will still be laughing after
> Every one of us disappears
> But never forget her laughter
> Is the laughter that hides the tears.

'Next time you have a night of passion under the bridges of the

Seine, sing that one. It has the Queen Anne ring.'

'I'll remember.'

'Don't be frosty with Glinda. What did you sing?'

'I'm embarrassed . . .'

'Don't fool me.'

'"I get no kicks from champagne."'

'A la Sarah Vaughan?'

'A la Sarah Vaughan.'

'Shakes, swoops, wobbles, and all?'

'And all.'

'Oh, my peewee. To have missed that! You wouldn't reproduce it for me, now, here?'

'No.'

'Just as well. We'd laugh so much we'd both pass out. "But I get a kick out of you." And Mark will no doubt get a kick out of you in every sense. He's had quite a few kicks already, poor Wonderboy, and God knows there must be worse – oh, and better – to come.'

I started to laugh.

'I don't trust that laugh. Glinda knows that laugh.'

'There is worse to come – a letter from you.'

'You cheat! You know I never write letters, and when I do there is no punctuation or spelling! Adolphe writing to Charles from Venice for the plot's sake! I love it, though. I thought I was just going to be banished to Venice while you and Wonderboy dilated each other's hearts. So I am back where I belong – centre stage.'

'Next morning, a letter from Adolphe express, in a fat mauve envelope reeking of Guerlain.'

'Guerlain! I hate Guerlain! It must have been Benares Frankincense. Are all my odours wasted on you?'

'Darling,' (it began), 'don't be surprised I am writing. I'm a creature of iron whim, as you know. I met Anna with THAT MAN two days ago, at Nico's on the Zattere. It was bound to happen, my meeting her I mean, for all the toupee and dark glasses and my

165

trying to walk without the famous wiggle. Anna looked ill, dramatically hopeless, with great fat greasy black bags under her eyes which could only partly have been helped by artifice, and was febrile and funny and febrilely funny. Of course the Lecture happened. I knew it would, but at least she had the savoir vivre to wait until the profiteroles.

'Which brings me to you. I see you growing impatient. Was it Rochefoucauld who said no one can bear the conversation to stray too long from themselves? Anna told me about Your Man. Goodness me. I got the lot out of her − the past, the present. Yes, yes. She isn't at all convinced by your "All's well with the world" performance on the phone.

'Here is where I put on my white wig and lorgnette and peer at you and say, be careful. I saw you were ripe for some sort of disaster at the party − you looked so peeled. When you look like that anything can happen. You must protect yourself. You have much to give everyone (this is the flattery part). You can't afford to give it all to some neurotic half-homosexual Married who will love you and leave you and scoot back to the car and kids when he's had his how's-your-father. You'll have to face one thing soon, and face it hard and long and good. DON'T WASTE YOUR TIME ON ANYONE. What does it say in Ecclesiastes? The time is coming when we shall work no more. Exactly. Work is the thing (I who have done so little) − work and art are the thing − and not all this passion business. You've had that. The twenties are for that, and you've had your twenties. Shine, but don't burn. Be as frivolous as you can. You've got enough Russian in you to have you floating down the Seine in a sack in no time. Always have three at a time: one young and mad; one safe and married; one old and rich. Three is the perfect number. It isn't the number of the Trinity for nothing.

'Maybe, of course, you don't want to survive. There is a lot to be said against survival. You get uglier, your friends die, Arabs or Mick Jagger buy the chateau you want to stay in. But you live to see the world free of illusion (free-ish) and you live to find some of it good (as God is supposed to have found all of it − which must be a mistranslation). And you live to love new friends as I love you, that is, if you are as intelligent and sweet-natured as I have proved to be. And as lucky. Looking at Tiepolo and eating squid once a day at Montine's is quite enough for me; I can't help thinking it should be enough for everyone.

'I must go. The dawn is unshadowing the Rialto. Good luck. I shan't be coming back to Paris to look after you. I'm off to Africa for a new film and a new tan. This new film I am confident will be my worst. Lots of lions, at least. A divinely beautiful and stupid

American is playing the lead, and most of my time will be taken up with seeing he doesn't get syphilis from the locals and cutting his lines to a minimum. The agonies of true art . . .

'Never less than three, remember. Repeat after me. Never less than three . . . Will all my wisdom have been wasted on you?'

I finished, looked up at Adolphe.

'Well, well, me to a tee. I offer you a survival kit tested in the most inhospitable climes, but do you take it? Do you hell! You wrinkle up your nose at it. You read it over and say, "How funny," and let it fall. Am I right?'

'You are right.'

'And you are right. Because you are you. A lizard is a lizard, a stone a stone, Charles is Charles. All life's comedy and tragedy is in that. And how could you listen to me with the Plot still to find its end? You could not stop the singing now, or the Plot would have stopped there, after all the suffering and Cole Porter. And Charles is addicted to Plot. You need Plot, as my New York friends need cocaine.'

Adolphe paused. 'How one has to love non-event to love wisdom! How one has to love the silence of long, empty, event-less days. Wisdom is wary of Plots; that's why wisdom is such a bore to those like you who want the soaring violins and the assignations with the Count or Countess (or both!) in the mid-night garden. Blessed are the Plotless for they shall see God.'

'Adolphe, really,' I interrupted, 'you railing against Plot. You of all supreme Plotters . . .'

'If you are trying to say that I am a paradox – I admit it. If you are trying to say I am a hypocrite – I admit it. There's a lot about my life even you don't know, and that would shock you if you did. But can the crocodile sprawled in the mud not look up at the stars? Can the blinded bird not remember the mountains she once flew over? Perhaps it is the very sprawling of the crocodile that shoots his glances to the stars, the darkness that covers the bird's eyes that makes her long to remember everything she has lost, and so recover it. What rhetoric! I didn't know I had it in me!' Adolphe started to do the Light

167

Fantastic and then stopped. 'You are the hypocrite! For not admitting how much of all this conflict you share! Down on your dirty English knees! Why would you be here if you did not already know what I am saying? That is why we are friends. That is why I am pouring you this minute another long cool glass of champagne. Drink up and drink to me and Plotlessness. And when you have – on with the Plot. The opera must go on. The opera shall go on, until all the worms are seraphim and the Adolphes are silent and the Charleses good. Heavens, I'm soaring. Of course I shall be silent long before you are good.'

'I know that.'

'Well, that is something. On with the Plot. What fun it is to orate! If only they had spas where everyone could give long wild speeches, there'd be no illness at all. I promise to be Plotless and not interrupt for ten minutes.'

Adolphe closed his eyes. I went and stood by the window, waited, and began.


Standing above Anna's table with the morning light falling in a calm square on it, I realised that, at last, I trusted Mark. I trusted Mark but I did not trust time. I was afraid of the disappointments it could still prepare for us. To trust Mark now, at last, was to make myself more helpless, not less; now there would be no anger or irony to hide in. Across the rue Furstenberg, in the opposite apartment, a boy naked except for a blue towel stood at his window looking down at the morning. He saw me and smiled shyly; I tried to smile back, but felt the muscles of my face tauten. Whatever happened between Mark and me now would bring suffering.

And Kate? Would she not be made to suffer by us? Had she not been made to suffer already? How could I ask for her husband's love without wounding her? What could I give him, without doing her evil? I understood that morning that there was nowhere I could hide from Kate. I knew how much she had given Mark and how much he had learnt from her; I knew how much he loved the children she had given him. I remembered how brave she had always been with me, not without flashes of anger or sullenness, but always, I knew, trying to understand me so that she could understand her husband, and allowing her liking for me to conquer whatever resentment she had. Or at least lie alongside it. Kate, I

168

knew was not grasping or stupid; I could not take refuge in any dismissal of her or any feeling that I alone could help Mark live his life; nor could I pretend that her love for him was more superficial than mine. I had known from that first glance at Kate and from all her words and actions afterwards that she loved Mark as intensely as I did. She had weathered him in a way I had not — weathered his failures and griefs, weathered his need for solitude and his need for me. I knew that there would be no other man who could give her what Mark had given her. I knew too Kate had the courage that comes from long love; she would fight for her love with every weapon she had; that fighting could wound us all.

Whatever Adolphe might say in his letter, there would be no worldly arrangement for our love that would not mock and denigrate Kate. How could Adolphe's epigrams help us, Mark and Kate and myself, facing each other and unable to turn away? I had always believed that the greatest sin was the destruction or mockery of love — how could I now participate in it? I myself had lived in a solitude bare of Mark's love for all the years we were separated — how could I think of consigning her to that? I could not hurt her without knowing at every moment how much I was hurting her. Neither could Mark.

I realised also that part of my love for Mark was his love for Kate; that I loved the calm at the heart of all his nervousness that came from his marriage to her, from the warmth of their life together. Mark, I saw — this was the greatest irony — was able to love me fully at last because he had been released by Kate into his true strength. It was to Kate in large part that I owed the simplicity of our days, to Kate's patience with a man who had needed reassurance to learn to accept his feelings. I realised that part of the fullness I loved and needed in Mark was that he was able to live roles I could not. I could trust Mark, I saw, as a brother, a friend, a lover, because he was also able to be a protective husband and father. I could receive his love without irony because I knew it was not a fantasy he would disown, but something that had ripened within him with all the other choices he had made. Mark's love for me was inseparable from his love for Kate and his children. His need for me was mixed with his need for Kate and his children, however we might both struggle to separate them in favour of a convenient clarity. His hunger for the tenderness and truth that a man could bring him was not to be divided from those that Kate and his children brought him.

Knowing these truths then, and knowing that I knew them more clearly than Mark could, was my pain and my responsibility; I had to try and be worthy of them and of the people caught in them.

Wave after wave of bitterness and anger closed over me that morning as I penetrated deeper into the place where love had brought me; waves of rebellion against what I was learning and what I understood Mark and I might have to do. But each time they threatened to close over and drown me I saw Mark's eyes looking at me calmly. I saw his face as I had seen it the night before. Grave and full of gentleness. There could be no retreat for either of us from what we knew, and felt.

Anna rang at noon that day from Venice. 'I'm spending my last shekels on talking to you. Is that wise?'

'Love is wisdom.'

'Not always.' Her voice had the raw, edgy, half-controlled quality it has when she has smoked and drunk too much.

'You were drunk last night.'

'Bravo. I gave the Buddhist a lecture he was not anticipating. Told him he was a fraud (true), a lousy lover (not true). He went on smoking calmly in the lotus position − *my* cigarettes, naturally − and said, "I am what I am; a rose is a rose; there is no point in struggling against any of it." I've got to get out of this. You're not saying anything because you know I know the answers and can't face them. I don't want to be wise. Please God, give me wisdom, but not until there are lines all over my face.'

'Enter a convent. Make it a nice warm convent in Yugoslavia, so that I could come and visit.'

'I'd be a good nun, actually. Marvellous at confession. Why did you lie to me last time we talked?'

'Lie to you?'

'About Mark. This telephone's costing me a fortune, so reply truthfully. Do you love him?'

'Yes.'

'Don't you want to run? You usually do these days. In the old days you'd stay and climb the cross and order the nails. Now you've grown shrewder.'

'I want to run.'

'Thank the Virgin. There's hope then. Second question . . .'

'Not sure I want to answer it.'

'Great friends are not allowed not to answer. That kills everything. Do you love Mark because he is unattainable? If so . . .'

'I'm just repeating the old dance to a different rhythm.'

'Yes. And there's something cynical about loving like that. As if you love like that so as not to be broken.'

'You lecture me like he does.'

'Answer me.'

'I am afraid for us, Anna — how could I not be? — but I am not afraid of him. You cannot imagine how new it is not to be afraid of the man I love.'

'I think I might just be able to.'

'I do not know what to do. I do not know what to ask for. I do not know whether or how much to ask. All I know is that I want this love to be done well.'

'Oh, my darling, you've got it bad, and that ain't ... What do you think he is thinking?'

'What I am thinking, but in his way.'

'Certain?'

'I have never been so certain of anything but that he loves me.'

'Do you realise this man has got you speaking like a minor Elizabethan? It must be love. You can still get out of it. You can say, "What he loves is a fantasy," and go on and despise him and hate yourself in peace. The neurotic's solution.'

'Anna ...'

'I'd be tempted. No, I wouldn't. Why do I always sell myself short? So, Charles, it's love, is it? Good luck.'

'What are you going to do?'

'I'm taking Hans to Naples. Remember that Clough line you gave me years ago? "As for hope, tomorrow I hope to go to Naples." Well, tomorrow I do hope to go to Naples. Hans is as pale as a frog, and I want to bathe in the clear blue off Posillipo. Then it will be farewell and a return to Paris, solitude and work.'

'Certain?'

'Certain. I have never been so certain of anything but that he does not love me. I can speak minor Elizabethan too. Slightly sadder in my case.'

'Not really.'

'That's what you think. Do you know the worst thing about the Hans business? He is not worth my tears. To have spent so much time with someone not worth one's tears. Anna's resolution for the rest of her life — not to cry over anyone that isn't worth it.'

'You're not crying now, are you?' Her voice had sounded suddenly small.

'Certainly not. That's for December and January.'

She hung up.


Adolphe cleared his throat. 'God, I love Anna,' he said.

'Then ring her up and take her out to dinner. She told me to tell you that if you didn't she'd never speak to you again.'

'I love Anna because she is good, brave and desperate.'

'Less desperate now than she was then.'

'Perhaps I should marry her,' said Adolphe. 'And leave her the apartment and everything. I'd like Anna to have the money to be happy in style.'

'Anna will have style whether she has money or not.'

'You're right for once. Anna makes me want to say silly things like, "She deserves to be happy," as if happiness is ever really deserved. Think how happy I seem to be and how little I've deserved it. Back to you, peewee. Back to L'Amoroso. All this suffering, as Caligula said watching the gladiators, is greatly to my taste.'

After Anna called, I walked for hours through the sharp dazzle of that late November day. I laughed as the taxis in the Boule Miche swept past, flinging up piles of dead gold leaves. The sky was cloudless, a white-blue stone; I tried to throw my mind against it and break it. No one that passed me, none of the students with red scarves or smart young wives with their gloves and wide glasses, seemed as real as that sky, that vast frozen emptiness which dwarfed the quais and boulevards, even the tall towers of Notre-Dame.

Towards three, when the sky was beginning to darken, I saw a clump of white crocuses in a small deserted garden near the Musée de Cluny. I gazed at them through the bars of a grille. How stupid of them to blossom when they would have no chance of lasting — and yet nothing in all the pomp of frost that ringed them was as beautiful as that stupidity. They shone in the menacing light brighter than any spring flower.

Adolphe began before I could stop him.

'Ah I did not think to see you
 Faded so soon, poor flowers
 You have passed away like love . . .

'*Sonnambula*, last act. My translation. Couldn't help it, darling.'

172

And Mark? What was he thinking? I sat in the dining-room of Anna's flat that afternoon in the late light, trying to enter his mind. If only I could penetrate his thoughts, feel what he felt. But it was impossible. Mark was the nearest to me of anyone yet his nearness made him mysterious.

I tried, sitting there in the half-dark, to rehearse all the possibilities of what he might be thinking, but the more subtly I did so, the further Mark withdrew from me. When I gave up trying to follow his thoughts, he was there beside me, so close I could feel the warmth of his breath on my face. But when I wanted to know, when I demanded of the afternoon, of the glass table, of the painted figures in the large screen against the wall – the man holding the sword, the woman with the blue ribbon round her neck – when I demanded of these the power to enter Mark's mind, he dissolved, and became a ghost whose presence chilled the room. I would have, I saw, to renounce my need to understand him. As I did so, I felt him sitting nearer and nearer to me in the darkness, until there was nothing between us but a thin smoke of absence one sharp breath could clear. I did not clear it because I did not need to. Behind it Mark was there; through it, the candour of his eyes and body warmed me.

Many memories that I had forgotten or hidden from myself returned to me that afternoon. It was Mark who brought them back to me.

One memory returned insistently. Four years before I had been travelling alone in India, and had stayed for a week at Mahabalipuram to visit the ancient Pallava temples along the sea-shore.

I had been walking by the sea all morning when, towards noon, without warning, the sky darkened and a storm broke out. Suddenly after the dead blue calm of the morning, the wind was lashing the palms, the sea was whipped by the rain's mile-long invisible chains. Great tridents of lightning were plunging again and again into the horizon. I had never in my life known such fear: the noise of the sea, the screaming of the wind, the flashing nearness of the lightning, all made me know that I was in danger. The beach at Mahabalipuram, about a mile from the shore-temple, is lined with scrub; I ran to a clump of bushes and cowered under them. The air had grown cooler, and as the rain swept down through the cracks in the small branches my teeth began to chatter. It was miserable crouching there, being frozen by the wind and rain, but I could not leave the bushes where I had taken shelter. I felt that if I left them and walked in the open, I would be struck by lightning.

Then something happened that I still do not understand. I became ashamed of crouching there, cowering like an animal. Why

173

should I be afraid to die in a storm like this when great trees were crashing to the earth in forests? Who was I to protect myself? As I watched the sea heaving and moaning, as I listened to the wind screaming in the trees, as I surrendered to the rain pouring over me, I knew that I had to walk out into the storm and give myself to it. I stripped off the cotton shirt and trousers I was wearing and ran into the storm naked. With one leap on to the shore, I lost all consciousness of danger. I began to dance by the sea, more and more wildly, as if my life depended on it, as if there were some pact between me and the storm that if I did not dance with all my body and soul I would be destroyed. It was not a ritual of appeasement I was enacting, but of union, of becoming so one with the storm that I could not be killed by it. As I danced I felt no hysteria, no sense of absurdity; I was calmer than I had ever been. I was as naked as the piece of forked driftwood I was brandishing.

As I danced, I turned to face the twisted clump of bushes I had been hiding in. From the bareness of the shore, they looked absurd. They were dwarfs in a cabal against a giant who could crush them at will. I began to mock them. Torrents of abuse, half poetry, half nonsense, poured from me. Then, the lightning struck. With a crackle louder than the fall of a house it struck a tree close to the bushes. The tree screamed, and fell across the place where I had been hiding. That safety should be the greatest danger, that dancing like a madman, naked, should be the only protection...

The night after I danced I had a dream. I was sitting by the sea. The sand was shining around me and the sea was calmer than I had ever seen it, so clear that I could see through it. I turned from the sea to see a figure walking up the long white shore towards me. It was a young man, naked except for a loincloth. He was walking slowly but calmly, and as he came closer I saw his face was thin-boned and beautiful. He sat down beside me. He said nothing and we did not touch. I understood that it had been painful for him to cross the sand in the heat towards me; if I touched him I would hurt him further. He began to speak. Language was so strange in that silence that at first I could not make out what he was saying; my mind had to return a long, harsh distance to piece together his words. 'Open your hands,' he was saying. 'Open both your hands.' I opened them, looking at him. Into one, he put the spine of a fish; into the other a white shell. The fish-spine glittered as if diamond dust had been scattered over it; the whorls of the shell moved with increasing lightness towards a centre of dazzling white. I said, 'Who are you?' over and over, hardly understanding what the words could mean. 'I am you,' he said.

174

I had woken to the shouts and garglings of the two businessmen who had the room next door, the ring of bicycle-bells in the street ... But for many days after, and now in Anna's room, I heard that silence by the sea. I saw the eyes of that stranger who had said he was myself staring back into my eyes. In India, that peace, those eyes, had dissolved, leaving me to my old self. Now, in Paris, I knew them again. This time the stranger had Mark's face.

That evening was startlingly mild after the cold of the day. I left the windows open on to the street, so that all the noises of the city could come into the room where I sat waiting for Mark to arrive. A door slamming, a car screeching to a halt, the cry of pigeons, a sudden break of laughter — each sound seemed related to a larger silence, from which it was born and to which it returned. Once before in Nepal I had heard this ecstatic music, in Pokhara, one summer, when I had taken a boat out on to the lake at dusk, and when everything, the sound of the oar in the water, the lapping of the lake against the distant shore, the wind in the trees by the lake, the white radiance of Machupuchare and Annapurna, had seemed inextricably interwoven. The serenity of that late afternoon had, I felt soon after, too sumptuous a background to be convincing. But this evening in Paris, sitting in the rue Jacob, hearing that music again, surrounded by all the objects that had surrounded me these last days — the elephants, the scraps of paper in the wastepaper bin, the glasses with the dregs of vodka and gin — I could not disbelieve it. Mark was walking towards me through Paris: I was filled with joy that I had known him, with gratitude for all the vicissitudes that had brought us to these days and their truths, and with acceptance of everything that he would bring with him. Whatever he gave to me and I gave to him would, I saw, be part of the evening and of the vast calm life that it stained only lightly, that it trembled lightly before, as the dark blue bead-curtain in my childhood summerhouse had trembled in the wind from the sea.

Adolphe applauded.

'Talking about childhood, peewee, I had an Irish nanny for a year when I was eight. She was fat and red-haired and called Miss Hennessy. She used to sing:

> "And you will be a wandering boy
> Whether you like it or not."

She was full of old Irish stories. Do you know the one about Oisin and the Great Music? No? It will help. Come and sit by me, then. Have you noticed how beautiful the night is?' Adolphe's great long window was open. Soft sounds from Saint-Sulpice came through it, and the warm night.

'Oisin was sitting with a group of other sages by a lake. One of them asked, "What is the greatest music?" Everyone answered in turn. One sage said, "The greatest music is the sound of a woman's skirts falling to the floor." We'd change that one, but we know what he meant. Oh, the whisk-whisk of boxer shorts once in an Italian train! August, 1936. Another sage said, "The greatest music is the sound of a stag belling across the lake at dawn." I'd choose Maria, mais quand même ... All the sages answered except Oisin, who sat apart from the rest – and here Miss Hennessy would always say "looking like sweet thunder", whatever that meant. Anyway, there he sat, looking like sweet thunder, "his great cape of many colours flung around the mountains that were his shoulders, that cape that had in it all the colours of the known and unknown worlds." Blessed Miss Hennessy! How her lips would quiver and her eyes flash, and her hand holding the gin-bottle tremble! And what did Oisin say when his turn came?' Adolphe stood up. 'I am Miss Hennessy now. I am red-haired, five feet six, plump as a samovar, and I smell of carbolic soap, gin, and lavender. "And what did Oisin say?"' There was a long pause. Adolphe's eyes glittered. 'Oisin said, "The greatest music is the music of what happens."'

Two car horns sounded almost together from different sides of the square below. Then, Adolphe cleared his throat and came over to me and held my head against him. 'What big ears you have,' he said, stroking them. So that's why you always wear your hair à la Chopin! My dear, they are elephant ears! Big enough to hear anything. You shouldn't hide them. They are one of the miracles of the world, like the leaning tower of Pisa, or my bottom!'

Something in Adolphe's voice shook me. 'You are sad,' I said quietly.

'Beauty is meant to make one sad. Anyway, I like being sad. It's a lovely wafty feeling, shiny as the moonlight between Saint-Sulpice's towers. Of course I'm sad. Our time together is about to end.' He tweaked my right ear. 'But not tonight. I can't face the end tonight. I'm not strong enough. The lightning on the Indian beach, that divine young man with the shell, and Miss Hennessy, have quite undone me. I don't think I could take you and Mark as well, doing whatever you are about to do. Not tonight. Tomorrow, after a nice hot bath! Can you come?'

'Of course.'

Adolphe looked down at me. 'Oh, pondsnipe, pondsnipe, will you remember what we have been?'

'How could I forget?'

'They all say that, honeypot, but they all . . .'

'Don't be morbid. It doesn't suit you.'

'If you forget me I shall haunt you.'

'You haunt me now.'

'How gallant! Six out of ten. Seven, even.'

I got up and kissed him. Adolphe walked over to the gramophone and put on a large black 78. A cackling squeaky voice began that I did not recognise.

> Why couldn't I have been Salome
> Or Mary Pickford
> Or Joan of Arc
> If I were Elinor Glyn
> Or even Anne Boleyn
> The future wouldn't look half so dark.
> Why couldn't I be Whistler's Mother
> Why did the gods decree
> That I should only be
> The Queen of Terre Haute?

'Cole playing. Me singing. Recorded in the late forties, at one of Greta's parties.' Adolphe opened his chiffon-sequinned arms. 'The Queen of Terre Haute . . . Not such a bad destiny after all.'

'You have had a wonderful life.'

'No. There are no "wonderful" lives, only cowardly lives and brave ones. You had better learn that soon. Fly away now.'

That night I dreamt I was sitting, dressed as Adolphe, at the Deux Magots. In the dream it was an early summer morning, like the one Adolphe had described on the day of his experience in the Musée Guimet, and I was dressed, as he had been, in an ill-fitting dark suit and dark glasses. I looked at my hands, resting on either side of my coffee; without surprise I saw that they were Adolphe's hands. Plump, beringed, but now with small brown spots all over them. I heard a child's laughter. I looked up. The Deux Magots was empty and there was no one in the square in front of it except for a young Indian boy, who was walking out of the door of the church of Saint-Germain towards me. I did not recognise him at first because he was in Western clothes. When he took out of his right trouser pocket a sweat-stained turquoise bandanna, I saw it was the boy who had rowed me on the Ganges at Mathura. He started waving the bandanna in the air and soon was encircled by jays. He spread out his arms and they alighted all over his body.

I closed my eyes. When I opened them again the tables around me were full and the noise had returned to the street. I looked to where the boy had been. Mark was standing there, in a white suit and open-neck shirt. He waved to me to follow him. Although he was about fifty yards away, I heard his voice as if at my elbow, saying, "You have to come now. There is no more time." When I looked at him again he was standing in sunlight, his shoulders and head shining, as if on fire. He started to walk. I followed him. He turned into the rue de Rennes. He was going to place Saint-Sulpice. Now I was walking behind him and we were not in Paris at all, but on the sand of the bank of the Ganges where, years before, I had seen the sadhu. A cloud of jays ringed us. A late afternoon breeze blew off the river to our right; an even light spread on the white sands before us and around us. Mark took his clothes off and threw them into the river; I did the same. Then between two small dunes in the distance we saw the sadhu. He was coming towards us naked and dancing. As he danced he stopped to gather driftwood, and rubbed it into flame. When he came closer I saw that he had my glasses on, but without lenses and stuck together with pieces of tape. He was dancing close to us now, throwing the pieces of flaming wood into the air and catching them again. He started singing. Now, as he flung up the pieces of burning wood, they hung in the air around him in the shape of a lingam. Mark turned to me and we linked hands. Then, together, we went naked into the burning lingam. I felt pain all over my body and a great calm. Neither of us said anything. When we had come through the fire, the sadhu and the lingam, the white sands, had gone. We were sitting, clothed, on the ground outside Mark's old house in Oxford. The grass around us glittered with breadcrumbs. Kate came out of the house to join us, in a blue dress, bringing oranges and wine.

# ·SEVEN·

'So it's your last day with Adolphe.' Anna and I were walking in the late morning sunshine. We stopped on the Pont d'Iéna to watch the sun dancing on the water. 'It's like a Bach fugue,' she went on, 'the light – thesis, antithesis ... everything finding its place in a counterpane of light. What a pun ... Quel beau rêve.'

'Perhaps it isn't a dream. Perhaps the man heard the real music.'

'The real music is the music of parting. You should know that.' Anna was wearing green that morning, with a yellow scarf. I stroked her hair. 'Perhaps we should get married after all,' I said, 'and have a large family.'

'I shall marry Papageno, not Prince Hamlet. To the daughter that is like me I shall make you godfather.'

'Not the son?'

'Not the son. Anyway, we don't need to get married.' Anna took my hand. 'I know exactly what you are feeling. I know how empty you are at the end of a book. I know how you will miss these evenings with Adolphe. I feel your sadness, here, in my chest.'

She took off her shoes, shook out her hair and began to run. 'This morning,' she said, 'it's too beautiful to be sad.'

Fifty yards later, she stopped, laughing, out of breath. I caught up.

'I'm too old to behave like a heroine out of Angela Brazil,' she gasped.

'No, you're not.'

'Believe me, I am. And today I don't give a damn.'

We were at the end of the bridge. Anna had almost run into a young, dark-haired man in a blue suit, who had stopped to look at her.

'If he had a hat,' I said, 'he'd raise it to you.'

'But he doesn't. Do they ever?'

I had asked Anna to come with me that morning to the Musée Guimet, without telling her of Adolphe's great adventure there. She said she would come with me only if she chose the things we looked at. 'There is only one thing I really want to show you,' she had said. 'When I'm feeling really cracked I often cross Paris to see it.'

Anna did not lead me to the dancing Shiva in the Indian room; she led me to the Tara, Buddhist Goddess of Compassion, that is at the centre of the Khmer section. She is carved from a quiet gold stone and is kneeling, her legs slightly spread out. 'She gives everything,' Anna said, circling her, 'but she has dignity, because she is patient. For her the giving is the joy, not the taking. She kneels to give and by kneeling frees and blesses all those who receive. You know, when I first came here three years ago, I hated her for being so submissive, so serene in her self-abandon.'

'But now?'

'Take that irony out of your voice. But now I am beginning to understand her. She has found herself in love; she has become love.'

'You sound as if you were praying.'

'I am.'

'She has found herself in love; she has become love.'

'Say it slowly. It is your prayer also, although God knows you fight against it.'

I wanted to say something sharp and witty, but Anna put her hand over my mouth. 'Not today. You don't have to defend anything today.'

I felt tears rising. 'You're going to make me cry. I can't stand it.'

'Go on,' she said. 'Be a big boy. No one will hold it against you.'

We held each other.

'We have made such a mess of our lives,' Anna said. 'But they are not over yet. Not to grow bitter, not to grow cold. Not to let the heart grow old. How frightening it is.'

'Don't, for God's sake, lose your irony.'

'I'm much too contradictory not to keep everything. Irony can be love too. You should know that. It doesn't have to be killing and English. You know what I always do when I come here?'

'Don't tell me. You dance the tango around her, when the guard's not looking. You read her Jacques Prévert's script for *Les Enfants du Paradis* – Anna as Garance, praying for all those who misunderstand her.'

'I put my hands on her eyes and then put them to my eyes.'

'But hers are closed.'

'That's what you think.' Anna, before I could stop her, touched the Tara's eyes with her hands and then put them over my eyes. 'What do you see? she asked me softly.

'I see the water dancing on the Seine as we crossed the bridge this morning, and I hear Bach.'

'That's a beginning,' she said. 'Liar.'


'Don't look so Wagnerian,' Adolphe said, from the top of the stairs. It was only when I was in his drawing-room that I noticed Adolphe was not dressed up. He was wearing a crumpled white shirt and baggy black trousers. There were no rings, no bangles, no wig. He had spread a khaki cloth across the wall with the photographs. One solitary tall white lamp by his sofa cast a soft light. 'Today,' he said, 'I thought we should meet in an empty space. I have some things I must tell you.'

'Tell them then.'

'Don't be so impatient. First you must read me the end of your book.'

'Adolphe . . .'

'No, I am not going to tell you now. It is not the right time. What did you do last night after we finished?'

'I went home and slept.'

'How boring. *I* picked up an Egyptologist.'

'Congratulations.'

'I decided I had to walk by the Seine. Not what you are thinking, swivel-hips. I'm long past writhing under bridges. But I love to be in that seedy ambience – the boys with their too-tight trousers wandering up and down like extras from *Nosferatu*, the little black ones with their fuzzy hair, the fake sailors, fresh from the Flore. I serve as early warning police system. I can make the most piercing owl sounds imaginable.'

'The Egyptologist?'

'I'm getting to him. I was sitting by the river, minding every one else's business, when this funny thirty-five-year-old man in a green plaid shirt and black trousers came and sat next to me. He started to stroke my neck, which was sweet of him, but I said I was past such frivolities and wanted conversation or nothing. He asked me who I was. I said I was a world-famous film director and that on no account could I give him my name. He giggled and said people were always telling him things like that here. What did he do? My dear, he was an Egyptologist. I could tell he wasn't lying by the strange light that came into his eyes when he said "Egypt". I had an uncle who studied Indian things, and his eyes had the same eerie glow.

'So there, with the bad little and the bad big boys circling us and each other, we had the most lofty conversation about Egyptian civilisation. He talked about Anubis and Osiris; he told me details of the funerals of cats, how men shaved their eyelids in mourning and women threw lemons over their left shoulders. I asked him if there had been bridges in Egypt under which the same wicked things went on. He looked at me. "The Egyptians accepted everything as sacred – every small animal, every act." "Very sensible of them," I said. By this time the Louvre across the way was looking like a pyramid and I quite expected some delicious slaves got up like Charlton Heston in *The Ten Commandments* to come out from under the Pont Neuf. My pick-up said in a hushed voice, "The Egyptians believed that this world was an exact mirror of the divine world, and that behind every human action, every human love, there was a divine one. At any moment, the veil between the worlds could be torn." I said I had always believed something similar in a vague kind of way, and had seen a few rents in the veil myself. What was he doing there, peewee, talking to me like that?

'I walked up to Notre-Dame with him and we parted in front of the cathedral. I walked on and turned to wave to him. But he had vanished – poof! Was he an angel, do you think, Azrafel or Gheherubin taking an evening off to saunter and instruct? For an hour, as I walked home slowly, everything looked Egyptian. Even the clochards seemed to have head-dresses. Perhaps you and I were priests at the Temple of the Sun who got expelled for chatting too much at siesta time. You, peewee, tell me your dream last night.'

'How did you know I had one?'

He smiled and said nothing. I told him the dream.

'Quel rêve! The Burning Lingam! My goodness. They'd never have allowed me to get away with that in Hollywood in my day. Both of you naked. Paul Newman and Monty Clift (that's flattering you) and me, of course, as the tape-spectacled sadhu. My last, only, best, Oscar-winning part. Imagine my speech at the Academy Awards! Halting, ceremonious, studded with imitation Shakespeare like Larry Olivier's, wiping the one dignified but glistening tear from my right eye, staring at Shirley Maclaine as if to say, "Get that, Shirl! You're not the only one who's been round the world on a magic carpet." Bergman of course will direct. It will finish off his career.'

Something plaintive in Adolphe's voice struck me. But when I looked at him closely he was smiling. 'But we aren't here to discuss Egypt and the Bergmans of this world. We are here for the Final Steps to Golgotha. I imagine it is going to be Golgotha, isn't it?'

'Wait and see.'

'The whole day long I was wondering whether or not we should have music tonight. And I decided, let's go for it. One can't be too Spartan, even at endings. Or at least I can't. I realise that Emptiness is Form and Form is Emptiness, but I still need my emptiness a little decorated.'

I braced myself. 'What have you chosen?'

Adolphe looked reverent. 'The end of *Sonnambula*. We have had "Ah non credea mirarti", in my wonderful rendition. Now we must have Maria singing "Ah non giunge". I want it in honour of a memory of Edinburgh, 1958, when the Great She sang Amina, and arriving at those last bursts of happiness walked to the edge of the stage as all the lights in the house came on. Oh, pondsnipe, would that thou hadst been there! You were peeling the legs off grasshoppers somewhere in the Deccan. She came to the footlights in a divine white dress (how I envied her that dress! How she hated having her waist squeezed to get into it!) She came to the very edge (God, I remember thinking, she's as blind as a bat, she's going to walk off into the second violins), stretched out her arms and raised them to the gods and sang, as I have never heard anyone sing before or since, not even her, with every brilliance, every nuance of grief and joy. She seemed to be singing not just for us, but to Life itself, to Life and Death as well (Maria was always singing to Death too). She was blessing the whole damn thing, darling, all the perversity and all the beauty, from a clear, wild, exalted, fiery heart. I was trembling from head to foot. I am trembling now – feel my arms. I went to see her afterwards, in tears. Do you know what she said? "Well, I did it that time. Eat dust, Rosa Ponselle!" and took a vast ham sandwich out of a plastic bag. No, Charles, this is the sound for every ending. No story is complete without it. And for you, there is so much to come.'

'For you too.'

Adolphe walked to the gramophone. The voice of Callas, taped that night so many years before at Edinburgh, filled the room, rising higher and higher, threatening always to break, to shatter, under the pressure of its own ecstasy, but, miraculously, soaring on and on.

Adolphe clapped. 'Maria, you've been dead years and you're more alive than ever. Now to you, peewee. The Beloved is coming across Paris. You have had three drinks, cleared your throat, practised a few scales, slanted your eyes to look like Maria's.'

'No mockery.'

'Ah, we are for the serious part. Is it at our serious parts that the gods laugh most? Actually I don't think the gods laugh. They smile, like my Buddhas. I've been practising that smile for the last decade, day in, day out. Some days I make it. Other days I hate it. It seems so terribly serene, if you know what I mean. The good honest cruelty of a let-them-get-on-with-it-the-idiots laugh might be better. I find that much easier, of course. I can laugh like a hyena on heat, as you know, or like some unknown African monkey. Do you want to hear my African Monkey laugh?'

'My dearest Adolphe, I have heard it.'

Adolphe gestured to me to stand by the window and sat on the sofa, cross-legged, his hands folded in his lap and shining in the lamplight.

'You look almost holy, Adolphe . . .

'The right lighting can do anything.'


'For once you are not late,' I said.

It was seven exactly when Mark rang the bell of Anna's flat. He stood in the doorway silently, as if unable to move or talk. The light on the landing went out, leaving us together in half-darkness. I could see his face. His eyes had dark rings of sleeplessness under them; the lines around his eyes were drawn. He was wearing an old blue pullover I remembered from Oxford.

'Aren't you going to come in?'

From the flat across the rue Furstenberg came waves of Telemann. The violins chugged away monotonously; a flute rose and fell without meaning. As Mark moved into the faint gold light of the narrow hall, I saw his hair was tousled and dirty.

'Can't you shut out that music?' His voice rose with nervousness.

I shut the window and turned to him. 'You look as if you have been in a fight.'

'A fight? You forget, I am the one who keeps his hands clean. Isn't that what you are always saying? Skip it . . . I've been trying

189

all day to write that article. I hate what I write. It's so bland: "Adolphe, the famous film director, sat in a red silk pyjama suit, sipping a Martini." That kind of stuff. Just Latin prose translation tarted up. Nothing original. But that's not the real reason I look awful.' He looked at me. 'You don't look that good yourself.'

'I feel all right.'

'Good for you. I didn't sleep last night. Usually I sleep just as you would imagine I sleep — like a child. Kate says it's obscene, the way I only have to hit the pillow . . .'

I looked away.

'Sorry,' said Mark, rubbing his eyes. 'It isn't the time to mention Kate. I thrashed about until dawn and was just about to sleep when the maids in the hotel started to chatter in the corridors. I say "chatter" out of courtesy. They were screaming and laughing like furies. My furies would be Parisian bonnes, wouldn't they? Nothing really grand with fangs and sweeping cloaks — more your style. You'd be rather a good fury yourself with your hair swept back and an opera cloak . . .'

'I have no desire to be a fury this year. I'm practising the more domestic skills, such as doing the washing up once a week, cleaning my typewriter with turpentine before the keys get so clogged I can't make any letters. You can imagine.'

'Domestic skills are things I don't need to imagine,' Mark said, laughing a frightening short laugh.

'I'm not going to stand here talking about furies and typewriters. Have some wine.' My hands were unsteady as I poured it out for him. 'It's the new Beaujolais,' I said brightly.

'The new Beaujolais. What have I done to deserve anything so wonderful as the new Beaujolais?'

'Have you been drinking?'

'You're scared I'm going to turn into an alcoholic. That would really blast your picture of Mark the Hero, wouldn't it? Don't worry. I've seen my mother falling downstairs and being sick in flowerbeds. It rather puts one off, you know.' He said the last sentence in an exaggeratedly upper-class accent. 'Let me tell you about the time when my mother took off all her clothes at the village fête and turned somersaults on the lawn.'

'Real somersaults? Springy ones?' I was laughing. Mark's face relaxed.

'Springy ones. At sixty. So drink doesn't kill everything, you see.'

'It kills the brain cells, but not the right brain cells. One of Anna's jokes. Have some more.' We were still standing in Anna's study. Mark took the glass from me and drank it in one gulp.

190

'How much does one have to drink to feel really good about oneself?'

'I've never found out.'

Mark took off his pullover and folded it across a chair. He folded it with surreal slowness, as if he had never done so before. He seemed, standing there, to be intensely fragile, his face drawn and raw like a sick child. I went over to him and put both my hands against his chest as if to steady him. He closed his eyes and put out an arm to the glass table as if to prevent himself from falling.

'Mark, what's up?'

'What's up?' he repeated tonelessly. 'What is up? That is an interesting question. We could discuss it from a variety of angles. Remember those hilarious philosophy lectures in Oxford? What is up? One can go on like this for ages. One has.'

'For God's sake.'

'How are you stressing that? For *God*'s sake! For God's *sake*. Worlds hang on stress, you know. Skip it. I learnt 'skip it' from American films. Skip what? Skip everything. I've been very good at skipping it.'

'Your self-disgust is boring.'

'I'm so sorry. I'd forgotten it was only you who was allowed that role. I keep forgetting my place. I must make notes in future before I see you. No drink. No self-disgust. No jokes. What's up? You know bloody well that everything is up. What you start, Charles, you finish. If you know what I mean. In all senses of the word finish. Complete, polish, kill.'

'The same could be said of you. You finished a lot of things for me for a long time.'

We stared at each other with hatred.

Then I said, 'Don't stand there like Ivan the Terrible. I can't bear it. Come into the drawing-room. Let us repair to the drawing-room. Repair is the right word, since we seem to be looking for right words. Sit. Repair. Breathe in and out. We have time.' My voice shook.

'You really think we have time? Time is what we don't have. Everything else but time.'

'You sound like an undertaker,' I began, but the sadness in his face stopped me. 'I love you, Mark. I've loved you badly and selfishly but I do want to love you well now. Help me. I seem so often to be saying Help me. I don't wish to harm you.'

'Oh, for God's sake, Charles, don't be Hindu. We will harm each other. We have harmed each other. People always harm each other.'

'I want you to know I trust you.'

191

'You must give me some of the drug you're taking. Then perhaps I could trust myself.' Mark sat down and leant against the back of the sofa. He had cut himself shaving and a small trickle of dried blood ran under his chin. I licked my fingers and rubbed off the blood.

'That's what Kate does sometimes.'

I didn't reply, surprised I was happy I had done what Kate would do. Mark said nothing for a long time and I sat in the lamplight by him and watched him. He stretched out his hand, looking for mine. I held it. I thought how strange it was that we, who had never slept together, should yet have, beneath everything, so old a tenderness between us, the tenderness, almost, of those who have been married a long time. This intimacy was what the years had cheated us of.

'You look so far away,' Mark said, stroking my cheek.

'I am remembering one of our first meetings in Oxford. Our third. We were sitting in that dark little coffee-house. I was talking, as usual, and you leant across the table and took both my hands in yours. You sat there, daring me with your eyes to take them away.'

'Did you?'

'You don't remember?' I laughed. 'No, I did not. I was astonished at your boldness, there in front of everyone.'

'I should have kissed you. I wanted to. If I had been really brave I would have done. Did you stop talking?'

'Yes. We sat there as we were sitting a moment ago. It was raining. It was always raining that winter. We sat until the rain was ended. You said, "When two men really love each other, they should sleep together."'

'What did you say?'

'I said — I surprised myself, I did not know I thought this — I said, "It is not enough to sleep together. They must re-invent love. What does sleeping together matter if they remain separate? They must give themselves up to each other, merge, risk being transformed."'

Mark smiled, 'Did I look scared?'

'We were both scared. We studied the table-mats very carefully, I remember.'

There was a sudden sharp silence. Mark opened his shirt.

'It's hot in here. Why don't you open a window?'

'And get some more Telemann?'

'Let's risk it.'

I opened the window slightly. The music had ended. A cool wind filled the room. Mark stood behind me, and as I stepped

192

backward pressed me against him.

'I lived through the whole of my life today,' he said, 'lying on that bed in that sleazy hotel in between bouts of writing. Nothing was real around me. I had to touch the table I was writing on to make sure it was there. Being a French table, it was. Nothing made sense except what I was remembering.' His voice went on hesitantly. 'About three years after we last saw each other, I had a dream about you that frightened me. I had forgotten it until last night. In the dream, I was waiting for you in the coffee-shop. The floor was covered with white sand and the sound of the sea came from beyond the open windows. The shop was empty and filled with sunlight. You came in, dressed in white Indian clothes, bronzed and thin, with a silver necklace. You were quiet and looked at me a long time without saying anything, as if you had come over a long distance. I did not know what to say. I was feeling guilty, angry. You said, "I have brought something for you" and took out of your pocket a small silver bell. You held it out in the light and it glittered. I was afraid to take it, as if it would burn my hands. You said, "If you ring it, it says your name." "My name?" I was baffled. I rang it and the strangest sound I have ever heard filled the room – not a word exactly, certainly not a "name", but a high ringing hum that merged with the sound of the sea, the light on the tables, the shining of the sand – a sound that seemed at once to come from the bell and from all the things around me. I shook, and had to hold on to the table. I was angry with you for not having warned me that the sound would disturb me. You stood with your back to me at the window, looking out towards the sea. I went towards you with the bell. You turned.' Mark paused.

'Without meaning to – or so I thought – I dropped the bell, just as I was about to hand it to you. It fell very slowly in the air, but I could not retrieve it. I stood there, hypnotised, watching it hit the floor. This time the sound it made was terrifying – a whirlwind of a sound, with winds in it and violent waves and a hundred thousand noises of the city, of trams screeching, of bicycle bells, of horns. The sound grew wilder until I felt it would break apart the whole world. I woke up sweating and went into Paul's room and held him asleep against me. All last night and today I have heard that sound again.' He stopped. 'I have so much I must say clearly.'

'I am listening.'

'I know,' Mark said softly, releasing me. We faced each other.

'I have cheated both you and Kate,' he said. 'I have loved you both and starved you both. I have understood that my life has made me like that. I want to change. I have said that before, I have even thought I meant it. But you do not really mean it until you want change as a drowning man wants air, or a person trapped in a burning house wants to run out into the daylight. I want to change and only you can help me. Even as I say it there is a part of me that wishes it were not true because it complicates everything. Kate has given me all she can but it is not enough. Kate moves me, but she does not reach me. It's not her fault; nor is it mine. I want to live my real life. I'm going to leave them.' He raised his hands in the air, and let them fall.

What he said so amazed me I could not take it in. 'Leave whom?'

Mark burst into laughter. 'I can't believe you said that. I am going to leave Kate and my children. I am going to go back home tomorrow and tell Kate everything.'

The enormity of what he had said at last struck me. I went forward to him instinctively, as if to stop him from falling over.

'I don't just love you, Charles. I need you.'

I said nothing.

'Whatever is best in me — and God knows that may not be enough for you — lives here with you, in you. I can help you too if you will let me. I have grown enough to be able to.'

'You have helped me.'

'Let me finish. If I don't say it all now I may never say it. How is it that I have said as much as I have? You have given me the courage.'

'It's your courage.'

'Will it hold out?' He smiled grimly. 'I do not trust myself as much as you trust me. If you knew how many lies I have told myself.'

'Everyone lies.'

'My lies have been so large and so cruel — to you, to Kate, to myself. That's not important. What is . . . I don't have to explain it to you. We've lived it together. These last days . . . Everything has been here. What else can these days have meant but that we must be together, whatever it costs? Don't think I haven't wanted to get around that.' Mark leant his forehead against mine. 'I can't ask you to be my lover, to meet me at restaurants, to snatch weekends. You would refuse. You are too proud. I can only offer you everything or nothing; that is all you could want. That is what we deserve.'

'You don't know what you're saying.'

'I know what I am saying for the first time in my life. I will leave Kate and my children and live with you, if you want me. If you can forgive me.'

'There is nothing to forgive.'

'I am saying to you that I have understood, about our love. I have seen it. I have seen it is the one complete love we will ever be

194

granted. I'm prepared to live it. I don't know how I will find the strength, but I will if you love me enough to help me. Do you despise me so much that you cannot believe I can change? What more can I do to prove myself? I have fought you, I have endured you, I have exposed my life to your ridicule. I am offering you everything I can offer anyone.'

I put my hands around his waist and held him to me. He was shaking. His strong body seemed suddenly brittle as if it were made of balsa wood, and any sharp movement could break it. We were silent, knowing what had to be said next. I listened to his nervous breathing in my ear.

'And Kate? What about Kate?' I said.

Mark gave a low groan and let me go. 'Kate will have to understand,' he said, looking away, trying to make his voice hard, and failing. 'Kate already knows somewhere. Kate will understand.' As if in a trance, he knocked his forehead with the knuckles of his right hand.

'Understand what?'

'That she and I are not enough for each other.'

'You are enough for her.'

Mark winced. 'That she is not enough for me. It sounds cold, said like that. It is cold. She will have to understand that I love you and need you more than I love and need her. There's no way of saying it that is not terrible.'

'No.'

'To make Kate suffer any more than I have already is the last thing I want. And my children . . . But I am prepared to be guilty for us. I am prepared to take on anything.' He paused. 'You wanted me, Charles. Now you have me.'

I said nothing. Then I said, 'I was not talking only about you and Kate. I was talking about me and Kate.'

'Don't be noble. Don't be moral. I couldn't bear it. One way of being noble is to choose love and fight for it and pay what it costs. God knows you've said that often enough.'

'I'm not being noble. If there was any way I knew of keeping you I would keep you. But there isn't. You know that. You knew that, even as you said what you said.'

I shook him. 'Look. You must look and see what I see. And you must see it with me, otherwise we are lost. Kate will always be with us wherever we go. There is nowhere we could hide from her. She will always be behind your face when I look at it; she will always be standing behind you in the shadow when you open the door; when you call out to me I will hear her listening. She may not even want to haunt us; she may really be "noble" enough to wish us well, though I doubt that. How could she lose you and not want me dead? I know what it is like to lose you. Kate's pain will penetrate our love and make it evil. It must, because neither of us can escape it. She has loved you with everything she is. I knew that the first moment I saw her. I knew and tried to forget, but Kate is too real to be forgotten.

'If there was a way of making her suffer, even extremely and for a long time, without knowing it myself, I would consent to it − to be with you, to have you with me. Perhaps there is no suffering I would not inflict if I did not have to know about it. But I do have to know about it. Kate is so much a part of both of us, and so much a part of my love for you, in ways I do not know how to explain. If I caused her the suffering I knew I would be, breaking her marriage, I would be frightened for us all the time, frightened that we had taken the only truly beautiful thing that life has given us − the love we have − and used it to kill someone else.

'You know we have been given something so great we both nearly break under it. You know that. We have been given something so enormous we have to be worthy of it. I hate that bloody word, but we can't totter round it. We can't and be true to what we are. What we have been given is not in time. It really is not. These days have been in some other dimension for which there is no name. We know that. That's why we have been trying so hard to put names to it. We are frightened of what we know. It *is* frightening. But if we try to claim what we have been given, if we try to drag it into time, if we try to possess it, it will change − it has to − into something monstrous. Our whole love will become that sound you described when you dropped the bell − cacophonous, full of cruel noises. I'm not strong enough, Mark, to bear the breaking of our love like that.'

Mark smiled strangely, touching my collar. 'Very impressive, your aria, but it's a lie.'

'I meant every word.'

'You always think you mean what you say. It's one of your worst faults.'

'It's not the time for epigrams.'

'I don't know. An epigram or two . . .'

'For God's sake!'

Mark punched me in the stomach, hard enough to make me gasp. 'What about my sake? What about our sake? You don't want me, you bastard, you want your bloody loneliness.' His face was bony with rage. 'That is all you have ever wanted − your solitude! You plan emotions as other people plan journeys, mapping them out in advance, taking all the latest inoculations. You want to be the one who does not stain life. I despise that ideal. It's too easy. It's safer even than the game I have been playing. You talk about love, but you have no idea what love means. You talk about what love costs, but you have no intention of paying its price. You want to talk about paying it. You want to write about paying it. I am not one of your books. I am here. I am asking you to give me and yourself a life, and you refuse, not because you are good but because you are afraid.'

'I am not afraid.'

'Don't lie to me. It's boring when you lie. It demeans you. Good word, demean . . .'

'Stop it.'

'I'm not going to stop anything, I warn you. I am going right to the end.'

'I hate my solitude. I rot in it . . .'

'When I was away, and unreal, you wanted me. Now I am here, you don't. It's too dirty, this reality, too ordinary. I sweat, I snore. In the mornings, when I have been drinking too much, I have bad breath. My socks smell. As a child I had to use that funny foot-spray that came in yellow plastic containers. My hair is receding. Slowly, but receding. In ten years I will have a bald patch the size of an ostrich egg. You have always thought I held the cards — because I was handsome, married, able to "play" with your love, as you believed. You have never understood how many "cards" you hold. You have your solitude, you have your work, you have your odd beauty that your vanity will keep bony. You have India to hide and have lofty emotions in, against waterfalls, mountain ranges — There are moments when I am jealous of you, helpless before all the arrangements of your life. What have I to give you except myself? And if I give you that, will I take away the one thing you ever really wanted from me — a vision of me that you could use for your own purposes? A bad exchange. I wouldn't accept it if I were you. I've a smell and a price. Vision is fragrant.'

'It is not. It is frightening. You say I do not want to pay the price of our love, Mark. I am paying it. We are paying its price together. It is worth it.'

'Worth what? Nothing can be worth it that separates us. You have a faith I do not have. How will I go back to my life when I leave you? How will I bear it, knowing what we have had?'

'And Kate? Paul?'

'You still do not understand how much I love you. One day you will, and when you do . . .' Mark stopped. 'I know our situation is hopeless. I know what you mean about Kate. I knew it even as I was bitter with you. I had to show you everything, to give you everything — to show you that I want, will always want, to give you everything. Charles, you are still not being honest. You are not giving me everything. You are not giving me as much as I am giving you. You have to try to. You have to, to make this bearable at all.'

I started to speak.

'Don't talk yet! You must know yourself. You say you trust me. But you do not. You do not know what trust is. If you trust anything it is your solitude and the work you do in it. I have known that for a long time and not dared to face it. Neither have you.'

'I'm not . . .'

'Be quiet and listen.' Mark came to me and put his hands on my shoulders. 'I will try and say what I want to without bitterness, as clearly as I can. You must not lie to me now, even unintentionally. You must not lie to yourself.'

'What lies am I telling? I do not know what they are.'

'I don't think you do. That's what makes me almost hate you. You are lying to yourself if you think it is hurting Kate that stops you letting me love you. You are lying to yourself if you tell me that you would give up everything for me, even your solitude. You need your solitude, as a drowning man needs air. It's a desperate need in you, and more ruthless than you know. You do love Kate in a way and you would hate to hurt her. You do also, I know, love me. There is one thing still that you do not love me enough to do.'

'Mark . . .'

'Be patient,' he said, with an odd calm in his voice. He stood close to me, and opened my shirt. He put his hand over my left breast and closed his eyes. Then he leant forward and blew gently into my eyes. I had never seen him like this. I was frightened. His hand closed over my breast, and then let it go. 'You do not love me enough to share with me your need to be alone, your fear of loving anything better than your aloneness and your work. Not fear — that's putting it too gently — your terror. There. It's simple, you see. Great terrors are simple. Your solitude is your one hope. That's what you know, although you don't admit it. Everything else is a game to you. You know the only place you will be whole is in the desert. You run there every day. You are running there now. I can see you running in your eyes, further and further back. You are a fool not to know these things about yourself, and you're a fool not to share them with me because I am the one person you can share them with. I can bear them, even if they take you away from me.'

He laughed. 'It's strange. You loved me for what you also hated — my capacity for life, my promiscuity, if you like, what enabled

198

me to love Kate and my children. I hate you for needing your solitude more than me, but I also know that that is why I have loved you — because you were solitary, because you had work to do that you believed in.'

He stood, swaying, despairingly. I started to reply, instinctively, with something evasive and caustic, but stopped myself in time. He was right — I had been lying; I had been lying for years and not known it. I felt ashamed. I felt a fool, a spoiled, stupid child, who had played games with my own and others' lives. I did not even have the satisfaction of playing games I understood. I had written plots without knowing why. I had organised dénouements, or tried to, without knowing what ending I wanted.

Suddenly the dream I had had in India returned to me. Like the man in my dream Mark had come across the sands of his life to give me the gift of myself, the fish-spine of self-knowledge, the shell of solitude. I had in India believed these to be tender gifts; now I saw them as they were, fraught with responsibilities I was only just beginning to understand. Yet, looking across at Mark, seeing in his eyes and hearing in his voice the love he had for me, a love which was not a fantasy, as mine had partly been, I felt that the joy of my dream had not been false either. He who gave me these gifts believed in my power to endure them, and gave them as a brother and a lover without malice and with faith.

I never loved Mark so clearly as in that moment; I never wanted to surrender my solitude so much as in the moment I saw its full egoism and necessity revealed to me. I saw what I would cost him and cost myself. I saw too — and this was what nothing I had ever lived could have prepared me for — that he forgave me. Being forgiven for what you know you have done badly is hard to bear; for a moment I was tempted to hate him. The moment passed; and that it passed was not my doing. It was his love that pulled me past myself even then. I saw there was no part of my grief that he did not want to understand, and cure, if it was in his power to do so. It was not — that he knew too. But that he wanted still in that moment to help me, filled me with wonder.

'I have not deserved you,' I said at last. 'Thank you.'

'Those words mean nothing now.'

In the stillness that followed, each sound from the street — every screech of tyres, the voices of two young men, laughing — seemed charged with power.

'We sound as if we are saying the Requiem Mass,' I said.

'We are.' He turned to go.

'Don't go,' I said. 'I'm afraid of being alone.'

Mark smiled wryly.

'Stay the night. Let's have one night together.'

'Like in a Victorian novel?' he smiled. 'One night, and then farewell for ever. We mustn't overdo it.'

I took off my jacket and laid it on the sofa.


Adolphe started. 'Well, pondsnipe, this is . . .'

'Adolphe, let me finish.'


We lay naked in each other's arms till dawn, when I fell asleep. When I awoke, he had gone. He had left a letter for me on my typewriter in Anna's dining-room.

'I am sitting where you sit all day looking out at your view of the yellow shutters, the classical windows opposite with their iron railings. I wish that you could see those railings now, painted with a light which makes them almost feathery. But they are not. You and I know they are iron, and the window-sills not made of the rice-paper they seem to be, but stone. But we know too that it is the light which matters, this clear winter light that transforms everything without deforming it. I'm going back on the night train to London. Once, years ago, you said, "If you ask life to help you, really ask with all your heart, it will." I hope so. I need that help now, and everything in me is asking it.

'Regret nothing. I do not. I found with you the courage to choose you beyond anything and the greater courage to lose you, so as never to lose you. I shall never lose you now, not to time or death, not to any other parting. You will be with me always, in all the journeys I make.

'And I've finally seen you asleep. For years I used to think that you never slept, never stopped talking. Now I know you do. I am glad to know that. You look funny when you are asleep, like a lion cub with a retroussé nose. And when you sleep you turn away, far away, into yourself, alone. That too I am glad to know. For I see you find something there that no one else can give you.

'Don't come to the station. Sit where I am sitting and read this and feel my arms around you and my breath on your neck. Remember that day you read the Song of Songs to me? It was in the coffee-shop; you read it too quickly as usual, glancing around to see if anyone was laughing at us. "This is my Beloved and this is my friend." I know now what those words mean, and the knowledge is startling. I feel I am saying the first words in a new language. I shall stutter in it for a long time, but the love I have known in you will help me speak it clearly. You speak it clearly too, for me.

'I shall not re-read this letter. I am too afraid my fear and anger might "correct" it. Let it stand. It is what I wanted to say. I love you and believe in you.

'Dressing quickly, I forgot my socks, but I'm assembled now. You wouldn't have wanted my grey socks. Not your colour. Be brave in all your colours. Renounce none of them; make them all dance together. I will dance too, in mine. I am dancing now. Listen and you will hear me.'

Underneath he drew two large, shaky circles, touching.


I drank all day. I wandered from room to room. I rang friends in London on the pretext of nothing in particular. I heard myself laughing too much, too harshly. I sat at my desk where he had sat and typed nonsense, scraps of poems, the beginnings of pompous business letters – a stream of words, phrases, to stop me hearing the wail in my mind. Everything I did – the way I held a cigarette or raised a glass to my lips – seemed forced. I longed to scrub out all my gestures, all my words, and begin again, but that longing itself seemed cheap, the longing of a coward who could not face his life. I tried to rehearse grief so as not to feel it. Afraid of what I would feel when the drink and hysteria had worn off, I tried not to think of him, for when I did I doubled over as if I had been kicked in the stomach.

Mark's train would leave at nine, the flat calm voice on the other end of the phone announced. At nine. It was eight-thirty. I still had time to get a taxi . . .

What would I do or say? My face and eyes were ugly with drink. I could not trust myself to speak without blurring. I was desperate to see him, but I knew that it was a selfish desperation, and one that could only harm him.

Nine o'clock. I imagined the voice on the phone anouncing the hour. Fate has a calm flat voice, announcing everything – the fall of cities, the growth of some quiet cancer in a young man's chest – in the same tone, without even the grace to sound tired. The train would be leaving. I saw his drawn face at a window. Was it really necessary, to have given up all that we had given up? Was there no way . . .

There was no way. I knew that. None of the words we had said or written mattered; the only thing that was real was that he was going and that we would never see each other again. What would our lives be like without each other? What could restore what we were now losing? All the half-wisdom I had gathered from my life in these last days deserted me. Everything we had said repeated itself in my mind, played at a surreal speed at which it all sounded garbled. Had everything we had done been tricks our vanity had played on us? The enactment, not, as we struggled to believe, of some desire to save love, but of a secret cowardice and hunger for parting? Every irony became clear: I knew too that time would take even this pain from us. His eyes, the lines of his face, his shoulders, the warmth of the furrow between his breasts. Even as I invoked them I saw them fade, darken, dissolve. Even his words, his brave words, I would one day have no way of hearing, or would hear only as if across a ravine, or as if spoken by the voice on the station telephone, flatly, almost meaninglessly.

Towards midnight, I went down to the river and sat by it. Images of a life Mark and I would never have came to me, more vivid than the dark sluggish water or the stone quai. I saw Mark in London, walking up a street with me to visit a friend in Chelsea with his black overcoat and silver wool scarf; I saw him in India, reading, in a white lungi on some steps by a river; I saw him standing half-naked, smiling, opening the door of Anna's flat; I saw us together, as we had been, in Oxford, but older now, sitting by the canal in summer. I saw each image as if it had already been lived, as if each were notes in a long drawn-out phrase life had already played. Then, slowly, with a strength I did not know I possessed, and a patience that was not hope but something more ancient, I found myself giving the images up, one by one, holding them up in that freezing air like photographs and burning them. I would live without them and without him. That is what he wanted for me, the courage to choose my aloneness instead of running from it into false hope; that is what he had wanted for me and what I now wanted for him. His love wished to set me free even from itself; I would try to honour its courage. I invoked the strength we would both need now, and for the years to follow, from the stone around me, from the wind and the slow noises of the river. As the moon rose higher in the icy sky and its light broke, regal and menacing, over the water, I felt, without knowing why, with a clarity indistinguishable from despair, that we would both receive what we had asked for, receive it and survive it.

Anna rang three days later.

'It's over! I'm coming back in a week. Sans Hans. More of that later. How is Brando?'

'Brando has gone.'

'Was the end dramatic?'

'When is it ever not? Will any of us ever have a relationship that is not out of *Gormenghast* and *The Brothers Karamazov*? A nice dull affair, with lots of cuddling?'

'Cuddling? That is my least favourite word in the whole language. Together with "necking", and that ghastly American expression "making out". Making out what? I've never made out anything. It's all opaque to me. Was it . . .'

'I don't want to talk about it.'

'You will. I give you seven days. The mystical seven. I can't wait to see you. What shall we do on the first night I get back? Go and hear Brendel at the Pleyel? He's playing the *Pathétique*. That's not a good idea. I'll sob all the way through and so will you. It will have to be something frivolous. Remember my art teacher, who said he wanted as an epitaph, "Profondamente frivolo"? I'm invoking his smile these days like crazy. I shall never quite make it, though, on the frivolo stakes. I shall always believe in Love, capital L. Am I wrong?'

'You're an amoureuse. It's your glory, your fate, your perversion, your wisdom.'

'And the ruin of my bank-balance.'

'And the ruin of your bank-balance. Think of the epitaph, "She ruined her bank-balance for love."'

'It would sound better in Latin.'

'Everything sounds better in Latin.'

'And what about Hans?'

'I'm working on my farewell speech. I plan to say farewell this time to farewell speeches, so this had better be the best one. I will begin by thanking him for the conférences and the nuits d'amour. I will say that bit in French because it is easier to lie in a foreign language. Then, en anglais, I will say, "Dear Hans, this is, as they say in forties American films, the moment of truth. I know you believe truth is completely relative – at least, I think that this is what you believe – but this truth is my truth, so stop eating and listen. In fact, let's begin with eating. You eat with your mouth open. You steal my cigarettes. You say sutra with too long an 'ooo'. Greater sins I could forgive you, but life is an affair of trivialities and those trivialities drive me bananas. I'm not a particularly sentimental type (lies!), but your lack of 'charm' is spectacular even in my experience. Imagine, for example, the cheering effect a bowl of roses might have had in the dingy hotel rooms we've been staying in. To be greatly good, Shelley said, one must imagine greatly. But there are some things. I suppose, that cannot be taught. I may throw in a little Blake too. The "Kissing a joy as it flies and living in eternity's sunrise" bit. But I'm not sure he deserves Great Poetry. Oh hell, throw it in.'

'And how will it end? I want to know the ending.'

'Miss Fortescue at school, of the hairy legs and moustache, used to say, "A lady always finishes things well." There are two possible endings. In the first, I urge him to leave my corrupt female presence and give up the world, as he's always talking of doing, give up my cigarettes and free meals and go into a monastery. Only there, I urge him with tears sparkling in my lenses, will he truly realise what I have seen to be beautiful in him. I do not cry. In the second I just spit at him – *Carmen*, Act III – and make an exit with packed bag and overcoat flung neatly over my left arm. I should be above such cheap effects, but then some people don't deserve any better.

Charles, I'm so sick of men, myself, the whole thing. Would you believe me if I said this is the last time I sell myself short, the last time I run begging to a man for a few scraps of love, the last time that I pretend to myself that a man with no arms and no legs can dance the tango. Really the last time, for I have seen the madness of my ways and considered the abominations of my desolations and, cross my heart and hope to live, want to change, purify, complete myself? It was, of course, what I said last time, but this time I mean it. Which is what I said last time too, but maybe repetition does make perfect. I'm too old to play these games any more, and they no longer hold any surprise. I used to be surprised by the pain. And that can keep one going for a bit. Now I want to be myself. I want to keep my dignity. If I go on as I have been I will end up withered and spitting flame and picking up young men with knives in their pockets on the Métro. I'm not going to do that.

Do you know what is really strange? Listening to Hans drivelling on about his sutras and whatnot has reminded me of a part of myself that I had shelved. I've been thinking that I'll finish off the work I have to do for the States and go to India in the spring. I'm not going to float about in white saying mantras. And I'm not going to go walking in the Himalayas. I am going to be quiet. To take stock of my life. I thought I might work . . .'

'In a leper colony? Oh, Anna! Ingrid Bergman's dead.'

'In a hospital or a mission somewhere. Don't laugh. I want to do something for others. I don't care how banal it sounds. I want to stay in Paris, but I want also to leave it and return to it and to my life from a different angle. There. Such good resolutions. Aren't I a wise and good woman?'

'You are a wise and good woman.'

'Nothing is over.'

'If you go to India I'll send you food parcels. Pâté, truffles, Toblerone. Who do you want to play you in the film?'

'I'm going to change a lot and you're going to be very surprised.

Be warned. I do feel terrible leaving Hans, but I also feel freed. I'm standing with the sour smell of burning in my nostrils, but also with a kind of hope I never felt before. Hope is the wrong word. It usually is. But a kind of resolution. Tomorrow, of course, I might think something completely different. Adolphe, by the way, will soon be back in Paris, so we'll have someone to recite our tragi-comedies to. How he'll mock every detail. The film in Africa folded. He wrote me a cheerful note listing all the New York mafiosi who had lost millions. "Besides," I quote, "the American Adonis turned out to have such bad breath no lion would go near him." '

'Poor Adonis.'

'Poor lion.'

'I don't feel like facing Adolphe at the moment.'

'We must be brave and brave his mockery. Mocking us is one of his best pleasures. You don't feel very mockable, do you?'

'No.'

'Bad sign. Let's drink to something.'

'It's noon on a sullen December morning. The flat's dry ... Let's pretend we're drinking to something. It'll make us feel better.'

'To what?'

'Oh, I don't know. What about to life?' Anna giggled.

'Oh, my God, Anna, to life? Like in a Russian film, you mean, smashing the glass against the wall? I haven't got my Cossack moustache on. And I think I'd drop the glass from laughing.'

'Don't be brittle. You're too good at it. Raise that glass, honey. Raise it high.'

'You've been drinking already.'

'Of course I've been drinking already. Raise that glass.'

'Darling, these last days ...'

'Fuck your last days, the misery, the speeches, the sadness. Raise that glass. "Only in the hall of Praise shall Lamentation ..."'

'I should never have given you that Rilke.'

'"Nymph of the weeping spring ..."'

'Isn't Praise pushing it slightly?'

'Of course it's pushing it. That's the point. To push it. Raise that glass.'

'I raise the glass. By the way, I've broken three of your glasses recently.'

'Only three? Some things do get better — You're getting less clumsy. "Only in the hall of Praise ..."'

'I'm raising the glass. There's a white shining liquid in it. Could be water, could be ...'

'The wine of Apollo, the holy sperm itself. Raise it and drain it.'
'I raise it and I drain it.'
'Say you feel better.'
'Of course. Amazingly, miraculously, transformed.'
We laughed, Anna and I, and something in our laughter held us together, held us steady.


I stopped and looked across the room to where Adolphe was sitting on the sofa, his legs tucked under him.

'Is it over?' he whispered, leaning forward so far I thought he would fall over. 'Wasn't I good in hardly interrupting at all? Am I allowed to stretch my legs?'

*'Consummatum est'*.

Adolphe made several heavy breathing noises and ran to the window-sill which he used as an exercise bar.'

'Up two three ... the last Nureyev saw me do this he went purple with jealousy. "Such line! Straight and strong like a Turkish prick!" I said it was clear we moved in different social circles, but that I'd be thrilled to participate in any ballet he created specially for me. Not with that Ivanovna woman however.'

'So?'

'So what did Nureyev say?'

'So what did you think about my you-know-what?'

'I've never seen your you-know-what. I thought we'd agreed to keep everything clean between us, clean and airy; I never imagined ...'

'What the hell are you thinking?'

'I'm thinking about Princess Eugénie's tortoise.' He looked at me in triumph.

'What?'

'You think it's absurd that I should be thinking about a tortoise? I suppose you're one of those idiots who believe animals don't have souls? They have souls all right, tiny souls the size of those earrings Cocteau designed for Elsa. What a tortoise that tortoise was! Today is the anniversary of its death in the Cairo Zoo in nineteen forty-nine. Start at the beginning

... Princess E had a pet tortoise. I've researched for years and never managed to find out what she called it. I like to think it was Hector or Achilles, an heroic, Greek name. For it was an heroic, Greek tortoise, enamoured not of Princess Eugénie (who was adorable, though a little pinched in her opinion of Jews), but of freedom. When the Princess was opening the Suez Canal, the tortoise slipped its diamond leash and went free. It was caught and put into the Cairo Zoo, but there it was treated as the royal animal it was – inside and out – and lived to a ripe old age, perhaps one of the ripest old ages of this century apart from mine. Think of that valiant little animal, in the middle of all those fanfares and silk banners, walking away into the desert, turning away from cameras and champagne and hats of the softest osprey to a world of rock and light! A creature of the purest loneliness! A mini-Bodhisattva!

'I loved your you-know-what. It's not a load of laughs and has no role for an English Butler, and no special effects or extra-terrestrials (unless you count my appearance), and I doubt very much whether it will set Tulsa alight (what would?), and there's not nearly enough sex ...' Adolphe giggled. 'If you could see your face at this moment, your progress in humour would leap years. But one can't hurry anything in this life. Everything in its season. Oh, the wisdom I feel rushing through my vitals at this moment! The visionary wisdom! I need a drink!'

He scrabbled about under the sofa and drew out a bottle of Château-Lafite. 'It's my last! Let's drink it together!' He poured out two glasses. 'To you, tortoise! To me! To us. I want to say a thousand things at once, in panoptical stereo, if only such a medium existed. In the Cabbala it says the angels speak in a million tongues at once. Or is it a hundred thousand? Figures, figures. First, I love Mark. I didn't know men like that existed. Perhaps they don't, but what the hell. They will. Second, I love Anna's noble resolutions. Nothing is ever over. Yes, all of you will have a hundred transformations to come, because you are cracked enough to go on trying to love and understand something. Two cheers ...'

'Before you go on, I think I should tell you something.'

'Your banker voice. Go on.'

'I changed the book as I read it to you. These last days, our meetings . . .'

'You mean I influenced you?' Adolphe fluttered his eyelids. 'Why, Miss Dorothy, if I thought I was in any way interfering with the oh-so-delicate mechanism of your mechanism, I wouldn't have opened my wicked little mouth.'

'I learnt from you, about love, about solitude. There were many things I added to the last scene with Mark, many asides, passages . . .'

'You're not going to tell me which ones?'

'No.'

'I can guess, I think. Of course you didn't go nearly far enough, pondsnipe. But then the young never do. I'm glad you made yourself out such a monster, though. The beginning of wisdom. One should know one is a monster. Adolphe's first commandment. Adolphe's second commandment: One should know exactly how much of a monster one is, and why and wherefore, and either have a hell of a good time being one or try to change. Sorry for the moralistic ending. It's my generation — bred on Georges Sand and George Eliot, nannies with moustaches, tapioca . . .'

'What didn't I carry far enough?'

'You want a serious speech, don't you? One of Adolphe's lectures. You know, I once did lecture at the Ecole Normale. Barthes didn't speak to me for a year, he was so jealous. I had them in tears, my dear. I concentrated throughout on a particularly spectacular blond number in the front row. His watery green eyes gave me every inspiration. Well then, pondsnipe, I'll have another swig.'

He drained another glass of Lafite and did a few steps of the Light Fantastic. Then he recited:

'The Angel that presided o'er my birth
Said: Little creature, formed of joy and mirth,
Go, love without the help of any thing on earth.

William Blake.'

'Go on.'

'There must be dramatic pauses. When Barthes . . .'

'Go on.'

'Have I told you the one about reading "The Little Chimney Sweep" to Greta, and Greta saying . . .'

'Go on.'

Adolphe repeated, softly this time, with his head on one side:

'The Angel that presided o'er my birth
Said: Little creature, formed of joy and mirth,
Go, love without the help of any thing on earth.

Without the help of anything on earth. Love without the help of . . .'

'You're losing me, Adolphe. I obviously don't have watery green eyes.'

'I shall say it straight for once. I may faint from the experience, but I'll try it. One should try everything once. Mark, or I, or writing the book, or whatever, made you understand one thing at least – your ambiguous, ruthless need for solitude. Yes. Bravo. One and a half cheers. But it is not just to work that you need solitude, little tortoise. It is for something more important – not just to accomplish your slim little novels and write your poems – something more important and baffling and wonderful and astonishing, in that or any other order. (I'm enjoying this.) Greta and Maria be with me! I'm nervous. I have so much to say and words are so slippery.' Adolphe took one last swig of the wine. 'I'll die an alcoholic,' he said with relish.

'You lived drunkenly – c'était ta gloire.'

'Never quite drunkenly enough. No one lives quite drunkenly enough. Mark unmasked your lust for solitude, but he could not take you further. You need solitude not merely to work from, but to perfect your soul. You need solitude not merely to polish your phrases, but to clean the mirror of your muddy and misted heart. You need solitude so that you can at last come into the heart of reality and dance there, at the heart of the paradox, the rose of paradox that flowers only in solitude. I hope you're taking all this down, little tape recorder, I wouldn't want my celestial inspirations lost. You need solitude like Princess Eugénie's tortoise needed the desert – to find the clear light then, the independence from which to survey the world without rancour. You need solitude, peewee, to learn love – not the love you have wanted so much but another, more difficult, more silent, more universal and over-flowing love, the love of Teresa and Francis and some of the fat old women in the rue Mouffetard, the love that has no name, no goal, that gives itself to everything because it must, as the flower must give its stunning perfume.

But don't come to me to guide to this love. I know what I have failed to realise. I know I have failed and why and where. But you, for all your vanity, pigheadedness, lack of true humour, selfishness, arrogance, cussedness, affectations of manner, for all your horrid and glaring etcetera, etceteras have a deeper chance than I ever did of finding that inner thing – whatever the hell it is – and of dancing from it and radiating it to those whom you meet. Take what Mark gave and go further; take what Anna gave and go further, press deeper, press onward. (God, I'm sounding like a scout-leader!) Take every-thing that I give and go further than I can even think of going or even know how to say. Onward to Sirius! Am I misquoting? Who cares? What I mean is, tortoise, don't fool yourself. Your destiny is love. "Without the help of anything on earth." The loneliest. That should thrill you. And don't think you will get any real help either. You won't be able to run into a monastery; you won't be able to hide your head under prayer-books or in a discipline; you won't find anyone evolved enough to teach you the love you need to learn, not even me. No, it will be all stumbling and fretting and wandering in the dark. I do not wish you renunciation – that's too easy – but the real plenitude in which all opposites are reconciled and where the lion lies down with the Chihuahua, Zsa-Zsa with Maria and Astaire

210

with Garbo. God knows you will have a hard time of it and a long mad journey. I only hope you don't die in the Cairo Zoo.' Adolphe sat down on the sofa, mopping his brow.

'What should I do now?'

'What a vulgar question! I'm shocked. There is nothing to do. You can't run off to India and have visions by the sea. It is not an Eastern love I am talking about – not the high serene thing at all, not that floaty-beyond love at all. No. And I don't suggest you plunge into domestic bliss either. Not that there's much hope of that. You're about as good at DB as I would be at climbing the Eiger in tennis shoes. There is no solution for your problem, no path for your search, no possible way to go. Nowhere to go, in fact. Just go on. Live your life. Be faithful to what you know. Turn your toes out when you walk. Clean your teeth. Wear slightly nicer shirts. Get your hair cut more often. Read the Persian mystics. Keep your mirrors clean. Oh God, you're not going to make me give you advice? No one can really give anyone else advice, not on matters like these. You will find what you need. Your solitude lived honestly will unveil to you what you require and what is required. There. That gets me out of everything and sounds pretty sonorous to boot (I love the expression "to boot"), but it happens to be almost the whole truth. Who knows what life holds for you? You might even be happy (gasp!) sailing the Aegean in Bermuda shorts. Limit nothing. Love without the help of anything on earth. But if the earth does offer you some small help, don't refuse it because you've read Blake. Embrace it. "For there is help and you have hands . . ." And such funny tapered greedy little hands too, flame-hands that can hold and burn up a lot! Spread them out, my little potato, spread those hands out!'

Adolphe sprawled out on the sofa. 'I feel quite weak from all this wisdom! To think I know so much! It's overwhelming, what even the most frivolous life can produce. With a little help from Château Lafite, your eyes, your operatic prose. Bless you for the opera, pondsnipe. It was lovely and painful. Just as operas should be.'

'Bless you for your opera. It has not been painful at all.'

'Learn from it. Sing it yourself, tomorrow. Love is a torch. Here, quick, catch it. I'm passing it to you. Don't drop it. Keep it flaming. And I mean flaming. In every sense of that word. Flame as I have flamed, and a lot brighter. I love you and I believe in you.'

'I love you and believe in you.'

'Well, now that touching little exchange is over . . .' Adolphe stood up.

'What a time we have had. My eyes are tanking up. We're like two old actresses backstage, but at least it's not England, so we don't have to reach immediately for our handkerchiefs. Let 'em fall . . . Darling, I told you I had something to tell you . . . I have a confession to make. Listen carefully. It isn't time, but when would it be?' He took my hand. 'I have told you only two lies in our whole friendship. That is probably a lie, but if so it is unintentional. I lied to you about the doctor and I lied about the dream about Mark. You may spank me severely if you wish. Not too, or I might enjoy it.' He giggled. I looked at him in bafflement. 'Oh, pondsnipe, one has to explain everything to you. That's part of your odd charm, of course. When I went to see that doctor three days ago he told me something I already knew. I am dying.'

'Dying?' I repeated the word foolishly, dazedly, unable to grasp its meaning.

'I have had cancer for fourteen years. It began soon after the incident with the Tibetan priest. It was the price I paid for my new life. Everything has its price, as every washerwoman knows. I have never regretted paying it, pondsnipe, never, not for one moment. It's not nobility. I just knew that what I was being given daily, hourly, was something richer than anything I had known before. I prayed for only one thing. I did not pray for a lover, or great friends, or genius, or fame, or even Nirvana; I prayed to meet myself. I prayed that I would turn up. All my life I realised I had been waiting, not for the cocks and canapés, as dear Jean would put it, but for myself, my real self. I wanted to meet the shadow that walked by my side, that lived silently and in the dark to the edges of my life, that I had caught glimpses of, but as if reflected in a circus mirror – grotesque glimpses, glimpses full of terror. I wanted to meet him in the light, serenely, with humour. It has happened. I have met him. He is here. And now Death has no meaning for me, and no sadness at all. The doctor gave me a month. He said, "There is no hope." I said, "Thank God." He looked at me with astonishment. I said, "I have always found hope a great confusion." He collected himself. Doctors can face anything, even metaphysics, if the patient is paying enough. He studied the tiny lines on his platinum cuff-links.'

'Adolphe . . .'

'Don't say anything. I know you love me. I know you will miss me. I know you will suffer when I am no longer there. Those are things I know. You don't have to say them. Everyone says those kind of things so badly. I should have given you time to prepare something simple and eloquent. Don't bother now.' He came and sat next to me and put his arms around me.

'I said I told you two lies. Here is the other one. I lied to you when I told you about the dream about Mark. In fact, I had it several days before I asked you to come and read your novel to me.'

I looked blank.

'Oh, pondsnipe, you are so dumb! It's delicious!'

'Help me then.'

'When have I not, you ungrateful piranha?' He pinched my left ear. 'In the dream Mark gave me a book. He gave it to me to give to you. I hardly knew Mark. We only met twice. Once at that party you describe so luridly and once when he came to interview me and I trotted out my usual epigrams. But I liked him and saw him. Perhaps it is hindsight, but I felt something, a soupçonette, of what he would mean to you. Of course, I didn't see he was going to be your Beatrice but one can't see everything.' Adolphe paused and studied the one small diamond ring on his left hand. 'What was the book he was giving me in the dream to give to you? I was baffled. I rang you and asked you to come over and read me the book I knew you had written and suspected was about him. I did not tell you at once about the dream, because I did not want to worry or scare you, and because I felt that our being and talking together would give me the clue I needed. The other afternoon, sitting at the doctor's, watching him study his cuff-links, and then start to write something on the white pad in front of him, I understood. Don't look so eager, you little ferret, or I might not tell you.'

He sat closer to me and hugged me. 'What bony ribs you have. How does anyone sleep with you and not get cut to pieces? I understood that the book that Mark was giving me to give to you was the book you had not written, the book you did not yet know how to write, the book, I flatter myself, that only I could help you write, if I loved you wisely and you listened lovingly. Mark was giving it to me because he knew that I had very little time, and by helping you into yourself I would also be realising something in myself, giving you myself, my selves rather, to be precise. In giving to you everything I could, the whole book of my flightiness and wisdom, I would be repaying, in a tiny but truthful way, the debt I owed to that Tibetan who saved my life years before. Wonderful what a handsome doctor studying his cuff-links can make one understand! There may be of course a thousand other meanings I cannot see. Let them float benignly about us, like putti in a painting by Tiepolo. I still do not know why I did not tell the truth about the doctor. I think it was because we were enjoying ourselves so much. I wanted everything we said and did to be unshadowed. Your concern would have put a mist over us and between us. So now, pondsnipe, I have given you the book – if you want it – and the ending, which, like all true endings (and ours is a true ending) is also a beginning. Basta. I've gone on long enough. Charles?'

'My dear friend . . .' The whole room seemed to tilt and slip away.

'Don't say anything. You'll only spoil things. Sit by me and remember what I have done for you I have done for myself, and often, my darling, my sweetest pondsnipe, I have had the absolute happiness, as now, of not knowing the difference.'